The Reprint

Nick Bruechle

Contact the author:
www.nickbruechle.com
nick@nickbruechle.com
facebook.com/nickbruechlebooks
@nick_bruechle

Production and proofreading by Hourigan & Co.
http://hourigan.co

ISBN 978-0-9953738-3-9 (pbk)

Set in Linux Libertine

To my wonderful wife, Rachel. Thank you for making a new man of me.

Also by Nick Bruechle

The Burnt Islands and Other Stories

Good Things and Other Stories

About the author

After thirty-five years in advertising having people telling him what to write, **Nick Bruechle** is now writing the stories he wants to tell. And he is the worst client he has ever encountered. Very happily married, he is a freelance writer, surfer, hausfrau and servant to two idiotic cats.

THE REPRINT

1.

"Okay, with the first part, we'll run graphics, animation and historic footage to show the event and the immediate effects, and we won't cut to live vision until you start talking about the operation going on behind you, okay?" Derren was, as usual, all business. The early morning chill was hanging around, and the crew was rugged up against it, except for Fleur, the on-screen talent. She was wearing a thin yellow woollen skirt suit and sheer stockings, and in between takes was shivering.

"Can't I do this in bits?"

"No I want the whole thing in one, with the sound effects of the machinery in the background. It's much more powerful that way." Derren's voice softened, and she approached the shivering young woman and gave her a hug. "I know you can do it honey," she said. "You know the material, and you know how important this is. Just give it a shot a couple of times and if we can't get it all in one take, we'll break it up. Okay? Don't forget, you can read from your script until we get to the part about the scavenging, because the camera won't really be on you until then. Okay everybody, ready to give it a shot?"

Toney checked that her boom mike was close enough but not in the shot, switched on the recorder, and gave the thumbs up. Jakob checked focus one more time, hit the record button and gave the thumbs up. Lars lounged against the electro-van that served as an outside broadcast truck – he'd set a small fill light but the scene was mostly naturally lit anyway.

Behind the reporter, a large front-end loader was gouging chunks out of the side of a huge, misshapen hill, dredging up clods of earth and grass mixed with heavy metal girders, remnants of walls, shattered glass, pieces of broken furniture and all the other detritus of a building that has long been reclaimed by nature, including, on occasion, pieces of bone and rotten clothing. A smaller unit was working on moving the larger items like joists and columns onto waiting electric trucks, and a swarm of professional foragers was working through the remainder, picking out and separating electrical wires and components, phones and computers, crockery, cutlery, books, bags, bottles, pieces of paper and everything else into neat piles. They were all wearing hazmat suits, and carelessly tossing the bones and pieces of putrefied flesh they found onto a separate pile, for burning.

"Twenty years ago today," began Fleur, "our world came to an end. A colossal geomagnetic solar storm had hurled an unprecedented coronal mass ejection directly toward earth, focusing its energy on North America, Central America and parts of South America, and it struck at precisely eleven thirty-one a.m. Mountain Time on Saturday, November 18th, 2017. In milliseconds, almost every electronic component, computer, microwave communication device, radar, transformer, power line, electricity distributor, transmitter, insulator and generator in the continental United States, Canada, Mexico and further south was damaged beyond repair by an overwhelmingly powerful electromagnetic pulse, an EMP. Cars stopped dead, planes fell from the skies, trains halted on their tracks and millions, billions of automated processes froze. The power failure was instant and complete, blacking out millions and millions of homes and offices, factories and shops.

"The death toll in that instant and the minutes that followed, in which vehicles, systems and activities everywhere crashed, causing explosions, fires, floods and structural collapse, was horrific. But it was just the beginning. Without electricity, and deprived almost instantly of plumbing reliant on pumps, transport, or any communication systems at all, millions panicked. Accidents occurred, fires raged unchecked, and savage violence erupted. In a matter of seconds, the banking and financial systems collapsed and cash became instantly worthless, the economy ground to a shuddering halt, and chaos enveloped our previously civilised world. As the systems that underpinned our infrastructure simply stopped working, the toll worsened. Hundreds of thousands of desperate victims died within the first forty-eight hours, many fled south or north – on foot and carrying only meagre possessions and far from enough food or water – in the hope of finding an unaffected area. Most of those refugees died somewhere on the road, either of starvation or at the hands of others desperate for their slender supplies.

"People in critical jobs abandoned their posts, and the destruction spread and multiplied. In nuclear plants across the country, plumbing and electricity failed, and failsafe procedures that depended on human supervision and management, or on backup systems that had fried in the EMP, crashed. This led to meltdowns, explosions and the unchecked release of deadly radiation that even today renders most of the former United States uninhabitable. Millions died of radiation disease, thirst and, again, eventual starvation. Many committed suicide. In many places across the continent the death toll reached a horrifying one hundred percent. Only in the so-called 'clean corridor,' away from nuclear power – Montana, Wyoming, Colorado and New Mexico – did people survive in any great numbers.

"By a miracle of geographical placement and fortunate coincidence, combined with hard work, determination and community spirit, the city of New Elysium has risen from the ashes of what was once known as Pueblo, Colorado. The two hundred thousand survivors who came to settle and rebuild in this walled city have collaborated to create a peaceful, harmonious and clean home, mostly by recycling the past. Here you can see EMP-protected computers, electronics and equipment from medical facilities, everyday items like fridges, cookers and generators, and even heavy earthmovers. All this came from the NORAD Defence Installation in Cheyenne Mountain, from the Buckley, Peterson and Schriever Air Force bases, or from other nearby military installations. Together, these vital machines provided the basic tools we used to recreate and improve on our previous society. That so many of the surviving and remaining military personnel have contributed to the design, construction and protection of our city has been a boon. Our new home is stable, happy, and prosperous.

"The waters of the Arkansas River remain clean and bountiful, our own community gardens and the plains to our east provide plentiful harvests, and our energy needs are met by a uniquely safe, clean and reliable source."

Fleur dropped the script from which she had been reading and looked directly down the barrel of Jakob's camera. Her wide eyes were white and clear, her perfect teeth gleamed as white as her eyes, and her freshly curled and styled hair jiggled softly in the gentle chill of the breeze. Her delivery was as flawless as her skin, and just as cool. Speaking slowly, with great care and enunciation, yet somehow conveying the emotion and gravity of the situation, Fleur spoke to the viewers' hearts.

"And today, we continue to build and enhance our quality of life using raw materials sourced from sites like this one on the outskirts of the former Colorado Springs. Nature has repossessed this once busy city, but our teams of recovery workers mine it for vital elements like steel, aluminum, glass and lithium. We retrieve the furnishings, accessories, devices, records and artefacts that the people here once held so dear, and we repair, reuse or recycle them. This site will provide building and other materials for New Elysium for another five to eight years, and when this is exhausted, we can move onto the much bigger site of the former Denver. We can survive for many, many years on sustainable recycling and reuse before we even have to think about turning to natural resources.

"It's a big job, and occasionally it's a sad and difficult one, but it needs to be done for the future of New Elysium. We've come a long way in twenty years, and who knows where we'll be in twenty more. This is Fleur Bilson for NETV."

"And cut!" said Derren. "Fleur, that was amazing, thank you." Her thanks were sincere, but her mind was already on the next step. She turned to the gentleman standing behind Jakob's camera. "Okay Mr Toynbee, we're ready for you. Jakob, tighten the framing a bit, Lars, do you need to adjust the lights...?" Lars shook his head. Meanwhile, Toney had handed Fleur a microphone and tested the levels. In less than a minute they were ready to go again.

"Okay roll it," said Derren.

Fleur looked down the barrel of Jakob's lens and began.

"I'm with salvage director Mr Alvin Toynbee at the site of the former city of Colorado Springs, where salvage operations have been under way for almost eighteen years. Mr Toynbee, thank you for taking time out from your busy day to talk to us."

"It's a pleasure Fleur," beamed Mr Toynbee. "It's nice to see some new faces around here."

"So, I've already explained to the viewers broadly what you do here, but I wonder if you could tell us in your own words?"

"Certainly, Fleur. We operate several different teams, and we search the site of the city to recover various items and elements that can be used in New Elysium. The loaders go in first, taking big grabs of the earth, dust, grass, shrubs and trees that have covered the part of the city we're working on since the event. Any large items like girders, panels, windows

– pieces that are usually melted down and recycled and don't have to be handled with much care – are attached to cranes or claws, and put onto the larger trucks.

"Usually what happens is that the first grab will remove the cover of what turns out to be a cache of smaller, more valuable materials, very often preserved in a kind of debris cavern. When that happens the workers go in and sort through by hand or with smaller machinery, identifying what's worth saving, what's junk and what needs to be handled with more care and respect, such as human remains."

Behind the camera, a worker could be seen hurling a thighbone onto a motley pile of bones, old clothes and other very human looking objects.

"Can you still find anything of value in this mess?" asked Fleur, incredulous.

"Oh, yes indeed," said Mr Toynbee. "Every day we find devices like phones, television sets, microwave ovens, radios, even cars and generators, all of them still working or maybe just needing some minor repairs. A lot of people didn't realise that, because of where they were at the time, like in an elevator, or just out of sheer blind luck, their electronic equipment – phones and computers and so on - still worked. They just couldn't connect or, because the power was out, they assumed the appliance was dead and abandoned it. We're still finding perfectly good generators that could have been put to good use, but people didn't think to try them, or, as I say, they left them behind when they abandoned their workplace or home. Some people used their generators for a day or so but then, when they ran out of fuel, just walked away from them. Most of those people lived within easy walking distance of gas stations that still have full tanks, and anyone with even a rudimentary knowledge of physics could have refilled their generators many times."

"You're saying that a lot of equipment survived the EMP but wasn't taken advantage of?" said Fleur.

"Absolutely. No doubt there are generators on nuclear reactor sites that could have been used to avert or at least delay meltdowns, but because the people in charge all ran away, they were never deployed."

"That's shocking," said Fleur. "How many deaths could have been avoided?"

"Well, Fleur, disaster preparedness authorities believed that in the event of an electromagnetic pulse of the magnitude that struck earth, the death toll in the United States would have been about two thirds of the population. As we know, it was much higher because of the nuclear devastation that followed the EMP, and because so many starved, or were killed in accidents and fires, or while engaged in risky activities such as looting, or even took their own lives rather than starve to death or attempt to survive the hard way."

Derren was signalling madly at Fleur to get back on track with the recovery operation questions.

"And what other important elements are you extracting from the remains of this city?" Fleur asked.

"Thousands of tons of building materials are being recovered every month, Fleur," said Mr Toynbee. "Bricks, timber, glass and steel I mentioned, copper wires, even cans of paint, fuels, gas cylinders and other very useful hardware items that have sat patiently under the rubble for years and years, unspoiled and ready for use. Actually," he grinned, "it's pretty much a treasure trove."

"It certainly seems to be," agreed Fleur. "Thank you again for your time Mr Alvin Toynbee, and good luck with your on-going operation, which is of such importance to the present and future of New Elysium. This is Fleur Bilson on location at the site of Colorado Springs for NETV. Back to you in the studio, Felicity."

Fleur dropped the microphone, shook Alvin Toynbee's hand and walked out of frame. The crew immediately started striking the set as Derren stepped in, thanked Mr Toynbee and said briskly, "Okay, let's wrap it up and be back in town by two."

Behind them, the rummaging and sifting continued, but they ignored it as they packed up the set. Fleur jumped straight in to the van and turned on the heater, rubbing her palms together and blowing on her knuckles. Eventually all the lights, camera, sound equipment and people were crammed into the electro-van, and Derren drove down the rough track toward New Elysium at breakneck speed. They were late for their next location, and it was an important one.

"You did a fab-tastic job out there, Fleur," said Lars. "The sound was so good – your delivery is so crisp these days."

Fleur smiled her coy, pleased smile and shrugged. "Thank you, Lars. You all did a great job today," she said to the whole team. Jakob grunted, Toney looked bored, and Derren didn't look up from the road. Only Lars looked appreciative, and probably too much at that.

"It's easy when you're so professional," he said.

"Oh god," muttered Jakob, digging his head deeper into his thick fur collar. "Are we going to do this all the way back to town?"

Lars looked annoyed, but Fleur took his point, and started digging into her little attaché.

"I should rehearse my questions," she said to no one in particular. "I'm so nervous about this next shoot."

"You'll be awesome," said Lars, then realising that he might have taken the ingratiation too far, shut up and watched the road ahead. The walls of the city loomed ahead of them, jutting out of the plain in tall, straight lines.

"It's like going back to prison," said Jakob in a gloomy grumble.

2.

They need not have hurried. Major Tom Flynt, the architect and builder of New Elysium, kept them waiting in his plush outer office for over forty minutes.

"Major Flynt will be with you in a short while," said his assistant, a very youthful, polished looking fellow with carefully styled hair and a dapper, sharply creased striped shirt, who had introduced himself as Garvin Wintz. "He is currently taking care of some very important business."

The office was situated on the top floor of the City Hall building, where Major Flynt was second in command only to Colonel Graves Martin, Head of the Military Council. The light and airy reception area was luxuriously decorated by local standards, adorned with some of the finest pieces of furniture and art yet recovered from the tentative digs in Denver, and the fashionable, refined and elegant Mr Wintz looked perfectly at home in it. While Jakob, Toney and Lars ferried equipment up from the van and stacked it neatly near the floor-to-ceiling window, Derren fussed over running sheets and production details, and Fleur chatted with the young assistant.

"Why aren't you in uniform?" she asked in a coy, coquettish voice, fussing with her hair, bunching it into a pony tail and then letting it fall free and shaking it as she spoke.

"Oh, I'm too young," said Wintz. His voice was unexpectedly deep and sonorous, and his eyes were a solemn, icy blue. He was older than he looked, because he appeared to have only a few years, if that, on Fleur but was in fact in his mid-thirties. "There is no United States army, navy or air force anymore," he explained. "It dissolved pretty much on the day of the EMP. The Major, the Colonel and the others in the Council keep their titles as honorifics of a sort I guess, but I was only fourteen when the event happened, so I was never a part of the military."

"Oh I see," said Fleur. "It's a shame because I'm sure you'd look great in a uniform."

"Thanks," he replied. Confidence radiated from him, and his piercing stare was mesmerising. "But I prefer civvies. I'm a bit of a fashion nut."

"I can tell," said Fleur approvingly.

At last, some time after the view of the city afforded by the panoramic windows had begun to pall on the crew – it was really just a boring grid interspersed with squares of green – the door to the inner office was flung open to reveal Major Tom Flynt. His uniform may have been aging, but it was crisply pressed, immaculately worn and as flawless a fit as the day he'd first put it on over two decades ago.

He invited his guests into his huge corner office. The entire west wall was made of glass and looked out to the distant Rockies – one of the few things tall enough to be seen over the city's protective wall. There was a full leather lounge suite along the east wall near the entrance they'd come through, and a huge model of New Elysium itself near another plate glass window looking out over the city. They were the biggest windows any of the crew had looked out of in many years.

Major Flynt eased himself into a simple leather chair behind a vast mahogany desk covered with orderly piles of paper and folders, his back pointedly turned to the distracting view, and said, "Now, how can I help you?"

Lars, Toney and Jakob immediately set to work placing their various devices around the model, which seemed like the perfect backdrop for the interview. Derren introduced herself to the Major and outlined her plan. Listening with the brisk inattention of one who is interminably busy, Flynt shook her hand with spirited vitality while ignoring her face entirely. He was already focused on his next target, Fleur.

"And you must be Fleur," he said in a charming baritone. "My inquisitor."

Fleur blushed and held out a limp hand, which he gripped with much less muscle than he had Derren's, caressing more than shaking it. "Go easy on me," he said. "I'm not used to being put on the spot."

Fleur actually giggled, much to the exasperation of Lars, who was watching the whole scene with distaste, and a heavy pause hung in the air. Derren broke it with her customary tact.

"We're privileged to have been given an hour of your valuable time Major," she said. Flynt's work ethic was legendary, and his achievement undeniable. The entire city of New Elysium had been his vision, and now that it was virtually complete in all but a few minor details, his triumph.

13

He tried, without much success, to appear humble, but only managed a smirk – albeit a handsome, urbane one.

"My god, he's beautiful," said Toney to no one in particular. As soon as they'd walked in she'd been captivated by his strong, tanned and taut features, his steely grey eyes and matching hair – which looked as if it was held in place by sheer force of will.

"What an asshole," whispered Jakob to Lars.

"Let's see how good he looks with this beauty blasting in his face," said Lars, holding up the head of his most powerful 2000-watt tungsten halogen spotlight, a nasty grin on his face.

While Major Flynt, Fleur and Derren discussed the nature and tenor of the interview, Jakob took shots of the city model from a few different angles and collected a few cutaways of the various diagrams and illustrations that lined the walls. Then, while the stars finished their niceties, he, Toney and Lars waited by the window overlooking the city. From up here it looked incredibly neat, homogenous and green. This was a new perspective for the crew. Down at street level, despite the care taken with planning and building, it was easy to see that every home, store, bar, café and apartment block had been cobbled together out of mismatched pieces of steel, timber, glass, brick and tile, so that up close it looked somewhat like a mishmash of styles, materials and ideas.

Eventually Derren indicated that they were ready to shoot. Jakob started tight on Fleur's face, the panorama of the city below a nicely defocused background. Speaking into the microphone that Toney had provided for the interview –

it's always more comfortable for the interviewer to hold a microphone so they can appear to control the dialogue by virtue of where they point it – she launched into her laudatory preamble.

As she spoke, Jakob gradually widened the shot to encompass Major Flynt and the model of the city, and there, for the time being, he locked off. Leaving the camera to run, he quietly picked up a second, much smaller unit and slung it over his shoulder so he could walk about the room getting close ups of both Fleur and Major Flynt as the interview progressed. These he could intercut with the shots of the model he'd taken earlier and, if necessary, stock shots showing the building of New Elysium, the parks, gardens, greenhouses and other features.

"In the twenty years of its existence, the last fifteen as a proper urban development with electricity, running water, real homes and a town centre, the city of New Elysium has accrued no greater debt than to one man," Fleur began. "He is the visionary who saw what the city of the future must be, and set out to build it. His exquisitely planned and boldly executed concept is now a fully functioning metropolis that serves as an exemplar to other cities around the world, a haven of sustainability, harmony, beauty and geometry. I refer of course to the architect and chief construction manager of New Elysium, army engineer Major Tom Flynt. It is a great privilege to be able to talk the gentleman himself on this important anniversary. Major Flynt, thank you for your time, and more importantly for making New Elysium the beautiful city it is today."

Flynt, who had been absorbing this praise with smug assurance, stared down the lens with an insouciant leer, and, turning his gaze to Fleur, said, "Thank you, Fleur, you're too kind."

"Can you encapsulate for us, Major Flynt, exactly what drove, what informed your vision for New Elysium when you first sat down to plan it?"

"Certainly Fleur, I'd be happy to," he replied suavely. Like an old pro, he turned to face directly into the locked off camera, realised that he could not hold that position for too long without looking arrogant, and turned again to his interviewer.

"The first thing that struck me when I contemplated what our future – now our present – would look like was that it must be nothing like our past. Our old cities seemed fine to us, even in some cases exceptional. But when the EMP struck it very rapidly became apparent that there was one attribute that they all, every single one of them, lacked, and that was what I call survivability. People in their wonderfully sculpted and faultlessly engineered skyscrapers starved to death because they were disconnected from the ground, disconnected from the very elements of survival that we all need – food and water. They had shelter, but that was all. Many of them couldn't get down to the ground or up to their homes without electricity, and almost every one of them starved or died of thirst very quickly once food and water were no longer on tap, so to speak.

"So when I took on the task of making a new city, I said to myself that never again should people be disconnected from food sources. Never again would we reach for skies in order to create the kind of population densities we once had to accommodate to make our cities work. This administration building, at five stories, is the tallest structure in New Elysium, and it is the tallest that will ever be built in this city."

He began moving a little to his left, toward the model.

"Sorry," Jakob said. "Can we stop there for a second? I need to move the other camera."

Lars was amused, Derren and Fleur were unfazed, but Flynt looked annoyed.

"Sorry," said Jakob again. He quickly adjusted the camera, and threw a look to Derren, who said quietly, "Okay, let's go again," to Major Flynt.

The Major smiled in a mildly deprecating manner, and seamlessly picked up his oratory. "If I could direct your attention to this model of New Elysium, Fleur, it may help your viewers appreciate what I was trying to achieve."

The model showed a vast square grid, symmetrical, rigid and inflexible, as though it had been planned by a military mind – which indeed it had. The wall around the city seemed, to Jakob, to be keeping people in, rather than protecting them.

Major Flynt waved his hand proudly over the model. "This is how I saw the city, and this is mostly how it has been built, with a few kinks and compromises to allow for the geography and topography. As you know, Fleur, there is no private property ownership in New Elysium. The city, which is also a state like the Vatican and Singapore among others, owns it all and apportions it to members of the community on an as-needs basis. This means that there are no 'rich' areas separated from 'poor' areas, we're all one big community regardless of income, family history, race or religion. It also removes the need to compete with neighbours for prestige and space, and more importantly avoids the need for people to go into debt servitude to own a home. The homes people live in are for all intents and purposes theirs, but they don't owe a lifetime of wages to a bank somewhere for the privilege."

The Major smiled a winning smile meant to illuminate his caring, egalitarian nature and his humble happiness at being able to achieve such an important victory for the people of New Elysium. Fleur smiled back admiringly.

"Now, the smallest units of community that we have," the Major continued, indicating the model casually, "are the local co-op blocks that are separated from each other by streets, which run north to south, and lanes, which run east to west. A neighbourhood consists of sixteen co-ops, bounded by avenues to left and right, and roads above and below. Sixty-four neighbourhoods make up a district, and the boulevards, which run north-south, and promenades, running east-west, mark out the boundaries of these districts. There are also of course our two Grand Concourses bisecting the whole city.

"Now, within the wider community we wanted to introduce small social units that represent a much tighter, friendlier and more co-operative connection. Something close to home, where everyone knows everyone else and they help each other. So the cornerstone of our society is the local block, the co-op, and I wanted to ensure that every resident of every co-op has the opportunity to, if necessary, almost barricade themselves into their home, or at least in their co-op with their neighbours, and yet survive."

Flynt left the side of the model and, with Fleur trailing behind him, walked to the wall. Jakob had to think quickly and follow with the portable camera so the microphone was within the correct distance to collect his audio feed. If Derren, Fleur and Flynt had choreographed this move while they were talking about the interview, they had not shared that information with Jakob. He gritted his teeth and tried not to grind them.

Flynt indicated a framed diagram of a typical co-op block on the wall, which Jakob had taken a static shot of while they were waiting. At least he had that one in the can!

"Here is a typical local co-op block, Fleur. Every co-op in New Elysium is the same size and dimensions: 315 metres per side, less the forty-by-forty metre chunk taken out at each corner for the local meets. Around the perimeter of these blocks, we place on average thirty-five individual dwelling and commercial lots of six hundred square metres each, with a few driveways into the interior making up the rest of the area used. Every individual lot is built with a one hundred square metre greenhouse and hydroponic facility on the property for the owner's private use.

"But you will have already noted, Fleur, that placing homes only on the outer perimeter of these large blocks," here his finger traced the outside line of houses on the block illustration, "leaves a large interior space in every local co-op – an area of some five thousand or so square metres. And this is given over, on every block in New Elysium, to the local co-op garden run by the residents of that block. The co-op garden consists of several large greenhouses with sophisticated all-weather hydroponic capacity, and a significant outdoor growing area where all kinds of fruit and vegetable crops are grown in the warmer months. The outdoor growing areas and the greenhouses, including the individual greenhouse on every home-owner's lot, are all irrigated from our reservoir and the river itself, with emergency supplies available from wells dug into every block."

Even with the aid of the image and the model, this was all getting very dry and dense, as well as being common knowledge to every New Elysium citizen, so Fleur stepped in.

"So this is the so-called survivability you have built into New Elysium," she said.

"That's right, Fleur," he replied. He'd become absorbed in his own handiwork, and had not noticed that Fleur was becoming fidgety. "Everyone gets involved in growing and preparing their own food, which depending on the season may be fruits, vegetables, herbs and so on, and any excess can be sold or bartered, so that some co-ops might have a small area in which they specialise in growing a crop out of season – say asparagus, or avocados, or my favourite, cherries – and sell their excess of these to neighbouring co-ops or swap them for a different produce. It's managed by committee and it encourages people to get to know their neighbours, and to take an interest in the running of the gardens. Most co-ops have chickens and a cow or two for dairy production and meat, with perhaps goats, sheep and pigs. Even the youngest understand where their food comes from, and are taught how to grow it and, when the time comes, how to butcher and prepare livestock. So if there should be another catastrophic event that wipes out our energy supplies, our government and the other infrastructure we all rely on, the local co-op will continue to provide sustenance for the people who all know each other and have a long history of cooperating with each other. Society won't just fracture and break down the way it did twenty years ago."

"And the parks?" put in Fleur helpfully.

"Yes, of course. As you know, no local co-op is further than three blocks from a huge park covering the space of two co-op blocks. If there is an emergency, we can turn as many as we need of these two hundred plus parks into further growing areas."

"That's a lot of growing area."

"Yes, it is a lot of growing area, Fleur, and quite probably more than we will ever need. Especially as over the last ten years we've developed substantial pasturelands and farming beyond the city walls. We now have several thousand people working out there, you know."

"It really is an amazing vision, Major Flynt," said Fleur in an admiring tone. She pointed to a large area at the south-west corner of the model, which was filled with square shapes indicating large, low buildings. "And this area?" she asked.

"That of course is our industrial centre, placed so that prevailing winds take any pollution – and our industries are very clean by world standards – away from the city. At over forty square kilometres, the land reserved for industry is quite substantial and we have a long way to go yet before we fill it, but business in New Elysium is booming." He continued to beam like a lighthouse. "Our energy generation plant, the cleanest in the world, is also down there," he added. "If there should be another tragic and catastrophic event like the EMP, we believe even our energy generation system will survive. So we really have built a bullet-proof little town here, Fleur."

"We have indeed, or should I say, you have Major Flynt. It is an amazing and beautiful place to live, and I am sure all the citizens of New Elysium thank you for your vision, your dedication and your talent," she said, looking not at the Major but the camera.

"The pleasure has been all mine, Fleur," said Major Flynt, also looking directly into the camera and offering a suave, toothy smile.

As soon as the camera had been stopped and the lights switched off, Flynt forgot all about Fleur and made a bee-line for Derren. He seemed to have noticed her during the interview, and from that point had hardly been able to keep his eyes off her. He took her hand and shook it warmly. "And it has been an absolute pleasure meeting you, Ms Tooley."

Derren returned his smile uncertainly, and for the first time the rest of the crew had ever seen, a blush of embarrassed redness coloured her cheeks.

"The city owes you a debt of gratitude, Major Flynt. One that we can never repay," she said.

"One does what one can," he replied modestly.

"What a slimeball," muttered Jakob as he packed his camera away.

"Okay team, let's pack up and get back to the station," said Derren in her brisk business voice, extracting herself from Major Flynt's seemingly never-ending handshake.

On the way back to the station, a minor fracas broke out between Lars and Fleur.

"Could you have been any more obvious, Fleur?" snapped Lars. A look of resigned exasperation appeared on Fleur's pretty, finely featured face.

"What are you talking about?" she asked flatly.

"The way you were practically pawing Flynt," said Lars. It was written on his face, which twisted and spat the words out reluctantly, that he didn't want to be having this conversation, mainly because he knew it would never work to his advantage to hassle Fleur like this, but he couldn't help himself.

"You're an idiot," Fleur snapped back.

"Come on, it was there for all to see," said Lars.

"Ewww, he is like old enough to be my grandfather. He must be your age!"

Lars was offended and deflated. "He's like a year older than me," he said.

"Exactly," said Fleur. She shuddered theatrically in her seat. "Way too old for me."

"You're miles off course, Lars," said Derren quietly, and just a little bit smugly. "I think you missed the real action."

"You mean you and the Major?" asked Toney, raising an eyebrow and leaning forward to eyeball Derren knowingly.

"Hah, no," said Derren too quickly, a shadow of a smile playing on her lips. "Fleur and the assistant. What was his name Fleur?"

"Um, Wintz I think," Fleur replied, quickly and with a pretension to vagueness. She fiddled with her ear lobe and looked straight ahead. Lars, taken by surprise and not knowing what to say, shut up.

"So, a couple of beers at Mickey's?" Toney said. Although there were local bars and cafes that served alcohol on virtually every street corner in the city, Mickey's was a larger establishment in the city centre, just a block or so from the television station where the crew worked, so they were regulars there. It was an easy walk, and situated on the big, wide Boulevard so there were always plenty of electro-buses to make getting home easy.

3.

"Another round?" Lars was, as always, enthusiastic about drinking lots quickly and encouraging his co-workers to do the same. The other members of the crew still held near-full glasses, but they all nodded and he went off to the bar.

The highlight of their long, tiring day had been the interesting, if slightly unnerving, outside broadcast shoot. Most of the residents of New Elysium didn't get beyond the city walls too often, if at all, and although the crew had all been outside the walls on assignments before, they'd never been that far from town. There was no regular public transport beyond the city limits, and given that private electro-car ownership was forbidden, it was difficult to plan an excursion. The idea of cycling out to the mountains did not appeal to many, particularly as there were still sick, deranged and dangerous nomads roaming about the countryside, according to the authorities. Yet they hadn't seen anyone but the recycling recovery crews at work on the Colorado Springs site, and it seemed odd that those crews didn't have armed guards or weapons or any other protection to hand if there were roving bands of brigands.

That aside, they'd been most impressed by the view. For the last twenty years, they'd had a wide sloping plain between them and the Rockies – and there was of course a wall obstructing their view of just about everything beyond New Elysium. So the closeness of the mountains to Colorado Springs had awed them. As the towers of rock dusted with snow had grown closer and loomed ever taller as they neared Colorado Springs, they had all craned their necks to get a better view. The mountains were so much taller, so much more real and majestic than they appeared from New Elysium. Their city, as snug and secure as it was, suddenly seemed small and too familiar.

So as they sat and drank, the conversation turned to the mountains and the scavenger work. It was full of joviality and excitement engendered by their big day out, though the easy camaraderie couldn't last.

Lars came back with four large beers, and placed them in front of the team: Derren Tooley the producer, Toney Kranz the sound recordist, Jakob Petersson the cameraman, and one for himself, Lars Enever the lighting gaffer.

"I hate it when the talent doesn't come to these things," he announced. "I mean, what are we, mutants or something?" This was his habitual rant.

"Lars, give it a rest will you," said Derren, voicing the thought in everyone's heads. "We all know you're hot for Fleur."

"Huh, as if," said Lars. "I just hate the way she thinks she's better than we are. We all work hard, we all do a great job, but she's the one on the screen, so she thinks she's some sort of hot shit. It just irks me is all."

"Lars, she's twenty-three years old," said Jakob. "She's ten years younger than you, and the rest of us have even more on her. Why would she want to hang out with us?"

"Because we're her work buddies, that's why," Lars said, pouting. "And besides, I'm only nine years older than her. And I hang out with you old hags, don't I?"

"Hah, because you've got no friends," said Toney. It was one of those eternal triangle things, where the people involved couldn't see it but everyone else could. Toney was hooked on Lars, but he didn't notice her because he had eyes only for Fleur. Admittedly, Fleur was a good looking girl, and smart, but it seemed to the others that the only reason Lars was so keen on her was because he was star struck. Whatever it was, every time they got together without the young presenter he took grave exception to her ignoring them, as though it was some sort of personal affront. Toney tried to remain good humoured about it, and gave Lars plenty of lip about it, but he never bit back. He always took it too seriously – Fleur was one of the only things he did take that way.

"Christ, she doesn't even remember the EMP," Toney said.

"I wish I didn't," said Jakob gloomily. Derren rolled her eyes at Toney. It was going to be one of those nights, then.

Of course, the EMP, or rather the aftermath, had been a horrifying, frightening event for all of them, as it had for every one of the relatively few people who'd survived it. It had been an ongoing spectacle of pain, starvation, violence, degradation and death that had lasted months, and then years. But they'd all come through it, and most had been able to put it out of their minds for years now. Some recover from trauma better than others, though, and Jakob was one of those who held onto the anger and pain it had caused him. Most of the time he was okay, sometimes even quite cheerful. But some nights he was maudlin and then, without warning, he would seethe and froth with fury – especially lately.

Lars, for all his generous humour and casual calmness – when he wasn't bitching about Fleur – sometimes fed Jakob's melancholy unwittingly. Derren tried to head him off at the pass.

"God, I remember it vividly," she said. "I was a young cadet journalist from California, on assignment in Denver. The minute it happened, I knew the world was fucked. Just like that. I knew it would be crazy to go back to LA, because the nukes at San Onofre and Diablo Canyon would turn it into a frypan. I said to myself, 'self, you've got to save yourself,' so that's what I did. I filled a backpack with food and water, grabbed a baseball bat from the sports reporters' office, and bolted. I ran downstairs, stole a bicycle, and pedalled my ass off for Cheyenne Mountain." She chuckled, as though she was talking about a drunken night out as a teenager. "Man, I had to smack some poor bastards on the head to get through. Everyone wanted that bike, but I wasn't giving it up. Lucky for me, when I got there most of the troops at Cheyenne Mountain were busy deserting, so there was plenty of room. Quite a few of us refugees turned up there; it was a real party for a while. And the soldiers and airmen that did stay, well, they looked after us. Still looking after us today, some of them," she said.

"Sounds like you did it tough, Derren," said Toney.

"Yeah I guess," said Derren, "but others did it tougher. I

was kind of lucky, I knew what I had to do, and I did it. And it made me the hard nut I am today." She laughed in a kind of hollow way, but everyone at the table knew what she meant. "If I had to do it all again, I would. What about you Toney?"

"Ah no," said Toney. "I was a fourteen-year-old girl at the time, and what I did to survive isn't the kind of conversation to have on a pleasant night in a bar. Even among friends."

"We all went through it," said Lars. "And now you've made it sound very juicy, you have to tell us."

"You first," Toney urged. Her dark fringe fell over her well-tanned face, and in the dim light they couldn't see that she was blushing. But Lars felt her difficulty, and he didn't push. Instead he launched into his own story.

"Mine isn't exactly bedtime reading either," he began. "We lived in Cherry Creek in Denver, next to the Country Club. Big house, Mexican maid, parents I never saw and who never really saw me. They dressed nice and went to a lot of parties, and my old man sold a lot of expensive real estate. I missed them even before they died. But then the EMP hit, and Carlita took off. Inside two days, things began to go pretty bad. Mom and Dad had no idea how to do anything, let alone survive in a place with no electricity, no plumbing, no drinks service or canapés. So on the third day, me and my old man watched my Mom put a .38 to her head and blow her brains out. He was supposed to take the gun off Mom, shoot me, and then do himself. We all knew he wouldn't do anything if he didn't see Mom die first. So he took the gun, but he didn't have the guts to kill me. He pointed the gun at me, gulped and said sorry, then put it into his own mouth and popped the back of his head off.

"Sorry old bastard, he left me there with the mess. A scared and skinny twelve-year-old, alone. I dragged their bodies out and buried them in the back yard, and for about a week I slept between the graves. I didn't want to go back in the house. But eventually it just got too goddamn cold, so I hosed their brains off the kitchen floor, cleaned up as much as I could, and moved back into my own bed. I ate dog food, cat food, cans of I don't know what. I got water – muddy, dirty, shitty water – from Cherry Creek, and I just sat there and waited to die. But I couldn't. I wanted to survive so bad.

"Then one day my salvation turned up. I was just sitting there watching the pool turn to green ice, wondering what it might be like to break through the ice so I could just lie on the bottom of it for a while, when this frizzle headed white-haired old dude walked into the yard. He was carrying a video camera – how it survived the EMP I don't know, but I suspect he had a faraday cage, the crafty old bastard – and he was going from house to house filming whatever he came across, and pilfering anything he thought was useful. I think he was as shocked to find me as I was to see him.

"He said, 'Can you carry a torch?' and I said, 'Of course.' He said, 'Excellent, you can come with me and we can do this at night-time too now.' And that was it, I went with him. We made a good team, Mike and me. He taught me how to forage properly, what was valuable and what, like money and jewels and stuff that I thought was worthwhile, was merely junk. He had a place in the foothills over White Ash way, and every day he trekked around documenting what had happened, and helping himself to whatever he needed. I wouldn't call it looting – nobody had any use for it any more. Pretty much everywhere we went was deserted, and there were plenty of gruesome reminders of what had gone on. Let's just say, my Mom and Dad weren't the only ones to check out the way they did, only most people didn't leave a skinny kid around to clean up the mess.

"He was more of a father to me than I'd ever had, old Mike, and he had a great nose for things that were interesting, useful or instructive. He made a comprehensive record of the aftermath of the EMP, and I helped him. I went from carrying a torch so he could video at night, to lighting things properly using equipment we'd found. 'Liberated,' he called it. But he wasn't infallible. One day he stepped on a rotten board in a rundown old shack – this was five years after the event – and cut his leg pretty bad. We didn't have any antibiotics or anything of course, so it got infected and he died."

Lars looked philosophical, the way he had all through his monologue. His eyes told a story of love and longing for the old man, but his face, as always, carried that studied nonchalance and equilibrium that made him such an easy man to be around.

"By then I was self-sufficient, and New Elysium was under construction, so I made my way down here and sold the stories we'd recorded to the TV station. I still don't know where Mike got that camera or the hard drives we filled, but he had a good line on them, and we never once ran out of disc space. Anyway the station gave me a job, so here we all are," he grinned. "And story-telling is thirsty work my friends, so here's the deal. Toney, you go get a round, and Jakob here will tell us his riveting tale."

Jakob quietly groaned, and drained his beer. He didn't look in the mood for talking, but he knew that when Lars had decided he was going to, resistance would be futile.

"So come on old feller, how did you survive and make it into this glorious new metropolis of ours?" Lars slapped him heartily on the back, and grinned at Derren, who grinned encouragingly back.

"My Dad was a prepper," said Jakob.

Lars looked delighted in a mischievous way, and he laughed out loud. "A prepper?" he echoed. "Ha, I never would have guessed. That's hilarious. A nutbag conspiracy theorist!"

"Yeah, I guess," said Jakob. "But it was no fun for me or my brother, growing up with that. Dad came home from Iraq in 2006, and he was kind of fucked up. He'd seen some shit, and I suppose done some other shit – he said we didn't want to know, and he was right. But he was convinced that Bush, and then Obama and the Clintons and everyone else, wouldn't be happy until they'd nuked somebody, anybody, and there was a list of candidates a mile long that kept growing. And that would mean the US getting nuked back, if we nuked the wrong people.

"So he bought a property out in Evergreen, and he started digging and he never stopped. For ten years he dug and he built and he collected stuff, and he built, and he dug some more. We had rooms and rooms full of water, food, fuel, batteries, weapons, ammo, everything you could possibly imagine. Five generators! And everything earthed, or shielded, or wrapped in tinfoil, because he was up with that shit about a nuclear explosion causing an EMP and he didn't want that to fuck everything up.

"We had seeds, a monster hydroponic set-up that grew everything you could want or need, freezers and refrigerators full of meat and vegetables, flat screen TV sets on the wall, I mean, it was a palace down there. So when the EMP hit, we just disappeared down our rabbit hole, and we didn't come up for months. We just bolted the doors, settled in to watch DVDs and eat dried foods, and pretended we were on some kind of weird holiday. Ben, my brother and me, we were going completely crazy, but my old man said no way, we are not going up until the last of our neighbours has run away, topped themselves, or died. 'I don't want to have to shoot anybody,' he said. I suppose he was right, but we hated him for it. We had no idea about how bad it was up here."

"Gee, sounds tough, man," said Toney, who had re-joined the group with fresh beers. "No wonder you're such a grumpy old bastard."

Jakob tried to smile, but it looked like a grimace. "Yeah, I guess I should be grateful, but I had such a shitty time growing up, I just never got over it. Do you know what it's like to have a dad who's crazy like that? Who runs around town spouting weird theories, stacks his pickup with giant economy bags of food and seeds and drives around telling folks they're all going to die? I got a lot of shit at school. I mean a lot. There was one kid, Errol Landers, I mean, that kid was an asshole. He never let up on me once. He called my old man a fruitbat, a crazo, a looper, a tinfoil hat wearing douchebag, a goocher, a bobo, a dumbass, a cracked out psycho – every nasty, crappy, hurtful name you could think of."

"All the things you were calling your old man, then," said Derren.

"Yeah but it's different when it's somebody else doing it," said Jakob defensively. He looked as if he was sorry he'd opened his mouth.

"Must have been rough when it turned out your old man was right," put in Toney, "and he saved your ass and kept you in luxury watching videos and chowing down on real food every night. I can see why you'd be fucked up about it." She'd always thought that Jakob was soft. She often found it hard to handle his wretched despondency, and now she was convinced she'd been right about him. He hadn't done it nearly as hard as any of them, but he seemed to be so much more affected.

"Great story, really great," said Lars. It was unconvincing, but they all knew that Jakob could be unduly sensitive at times, and he didn't want to risk a hissy fit. "So who wants to go back to my place and smoke some weed?"

"Ah, at last he begins to make sense," said Toney, throwing back the rest of her beer with relish. "Let's do it," she said before tossing out a gross burp.

"I'm in," said Derren, who demurely elected to leave most of her remaining beer.

"Jakob?" asked Lars.

"Nah, I think I'll stay here and have another beer or two, thanks," said Jakob. His shoulders were hunched and he was clasping his beer in both hands, staring at the amber fluid sightlessly.

"You look like you could use it, man," said Toney.

"More than the rest of us," agreed Derren.

"I'm good thanks," Jakob said in a tone that said he was not.

"Why the fuck not, man? Come join your workmates." Lars was trying to coax rather than command, but it wasn't working.

"Honestly, no," said Jakob. "I told Ellandra I wouldn't smoke anymore."

"You're kidding? You know she's your ex, right?" said Lars.

"Yeah I know. But if I stay off the pot, who knows?" Jakob replied

"Oh man," said Toney. "You're serious aren't you? You're deluded, she's done with you." This was not calculated to attenuate Jakob's now visible irritation, but she ploughed on, regardless. "Besides, you really seem like you could use it. You're looking kind of annoyed right now."

"Toney's right." This was Derren, trying to moderate and mediate, as was her way. "Doesn't Ellandra know you're a much nicer person when you're smoking? You get less irate, you take things much easier, you're even funny when you want to be – and that's even when you're straight. When you don't smoke, you think about everything way too much, you let little problems weigh you down, and it's difficult for your friends to get through to you." She meant well, and the friendly hand she laid on Jakob's shoulder felt warm through his shirt, but he shook his head.

"She doesn't see that," he said. "She sees the stoned me that's inattentive, messy, forgetful and distant. And she's right. And you're right too, and I appreciate it, but I have to try and do things her way for a while."

"I hope it's worth it, dude," said Lars. He finished off the dregs in his glass and slammed it onto the round table. "Come on ladies, I'm all yours," he said, putting his arms around them and ushering them toward the door. Jakob didn't look up. He sighed, lifted his glass, and took a long swig. When the glass was empty, he moved to the bar and ordered another.

Mickey's was quiet, dark and gloomy, just the way he liked it. The long timber bar was mostly deserted, with just one couple in deep conversation near him, and another lone drinker at the other end. The booths were empty, and now that his friends had gone so were the tall tables surrounded by bar stools.

Behind the bar, a bored young man sat writing in his journal. Normally he noted the antics of drunken patrons, planning one day to write a novel based on his experiences, and tonight he was documenting the desolate atmosphere and the desperate unhappiness of the lone drinkers. He'd been hoping that there would be more people out drinking, but even those who did go boozing on a Wednesday night usually hit it hard early and then went home to keep drinking, and probably smoke some dope.

Jakob planned to sit there and get just drunk enough to sleep the night through, without getting so drunk he'd have a hangover the next day. It takes good judgement and careful planning to carry off such a plan, but with several under his belt already, Jakob was already beyond that capability, and caring less about the possibility of a hangover with every drink. He wished he'd gone with his crew. He was dying for a smoke, and equally afraid of being alone with his dark thoughts. But he'd promised Ellandra – she hadn't asked him to, and even told him he didn't have to, he was a free man – that he wouldn't smoke any more. So here he was.

The young couple got up to leave, already intertwined and obviously heading for a place where they could get naked and completely tangled. The bar was deserted except for Jakob, the bartender, and the older fellow sitting at the other end drinking short scotches – who promptly moved over and sat on the stool next to him. Jakob groaned inwardly, sank his head onto his folded arms and reluctantly turned to his new drinking partner.

The man was about seventy, his face lined and hard, his hair a grizzly grey tangle. His hands, one of which was wrapped so tightly around his drink that he was almost white-knuckled, were marked with liver spots and scars. He ignored Jakob's pained look; he wanted to talk and the fact that his listener seemed unwilling to listen was of no interest to him.

"I heard your friend spouting off about the EMP. Twenty years coming up, eh?" he said. "Not an anniversary I'll be celebrating. After all, what have we done? We've tried to build another society just like the last one. What was the first thing we did? We found undamaged gadgets like video cameras and television sets, and recreated the media that misled us so poorly in the last days of the old world. We melted down all the gold and silver we could find to create money. Money, for fuck's sake! Although at least now it's tied to something physical, even if metal has no real value in itself except when you use it to build something."

"Fuck off," growled Jakob.

"You fuck off, if you want to," said the man. He grinned with a cruel, jovial insouciance. "I like to drink and talk, and I'm tired of trying to listen from all the way over there. If you want to drink here, you'll listen." Jakob wanted to drink, so he shut up and stared at the row of bottles behind the bar.

"We could have created a proper world," said the drunk. "A place without computers and people watching people all the time and greed and bullshit. Instead we chose to go right back and make the same mistakes. Why would we do that?"

Jakob looked into the man's watery, yellowing eyes and discovered an unlooked for intensity. He wasn't angry so much as involved, genuinely questioning the stupidity and futility of going backwards. And he was right. But that just irritated Jakob. He resented people being right just as much as he resented them for being wrong.

For the next hour, the older man raved on about how the founders of New Elysium could have built a society with a real connection to nature and to people, rather than simply a pale shadow of the old rat race. Every now and then, Jakob was forced to interject.

"Oh come on," he said with exasperation at one stage. "What we have now is no way like the old way. Crime is almost non-existent, people work together rather than against each other, the air is clean and poverty has been practically banished, it's a vast improvement on what we had."

"That's only because our population is so small," said the old man. "Any society that's in equilibrium will have a sense of harmony and community about it. It's when competition for resources and wealth heats up that it becomes the rabid dog it used to be. And because our new way is modelled on the old one, it'll inevitably go down the same path."

"It won't," said Jakob. "We're so much closer to nature. We grow our own food and we're connected to our environment. We work with our neighbours and we take care of each other. There's a real connection there, you're just being a cynical old fart."

"We're forced to cooperate with the halfwits that live around us, and we grow shitty crops that the majority votes for even though everyone of us thinks he could do a much better job if they just left us in charge," growled the old man. "It's not a society, it's a cluster-fuck."

Again, the man was right, but that didn't endear him to Jakob. He steadily downed beers until they became too much, then switched to neat gin. He knocked these back at a rather furious pace while the older man slurped loudly and often from his scotches, keeping up his lurching, mocking, disparaging rant. Eventually, Jakob got unsteadily to his feet and announced that he had had enough and was going home. The old man said that he, too, had had enough, and would walk Jakob out.

"For Christ's sake," said Jakob in an irritated voice, "can't you just let me go in peace?"

"Son, I have every right to walk down the street with you,"

said the old man. "Maybe you don't like me talking the truth to you, but it's a truth you need to hear. More important, it's a truth I need to get off my chest. So I'm going to follow you down the street and there's not a damn thing you can do about it."

Jakob stalked out into the biting night air, hunching into his overcoat and trying to ignore the old man shadowing him, annoyingly walking straighter and more energetically than he could. The chatter did not cease, echoing off the walls in the dark, deserted street, and pounding Jakob's ears relentlessly.

The old bastard's harangue veered bizarrely around; one moment it was inescapable that the old world would collapse because everything was so rotten and corrupt, the next it was a shame that civilisation had fallen, because people were so much better then than they are now.

"These new generations, they don't know what it is to be part of a wide world, to have a direction and common purpose. My generation, we were connected to each other. We cared about each other and we knew … so much. Everything was at our fingertips, and we could do anything we wanted to. We were ready to build a new world, and we tried. But then the century changed, and the world changed, and it hasn't stopped changing since then. And this new lot," he waved his hand to include everything around him, including Jakob. "They don't know what it is to build, only to imitate. This whole operation is a sham. A scam and a superficial joke. It'll never last."

At last, they were at the electro-bus stop. Jakob looked

cross-eyed at the timetable, which told him the next bus would be along in ten minutes. He was relieved that he would soon be rid of the old man. It was obnoxious when he didn't make sense, but it was repugnant when he did.

"Yeah, whatever old man," said Jakob pleasantly. "This is where I get off. Nice dreams."

The man grabbed Jakob by the shoulders and turned him so they were face to face. He prodded Jakob hard in the chest. "They think you're weak," he said.

"What?" asked Jakob, startled.

"Your friends, they think you're weak," the old man said. "A soft, whiny, self-absorbed punk. A drag. A downer. A sad, sorry little bitch."

"What would you know, you drunken old turd?" Jakob was ready to be offended but he tried to be offhand. Maybe the old guy was just drunk.

"Don't think I haven't seen you in there before," said the old man, and his eye glinted in the darkness. "You come in there with your friends, and they all put up with you because they think you're a pussy, but they'd be much happier if you weren't there. In fact," he prodded Jakob in the chest again, "I've seen them there without you, and they *are* much happier when you're not with them. Look at you. You agree to anything because you don't like to fight, then you get pissed with yourself so you turn all dark and moody, because you wish you had some spunk. Some kind of personality at all. But you don't, you're a sad jellyfish getting tossed around by the currents, getting sadder with every change of direction. You're fucking pathetic."

Jakob shoved the old man in the chest with both hands. "Back off man," he said.

"I don't have to do anything you say, you piss-ant," shouted the old man. "Run back home and cry yourself to sleep – that's what you usually do, isn't it?" He was holding his chest where Jakob had pushed him, but the younger man advanced again and pushed him again.

"I said back off."

"You honestly think that makes you look tough? Pushing an old man around?" said the old man. "I'm drunk and I'm ancient, but still I could beat you."

Jakob swung at the man's face; a wide, wild roundhouse that somehow connected. The soft, saggy flesh of his face gave way under the weight of the blow from Jakob's fist, and he staggered back. But immediately he stepped forward, shaping up into a loose limbed, broad-footed stance that looked ridiculous. Jakob was trying to look at his fist in the darkness. That punch had hurt. But the sight of the old man coming at him seemed to snap something inside of him. In a flash, Jakob was wading in, arms and fists flailing, beating the old man with a savagery that stunned them both, and overtook any sense of proportion or control that Jakob might have had, while at the same time robbing the old man of any ability to defend himself. The old man bent and cowered under him, but Jakob continued to pound his head, his ears, his face, the arms he had crossed in front of him for meagre protection. In just a few seconds, the old man went down completely, and Jakob stepped in immediately to kick and knee him. The man was groaning softly now, and Jakob was breathing heavily but saying nothing. The whole process had been remarkably quiet. There was blood on his hands and splattered all over his clothes, and still he kept on attacking. Even when the old man stopped making any sounds or movements, Jakob kept kicking and kicking, not even noticing that the old man was completely motionless. And then his energy stopped flowing. He looked down at the crumpled mess of clothing and flesh and bodily fluids beneath him, and with one last gasp of fury and hatred, he stomped his boot on the old man's darkened, bloodied face. He turned, staggering, down the street, wondering how he could get on the bus looking like that. He took a step forward, and a strong arm curled around under his armpit and around the back of his head from behind. He caught a glimpse of a White Hat, and knew he was in trouble.

4.

A familiar rumble and clank, the sound of the electric street-sweeper grinding its way down the street, woke Jakob. For a long moment, he didn't know who he was or where he was, he just lay looking blankly at the ceiling. But then he was properly awake, and looked at the clock ticking with rhythmic insistence on the bedside table. Already 7.00 am, and time to get moving if he was to be at work on time. And yet, he didn't move immediately. There was something odd going on, as though part of a dream was still intruding into his reality. He tried to remember what had happened the night before, but could recall only the location shoot in Colorado Springs and nothing more.

There was a shadow of a memory there, though. A phantom idea that something had happened, but he couldn't piece together what it was. He was drawn to check out his hands – they were fine. Strong hands, but soft perhaps, because his work was not, after all, manual labour. He got up and looked at himself in the mirror; he saw a man of reasonable looks, a few lines of care and gravity around his green eyes, but still the face of a young man with energy, good health and many years left. Some might even say he was handsome, and his eyes certainly had a penetrating quality. He smiled, and was pleased to see that there were one or two smile-lines present, though he was surprised at how smooth his skin was. He noticed that that persistent acne scar had at last disappeared, but otherwise his face was the same. Or was it? Did he look older? Younger? Different? Maybe, maybe not. It was too hard to tell. He stepped into the shower, uncertain and for some reason guilt-ridden. What had happened, and why did he feel bad?

Dressing for work, he found that the previous day's clothes were neatly folded on the chair near the bed, clean and pressed, it seemed. He had never, ever folded his clothes before bed before, but he must have done so last night. He couldn't remember, and it was weird, but there was no other explanation. He figured he must have been completely out of it, and wondered if he'd smoked any weed with anyone? It could have happened.

The electro-bus dropped him off at the studio at 8.15am, time for a coffee and to collect his thoughts. Everything still seemed a little hazy. The first person he saw was Lars, look-ing typically jaunty and unaffected by the previous night's depredations.

"Hey," he said, "how you doin'?"

"Yeah, fine I guess," was the answer.

"Man, you must have put away some serious booze the other night, to miss a whole day."

"What?" Jakob was confused and a little alarmed. "What do you mean, missed a day?"

"It's Friday, fruitloop. I'm guessing you were too hung over to come in yesterday. Or were you in the Tank?"

It was a fair question. If the White Hats – that is, the Military Council Security Service – found you asleep in public, or wandering around slobbering drunk or stoned, they'd take you to the Tank to let you sleep it off. In the morning, they would shower and feed their overnight guests, and send them on their way with a lecture on the health hazards of overdoing it. There was no arrest or misdemeanour or anything like that. Jakob had enjoyed their hospitality more than once, but he was fairly certain that had not been the case last night. Or the night before, for that matter.

"Nope," he said.

"Well, wherever you were, Derren is slightly pissed at you; I'd give her a wide berth today if I were you."

"Uh, yeah, sure, thanks man," said Jakob. Had he really slept the whole day and night away? It didn't make any sense. But then again, it would account for the fuzziness in his brain – he'd overslept and his head was still a muddle. He'd sort himself out soon enough.

Derren barged into the coffee room, a tablet in her hands and a concentrated frown on her face. "Oh, you're here," she said. "Lovely. Do us a favour, next time call us yourself rather than getting your brother to call. Or better yet, don't get too shitfaced to work the next day."

Jakob started to answer, but Derren was already moving on, consulting the running sheet on the tablet screen. "At least you didn't miss studio day, I suppose. We're taping in forty-five minutes; I expect you on camera one and ready to go for opener rehearsal in ten. Felicity is in makeup, and I have guests arriving in the green room. Lars, you set?"

"Aye, aye captain," said Lars.

Jakob quickly finished his coffee and scurried off to the studio floor to check the camera, clean the lens and do all the other little tasks that needed to be done before the recording light went on.

The show, to be aired the following Wednesday on the actual anniversary of the EMP, was all about the event that had created and defined New Elysium. The Colorado Springs report the team had recorded with Fleur a couple of days ago was just one part of the program, and among Felicity Fen's studio guests were Colonel Graves Martin, the head of the Military Council that still ruled the city in a temporary capacity; EMP historian Nellah France; the oldest survivor of the EMP; and, opportunely, Jakob's ex-wife Ellandra Mansoor, appearing in her capacity as Director of Public Health for the Military Council.

It would be a long, difficult day, and the live studio audience meant that there were few opportunities to go back and re-do things. Jakob had to focus on what he was doing, which meant forgetting about the odd thoughts ricocheting around in his head.

5.

Ellandra Mansoor was enjoying watching the television screen in the green room in the NETV studio. Normally she didn't care for Felicity Fen's weekly current affairs and talk show – it was just gossip and trivia, and in a place as small and isolated as New Elysium, the same faces and the same innocuous stories tended to cycle around and around. Otherwise Felicity would present stories cadged from media around the world, which Ellandra found trite and irrelevant.

Today was different, though, because the subject was the EMP anniversary, and much time and thought had obviously been put into the stories and the guests. Fleur's brief précis of the momentous events of that day, complete with powerful graphics and disturbing archival footage – much of it shot by Lars' protector, Mike – was merely the introduction, a sobering reminder of the terror, horror and devastation that the electromagnetic pulse had wrought on the previously snug, smug, secure part of the world they called home.

Ellandra had been 22 years of age on that terrible day, working deep inside the Cheyenne Mountain complex as a signals operator. When satellite, video and radio feeds from every part of the Western hemisphere had winked out as one, she had known that something awful was happening. It took a while to understand what that something was, and for news to start filtering in to the mostly undamaged NORAD network from other military installations that were similarly protected, or from parts of the globe that had been unaffected by the surge. The fact that almost every satellite above the hemisphere had been junked by the EMP had added considerable delay to the process.

When the reality had begun to set in, most of her colleagues had almost immediately deserted on the basis that there was no United States to defend at that point and because their families would need them. But Ellandra had stayed on. She believed it was her duty to stay in the facility, to keep doing her job as long as possible and to attend to the needs of the refugees who were already pouring in. Her natural empathy and her fiercely protective attitude toward the wounded, distraught and confused people arriving at the Mountain had led to her becoming a senior member of the refugee management team. Later, as things began to settle down and the focus shifted from pure survival to rebuilding, Ellandra continued her interest in ensuring the safety and wellbeing of the people she considered 'hers'. As her skills in the area had developed, her positive, determined management style had evolved, and eventually she had become the popular Director of Public Health in the new city-state.

On the screen, her boss, Colonel Graves Martin, head of the Military Council that ruled New Elysium, was sitting next to the historian, Nellah France, and facing Felicity. The interviewer was smiling broadly under a gaudy sign bearing her name, but the Colonel was doing all the charming.

"Felicity, we're a Military Council only in the sense that

most of us came from the military," he said, in response to Felicity's unexpectedly probing question about when 'democracy' would be restored in New Elysium. "The Council was formed shortly after the disaster of November 2017 because the former government had simply melted away. The state of Colorado had fragmented immediately, as did all of the other previously United States, as mayors, police commissioners and almost every other official disappeared, abdicated their responsibilities, or fell victim to the many calamities attendant on the main catastrophe. Only some pockets of the military remaining in Cheyenne Mountain and other defence bases in our region held together the necessary discipline, and even they were decimated by desertion. But those that remained at their posts eventually brought to bear their skills in medicine, engineering, construction, management and law enforcement, among other things, to start to rebuild our society. They became the Military Council."

"The Council designed the city and directed its construction, created the sense of harmony and civility that has made us so successful as a community, and instilled the security and discipline that keeps us on the right path. All that has taken us quite a while, and I admit my Council has been in power uncontested for a long time. But I believe we are nearing the time when I can at last take a rest, and allow a duly elected government to relieve my overworked, often under-recognised Councillors." He beamed broadly again, showing possibly the best set of teeth in New Elysium. Except, perhaps, for Felicity Fen's; she returned his smile with dazzling assurance.

"We have in the last decade or so, as you know, established road and rail trade routes through the only safe corridors available to us – south through New Mexico and to our north and north-west, traversing areas that were not permanently overwhelmed by radioactivity from the meltdowns of nuclear reactors. We've long been able to fly in medicines, foods and other necessities from places in the world that were not directly exposed to the EMP, and thus survived in much better shape than the United States..."

"That's right," cut in Felicity. "Sometimes we feel, as one of only ten viable communities in the entire continental United States, terribly isolated here in New Elysium. We forget that there are many, many countries that did not suffer the same dreadful fate as we did on that horrifying day."

"Well, of course, the loss of the United States did precipitate a global economic breakdown," said historian Nellah France, who had been looking for an opportunity to contribute to the conversation. "The US dollar disappeared, and a market of over three hundred and twenty million people evaporated overnight, so it was a truly world-changing event. Nonetheless, many other countries did escape relatively unscathed in the physical sense, and were thus able to rebound much more swiftly, with the majority of their populations intact. We, of course, suffered incalculable human loss – over ninety-nine percent of our population – as well as the contamination of over eighty percent of our lands. In this respect we fared so much worse than Canada, with only three nuclear power stations in its south-eastern corner, and Mexico with just the two reactors at Laguna Verde. Although the meltdown of those reactors did of course destroy Mexico City."

She paused, and Colonel Graves stepped into the breach.

"But to get back to what I was saying, Felicity," he smiled, "I feel, my Council feels, that our job is almost done. New Elysium is self-sufficient, thanks largely to the work of Major Tom Flynt in designing and building the city with its eminent survivability, and our burgeoning trade links certainly help us enjoy some of those luxuries we've all missed. Our community is harmonious, our energy is clean and renewable, and our future is bright."

"It has been a remarkable twenty years," said Felicity with a wistful lilt in her voice. Having been alive for just twenty-five years, too young to really remember the event itself, she tended to think of it in almost mythical terms. She had no practical concept of how the world had been before. But she found this no impediment in talking about it.

A production assistant came into the green room. "Three minutes please, Ms Mansoor, Doctor Hedley and Chief Berry. If you could follow me to the studio, that would be great."

6.

Seated on the chintzy lounge room set, with the single visitor's couch replaced by three white armchairs, Ellandra and her fellow guests faced Felicity and the studio audience. Jakob struggled to stick to the directions coming from the floor manager through his earpiece – resisting the urge to fill his viewfinder with the image of beautiful Ellandra. Despite the fact that she was six years older than him – and in the past couple of years the age difference had become more apparent – he still found her magnetically attractive. Her hair, a russet colour with lighter streaks, cropped short around her diamond shaped face, shone in the intense television lights. Her deep brown, intelligent eyes roved the scene slowly, taking in her co-panellists, the studio, and everything in between. She had always been perceptive, and the light smile on her face masked the intensity of her interest in what was going on around her. She looked briefly at Jakob, but instinctively knowing that to rest her gaze on him would appear to viewers as her boldly staring down the camera, she looked away just as quickly.

Felicity commanded his full attention as the commercial break ended, the red light on his camera lit up, and Jakob zoomed in on the host. Zeke, on camera two, would take care of the face shots of the guests as Felicity nominated them.

"Welcome back to *Felicity*," said the host warmly. Her plush, round face was encircled by a gorgeous cloud of soft, dark ringlets, offset sweetly by thick red lips that were constantly parted in a smile or a turned in a deliciously adolescent pout, and her grey eyes had that curious capacity to be both kind and cool at the same time.

"I'm pleased to be joined in the studio now by a panel of distinguished guests who are going to talk about some of the social aspects of the EMP event, and what it means for those of us living here today. Please welcome Captain Ellandra Mansoor, Director of Public Health in New Elysium, Doctor Malia Hedley, eminent psychologist and social commentator, and Captain Kieran Whitefeather, chief of the Military Council Security Service. Thank you all for coming." The 'applause' sign lit up, and the audience applauded as required.

"Let's get straight into one of the major challenges facing our community, substance abuse, and its relationship to the EMP event. I'll start with you, Captain Mansoor; does New Elysium have a drug problem?"

Looking her host directly in the eye, Ellandra smiled politely, but shook her head. "It's just Ellandra these days Felicity, I don't use my former military rank," she said pleasantly. "From a public health point of view, I'd say that New Elysium has what I'd call a troubling, but not intractable substance abuse issue. Of course, we don't like to see anyone impair their health in any way, and excessive consumption of anything, from sugar or salt, to alcohol or drugs, whether they are recreational or prescription, can have an adverse effect on the individual's wellbeing. It seems to me that, in terms of the substances being abused recreationally, the most destructive, prevalent problem is with alcohol. This is not new of course; it was the case long before the EMP. Abuse of alcohol can cause major health issues such as cancer, liver failure and various other diseases, and it can also incite violence, often of a domestic kind. That we have so few incidences of disease or alcohol-fuelled violence is, I think, a testament to the efficiency of our health services. Our most prevalent health problem is, as you know, Felicity, cancer, which is most often caused by the latent radioactivity in our environment," she added as an aside.

"The other substance of concern is marijuana, which is not nearly as damaging as alcohol, either in physical effects or in terms of the social issues that can arise from its use. It's easily available and quite popular, due mainly to the fact that a great many people grow it in their own greenhouses, and they can buy it very cheaply over the counter at their local grocery stores if they wish. That has been the case since before the EMP, of course, as marijuana use was legalised in Colorado several years before the event. And because it's so freely available, the black market for it is negligible, if it exists at all, and it doesn't generate any crime. So that makes it more of a health problem than a social one."

Felicity affected an interested, concerned look, pursing her lips to bring out the shallow dimples in her full cheeks. "And what about other drugs, Captain?"

"Please, call me Ellandra," said Ellandra. "Thankfully for us, the so-called hard drugs that plagued the country and the world at the time of the EMP – heroin, cocaine and amphetamine based drugs – are almost non-existent here in New Elysium. The precursor chemicals required to produce amphetamines such as ice and speed are practically impossible to procure, given the collapse of the pharmaceutical and chemical industries, and the difficulties of transporting heroin or cocaine across large distances and dangerous territories for such a small market mean that New Elysium is not on any of the large cartels' radar screens. Similarly, with so few pharmaceutical manufacturing facilities in New Elysium, even now, prescription drugs, which were something of a scourge in the old world in more ways than one, are not a serious problem. So in terms of public health, we're doing much better than some other places."

Turning to the chief of police, who was holding his white pith helmet as though it were a sleeping snake that he did not want to disturb, Felicity said, "Captain Whitefeather, do you agree with Captain Mansoor's appraisal?"

"Yes, yes I do, Felicity," said the captain. "As you know, the Military Council Security Service tolerates appropriately moderate marijuana use as well as alcohol consumption, and deal with intoxication by assisting the inebriates rather than processing them judicially. Our program, designed with Ms Mansoor's help, allows us to educate and, in some cases, rehabilitate habitual substance abusers. But there are, as Ms Mansoor says, virtually no other drugs available for recreational or personal use to speak of in New Elysium. Given that there is no private vehicle ownership, and strong welfare safety nets for those who cannot work, much of the danger and crime associated with overconsumption is alleviated, and our comprehensive surveillance network usually allows us to identify potential trouble before it develops into something uglier.

From a social management perspective, we have the situation well in hand. Every citizen in New Elysium knows that they are valuable and valued, and we don't like to lose anyone, physically or spiritually, if I may say so. We rarely do. Crime is not a minor problem here in New Elysium Felicity – it's non-existent. You know," he continued, "in the previous century a concept known as the 'broken window' theory was developed. This was based on the notion that signs of vandalism, such as broken windows at abandoned factories and so on, sent a kind of positive signal to antisocial types that a little petty crime, like smashing windows on empty buildings, was okay. This was believed to lead to the escalation of antisocial behaviour, as those permitted to get away with minor crimes moved on to larger and more damaging offences. By actively policing minor offences such as vandalism, fare evasion, loitering and so on, authorities would be able to create a norm in which only lawful behaviour would be seen as acceptable, and this would lead to a downturn in major crime.

Unfortunately, the 'broken windows' approach in reality led to the development of what some might call a police state, in which people at all levels of society felt intimidated and at times threatened by the forces that were supposed to protect them.

Here in New Elysium, we practice what we call 'clean windows' social management. That is, our White Hats help people rather than stand over them, and we talk first rather than issue orders and directions. We really are there to protect and to serve, and if necessary we will actually pitch in and clean the windows on our citizens' houses. The result is that not only are crimes such as vandalism frowned upon by every citizen, and therefore virtually unknown, we encourage and facilitate the involvement of every resident of New Elysium in keeping our city clean, well-ordered and crime-free. As a result, we really are crime-free."

"Thank you sir," said Felicity. "Doctor Hedley, if I can turn to you now, as the city's most eminent psychologist, do you think that New Elysium has a drug problem – or in fact an alcohol problem as it turns out – and what is to be done about it?"

Her gentle, dark square face set in an expression of gracious compassion, Malia Hedley blinked once or twice and laid her hands palms up in her lap. She looked first at Felicity, and then cast her eyes around the studio audience in motherly consideration.

"You have to understand, Felicity," she began, "that almost everyone alive in New Elysium today has endured a great deal of trauma. Certainly everyone over the age of, say, twenty-one, has seen and lived through some unspeakable occurrences. Many, sadly, have had to commit acts that they would never, ever have contemplated, or even imagined witnessing, in order to survive. Given the magnitude of the horror that they have seen, the fact that so many people choose to self-medicate is understandable. In fact, I would be surprised if the great majority didn't feel the need to engineer some sort of mental escape every now and then."

"Hmmm," hummed Felicity. "And what about the moral implications of that?"

"Well, my dear, you're young," said Doctor Hedley. "And perhaps you have a more rigid code of ethics than some of we older folks. But, again, given what so many of us have lived through, and the choices we've had to make merely to continue eating, or breathing, condemning certain behaviours, even if they are self-destructive to an extent, sometimes seems a little … high-handed to us. Morality becomes quite relative, even elastic, when your own life is in your hands, and it becomes easier to place such little things as getting high into a broader perspective. Although one isn't religious in any sense, it seems obvious that the primary basis for any moral code should be the one promoted by the Jesus fellow – do unto others as you would have them do unto you. Beyond that, everything else seems like petty rule-making for the purpose of control, no?"

Looking a little as though she had been betrayed by her guests, who she had hoped would give her some bad news and inflammatory statistics about the wanton behaviour of the citizens of New Elysium, Felicity tried to salvage controversy out of the interview. As it was, there was hardly anything to outrage anyone but the most puritanical of viewers, and the great majority of them had been dead for two decades.

"So the message to our younger viewers is, anything goes in New Elysium?"

Ellandra spoke up, but she wasn't defensive, just matter

of fact. "Oh no Felicity, not at all. It's just that we've learned, perhaps the hard way, that education is more effective in dealing with any number of social issues than prohibition. Our schools employ quite powerful educative strategies based on the potential mental and physical health impacts of substance abuse, rather than threaten our young people with the dire consequences of imprisonment. In addition, we have in place a range of programs and strategies that are designed to enhance the mental health and physical wellbeing of our citizens. I refer of course to the free daily exercise sessions undertaken every day in our many parks, our free swimming and aquarobics programs conducted in the ten large heated, undercover aquatic centres in New Elysium, subsidised workplace exercise, yoga and meditation facilities, and of course free counselling available twenty-four seven for all New Elysium residents. These are much more effective in turning people away from harmful substances than fear of arrest and detention."

"But what about-," began Felicity, but Captain Whitefeather broke in.

"I might add, Felicity," he said, "that thanks to programs like those described by Ms Mansoor, New Elysium is probably the most harmonious, crime free city in the world at present. Some of your viewers may be aware that, prior to the EMP, the United States had by a very wide margin the highest incarceration rates in the world at that time – more than seven times as many per head of population than places like Egypt, or our neighbour Canada. Now, we don't even have a prison here in New Elysium, we just don't need it."

"Thank you again, Captain," said Felicity, although she did not like being interrupted. "As I was about to say, what about the parents? Do we just let them get away with drunkenness and marijuana stupefaction? Isn't that a bad example to the children?"

"Actually I think you'll find it can be a compelling deterrent," said Malia Hedley. "Our kids see their parents self-medicating in this way, and occasionally losing control, getting sick, or suffering hangovers, and it turns them off the use of alcohol or drugs".

"We emphasise these negative aspects in our schools to help them evolve that interpretation," Ellandra added. "It doesn't work with everyone, but does anything?"

"And of course we don't just let people get away with anything," said Captain Whitefeather. "We just don't punish them for being unhappy enough to turn to intoxication. If we find them on the streets, we take them to the detox facility known as the Tank, let them sleep it off, feed and clean them up, and send them home. It keeps crime down, and spirits up."

Trying her very best not to appear too miffed, Felicity said, "Well, that all sounds very cosy, and with a little luck it just might work."

Ellandra tried a new tack. "You must understand, Felicity, that the people of New Elysium, we're all quite reserved and in a sense conservative. I think this is a legacy of the trauma we've all suffered – nobody wants to be the cause of any drama. So even when we do get drunk or stoned, we generally don't 'act out'. We get quietly, politely smashed, if I may put it that way, and we don't cause any trouble. That's why, in spite of the health problems that substance abuse does undoubtedly cause, there are few, if any, social problems around it. Ours is a private sorrow, I would say."

"And I would agree wholeheartedly," said Captain Whitefeather. "We forgive people for their excesses as long as those excesses remain personal and respectful. And on the rare occasions when people do 'act out', as Ms Mansoor says, we try and be lenient, supportive and accommodating rather than to criticise and punish them."

Felicity did not look convinced, but at least Ellandra's tone had mollified her somewhat. She smiled weakly and said, "I would like very much to continue on with this fascinating and important subject, but it seems we're out of time." Pursing her lips lightly again, and looking deeply into the camera, her cool grey eyes penetrating its very depths, Felicity said, "I'd like to thank my guests Captain Kieran Whitefeather, Doctor Malia Hedley and Director of Public Health Captain Ellandra Mansoor. After the break, we'll be joined by a business owner who is pioneering flights of live lobsters, shrimp and fish between New Elysium and Japan. Get ready to start enjoying fresh seafood again!"

The light on Jakob's camera went out, the floor manager stepped onto the set and started shooing the guests off their seats, and a couple of stage hands started bringing the guest couch back. As Ellandra stepped off the stage, Jakob intercepted her.

"Have dinner with me tonight?" he asked in a voice not quite pleading.

Ellandra kissed him lightly on the cheek and put her hands on his shoulders. "Is that a good idea Jakob? It usually seems to upset you."

"I think I need your help," he said.

"Oh?"

"Yes. I can't tell you now; we'll be back recording in three minutes. Please say you will?"

"Okay," she said. She usually gave in, tried to go easy on him and failed, and the evening ended up with him being sad. But he seemed to enjoy it in some perverse way, so she almost always agreed. She didn't have any plans, and she still regarded him as a friend. She just didn't want him to be her liability any more.

"Terrific," he grinned. "I'll see you at the Montana at eight?"

Ellandra nodded, and the floor manager's voice in Jakob's earpiece called him back to his camera. As Ellandra headed back to the green room to collect her things and have her makeup removed, he lunged after her awkwardly for a kiss, but missed. He went back to his camera unusually merry.

7.

The Montana was a quiet, dimly lit restaurant filled with tables for two. Early in their relationship Jakob had taken Ellandra there for a romantic dinner, and it had remained his favourite place to be with her, if not her favourite place for anything. He was already seated at the bar when she walked in, having his first beer for the day. She sat with him and ordered a mojito, and they made small talk about Felicity's show and the various guests who'd appeared on it.

"Twenty years," said Ellandra. "Such a long time and such a short time. So much has happened."

"We were together for about half of that time," said Jakob.

"Yes, I suppose we were," said Ellandra with a forced smile. "But we were both alone for about half of that time too."

"True. Did you know I've given up smoking weed?"

"Oh?"

"I've been trying to change Ella. To get better. For you." He smiled, but it looked like he was gritting his teeth.

"Jakob, you know I didn't ask you to do that. You're a free man, and you can do whatever you want, and if that includes smoking pot with Lars every night, just go ahead and do it."

"I want to be the man you married," said Jakob, trying to keep that pleading note out of his voice.

"That will never happen," she said firmly. "That person

doesn't exist anymore. Nor does the me that married you, if that makes any sense."

"I can be that man again."

"No, you can't. I appreciate the change you're trying to make, but it won't work. I watched you change once before, and I wouldn't care to do it again. Besides, it's not for me to say – the you that you are now might be a better man than ever, I don't know. All I know is that we won't ever be together again."

Jakob looked crestfallen, as always happened on these occasions. "It wasn't just you that changed, Jakob," Ellandra said. "It was both of us." She was being conciliatory, but he persisted in his pained look.

Just then, the waiter turned up and said, "Your table is ready Mr Petersson."

Ellandra stood up and said, "I don't think we need it, do we Jakob? I've said all I can say."

"No, please," said Jakob. "I really do need your help. I promise, no more talk about you and me."

Doubt written all over her face but kindness in her eyes, Ellandra nodded. The waiter headed towards a table and she followed. Jakob gulped down the rest of his beer and motioned for the barman to send another after him.

They perused the menu in extended silence, the only noise being the turning of pages and the sound of Jakob drinking his large beer rather quickly. At last Ellandra closed her menu, indicating that she was ready to order, and Jakob immediately closed his too. He'd been ready to order for some time. In fact, he always had the same thing.

The waiter appeared through the darkness, leaning attentively toward Ellandra. "The cream of potato and leek soup, followed by the roast chicken breast and sautéed vegetables, please," she said, handing him the menu.

"Buffalo wings to start, and then grilled sirloin, lean and rare with mashed potatoes," said Jakob. "And another beer thanks." He looked at Ellandra. "Shall I get a bottle of wine?"

She shook her head. "None for me thanks."

"Just a carafe of the house red then thanks," said Jakob. The waiter leaned across the table to pick up Jakob's menu, and as he walked away Jakob said, "I don't even know why I ordered that. I don't really feel like drinking."

"You always feel like drinking."

"But that's just the thing," he said earnestly. "Right now I don't. In fact, I feel really quite different."

"Jakob, if this is an attempt to convince me that you've changed, please don't bother." Ellandra was losing her patience.

"No, honestly, that's not it," he said. "Since I stopped smoking weed I've been having these incredibly vivid dreams. Lots of them kind of nightmares. But now I feel even more different than I have been feeling, and that's brand new. It's only today, to be honest."

She sighed and put her chin on her hands. "Really?" The tone was suspicion laced with sarcasm.

"No, seriously, and that's why I need your help."

"Oh?"

"Yeah. I think… I think I might have done something wrong."

Accustomed to these sorts of confessions, Ellandra did not change her expression.

"Oh," she said again, expecting some sort of declaration that he had not treated her as well as he might, or how he had not looked after himself as well as he should since they split because without her in his life he couldn't see the point. Or some other such tedious assertion.

"It's weird," he said, "and it doesn't make sense, and I don't have any evidence for it, but I think I might have committed a crime."

Suddenly Ellandra was attentive. Her eyes widened and she sat up straight, her gaze boring into him.

"What do you mean?" she asked sharply.

"Well, that's just it, I don't know," he replied. "It's like it's a dream, maybe one of my nightmares, but different. And I can't tell what it was I did or how I did it, but I get the feeling I hit someone, or broke something. I don't know." He put his head in his hands.

"Tell me!" she said with the kind of severity he rarely heard in her voice, even when she was exasperated with him. "What have you done?"

"That's just it, I don't know."

"Then how do you know you did anything?" she asked.

"Because it's like there's a shadow of a memory, or a dream. I can't get hold of it and if I think about it, it disappears. But there's a definite feeling that I did something, that just won't go away."

She relaxed and sat back, looking relieved. "So you didn't really do anything. It was just a dream, or a flashback or some other bullshit thing?"

"I can see why you'd think that," he said. "But there's something else. I lost twenty-four hours."

"What do you mean?" She was on full alert again.

"Just that. The last thing I remember is being in Mickey's on Wednesday night, and then I woke up this morning. I had no idea it was Friday."

"Oh Jesus," she breathed. "What have you done?" She closed her eyes, tried to take the emotion out of her voice. "Tell me everything you can remember," she said.

"Nothing," he said. "Just what I told you. I was in Mickey's on Wednesday night, and I got, okay I got drunk. Then I was in my bed and it was today. But when I woke up, I had a feeling my knuckles would be bruised and cut, but they weren't. And my clothes were clean and folded on a chair, and I couldn't understand how I would have done that. I was drinking gin," he added by way of explanation. "That's why I was hoping you'd help me. Maybe you could get hold of the surveillance footage from between Mickey's and the electro-bus stop on Grand Concourse West and Avenue I?"

"Shit!" she said. Just then the waiter brought the buffalo wings and the soup, so they were quiet for a moment. When he was gone, she looked at Jakob sadly, sorrowfully. "I don't think that will help," she said.

"Why not?" he asked, lifting a buffalo wing to his mouth.

"Because there are gaps in the surveillance."

"What do you mean?"

"I mean there are gaps in the surveillance. There just aren't enough people or even enough computing power to

71

record everything from every camera," she said, although even he could tell she was being slightly evasive. She looked down and picked up her spoon, stirred her soup but didn't eat any. "Sometimes they turn it off," she said softly.

"Why?" he asked.

"Jesus, Jakob!" she said. "This is not good. Not good at all! What have you done?" This last was said in a plaintive tone. But then the harshness returned. "I can't help you. There won't be any surveillance footage, and if there was, I couldn't get it for you. Just drop it."

He was stunned. She never acted this way. Even at their worst he had always had that sense that she wanted to help him, that she cared for him, that she felt sorry for him. Now she just seemed angry, and a little bit frightened. What was going on?

Ellandra stood up. "I have to go," she said. She looked at him, and that old mixture of sadness and pity had returned. "Oh Jakob," she said. "What have you done?" she repeated for the third time. "Don't answer that. Just forget it. Get on with your life, and I'll get on with mine. Don't contact me for a while, I can't look at you," she said. She started to walk out.

"Wait," he said, grabbing her arm. "If there are gaps in the surveillance, and you knew about it, why didn't you tell me?"

She looked at him with infinite sorrow. "Because people like you only behave if you think you're being watched, Jakob," she said, and then added, "and because I know the consequences of misbehaviour." She shook off his grip, and walked out of the restaurant.

Jakob sat for a moment, then reached for his beer, looked at it and put it down. He put some New Elysium dollars on the table, went straight home and sat in the dark, trying to figure out what was going on.

8.

The more he tried to grasp it, the more the memory – or was it the memory of a memory? – slipped away from him. He sat in the dark for most of the night trying to remember, or at least to work out a reasonable scenario, but all he got for his trouble was exhaustion and frustration. The facts were clear, and yet they were not. He had been at Mickey's bar and gotten drunk. He'd woken up not the next day but a full 36 hours later, with no recall, and an uneasy feeling that something had happened. There was no evidence to suggest that anything had happened, let alone what, how it had occurred, or what had happened after it. It was a complete phantom. Maybe a hallucination. Except for that missing time. And the fact that his clothes appeared to have been cleaned and folded, which was most unlike him.

Eventually he slept, but not for long or well, and was again awake early. He felt incredibly tired, but intensely wired, as though he'd had about ten coffees. It was like his brain was brand new, and was testing itself out, seeing what its limits were and pushing them. He went out to the greenhouse to work on his vegetables while it was still dark, to try and keep his mind off his mystery.

As early as he could without risking abuse and instant refusal of his request on the basis that he must be drunk,

Jakob called his brother. "Can we get together this afternoon?" he asked.

"Gee, I've got a lot on Jakob. Saturday is kids' sports day, you know? Lani has a game this morning, and Ben Junior has a big game this afternoon. I'm the coach, I can't miss it."

"Jesus, don't you get enough of coaching during the week?" Jakob had been prepared for some such excuse, but he was still surly.

"Bro, I coach at Clinton because it's my job. I coach Little Ben and his team on weekends because I want to. You can't ask me to do this." Ben was, for a man who believed strongly in discipline and self-respect – two qualities that Jakob often conspicuously lacked – remarkably tolerant of his younger brother's petulant tone and typically insistent demand that he drop everything and run to his aid.

"Tonight then?" asked Jakob. "I really need to talk to you. Something happened," he said.

Ben sighed. Something was always happening with Jakob. "Sure. I'll meet you at Mickey's at seven. *Don't* be trashed when I get there," he said, and hung up.

Jakob spent the rest of the day wondering what he would say to his brother, and sleeping. At five he got up and showered, dressed and caught an electro-bus to Mickey's, arriving around six. He ordered a beer and a subway sandwich, and sat watching the television screen blankly. He was alone in the bar, except for the barman, for the first thirty minutes or so, but then Saturday night drinkers started filtering in and the place became more lively. Barely noticing the crowd filling in around him, Jakob watched the screen, an ancient wildlife documentary showing the kinds of mammals that used to roam the United States, toyed with his beer, and slowly finished the fries that had come with his sandwich.

At seven, Jakob took the froth off his second beer, and waited. He was still less than half way through it when Ben arrived, bustling, at 7.25pm. "Sorry, Bro," he said as he enveloped his little brother in a bear hug, "been a long day, and the electro-bus was late." Ben was a big, solid, strong man; he would surely have played pro-football if the EMP hadn't come along when it did. "Beer?" he asked as he made a bee-line for the bar. Jakob looked at his half a pint, nodded, and quickly drank off the rest before Ben returned with two fresh ones.

He downed half the pint in one swig as soon as he sat down. "Fuck, that tastes good." He shook his head. "I didn't realise how much I needed that."

"Everything ok?" asked Jakob.

"Yeah, fine. Kind of," said Ben. "Just the usual – whining wife, bitching kids, shitty job." He tried to smile but it looked more like a grimace than a grin.

"Anything I can help with?'

"Not really, Bro, but thanks for asking." Ben had always been the tower of strength and fortress of silence in the family, but it looked as though some of his interior walls were beginning to crumble. His big, round face was tired and more lined than Jakob remembered it. His eyes, usually so full of life and fervour, looked dull and drained of colour.

"I just. You know, I thought – I really believed – that Little Ben loved his football," he said, referring to his son Ben

Junior. "But it turns out he only plays to make me happy."

"Bullshit," said Jakob. The game that his brother loved had always been the bond between Ben and his son, especially in the last couple of years since Little Ben, as everyone called him, had started playing. "He loves the game."

"He loves to watch, but he doesn't want to play," said Ben sadly. "At least, according to Kohl."

Kohl was Ben's wife, a beautiful, slim, athletic former sprinter with coal-dark hair and brilliant white teeth. If they'd met in high school they would have been high school sweethearts – as it was they'd met in the Cheyenne refugee camp a year after the EMP. Kohl's father was a prepper, like Ben and Jakob's dad, and, like Ben, her presumably stellar career in sports had been denied before it began. They'd instantly taken to each other, and the only surprise about their relationship was that they'd taken almost five years to produce Ben Junior, with Lani following two years later.

Ben had already finished his drink; Jakob finished his own in three gulps, and went to the bar for another. For the next hour and a half, Ben talked about his own troubles, and for a change Jakob listened. Ben Junior had not and, according to Kohl, would not tell his father that he didn't want to play ball. He would rather suffer and keep his old man happy. "Remember that, Jake?" he said. Ben was the only person in the world who called him Jake – at least, the only person in the world Jakob would let get away with it.

"Yeah I remember," said Jakob. "But we didn't have a choice, did we? If we didn't do things the old man's way, we ate shit." Their father had had a short, ugly temper, and it didn't pay to cross him at the best of times. Say the wrong thing at a particularly bad time, and the result was usually swift and violent.

"That's what worries me about Little Ben," said his brother. "What if he won't speak up because he can't? What if he's as scared of me as we were of the old man?"

"He can't be," said Jakob. "That's a flat fact. You're not the old man. He got broken in the war, man. He didn't know how to control himself. You're a high school coach – you keep a lid on your temper for a living!"

Ben laughed, but he shook his head. He was drinking more and faster than Jakob had ever seen him. And despite not having his usual appetite for booze, Jakob was keeping up.

"Surely Kohl's told Little Ben he doesn't have to play," said Jakob. "That all he has to do is tell you he doesn't want to, and you'll be okay with it."

"I don't know that she has," said Ben. "What's worse, I don't know if I would be. Christ, I wouldn't hit him or anything, I probably wouldn't even lose my shit. But what if it changes the way we are? Football is what we do together, man. Without that, I don't know."

And on it went. Ben grappled with his problems with his wife, his daughter Lani, who he did not understand even a little bit, and Little Ben, while Jakob listened and they both drank. It turned out that Ben wasn't happy with his job, and his marriage, while technically not in trouble, was a little cold, compounded by the fact that dealing with kids who were starting to feel their own personalities and search out their own identities was a lot tougher than he'd ever imagined.

"Shit, I'm sorry, Bro," Ben said after they'd spent a couple of hours in a huddle. "I came here to talk about your problems." He ran his hands through his hair and grinned sheepishly. "I didn't even know I was so fucked up about this stuff."

Jakob patted his older brother on the shoulder and raised his glass. "Bro, don't worry. It's made a pleasant change. Usually it's me that does all the talking – well, the bitching if I'm being honest – and it's kind of nice to sit here and drink and listen." They were both feeling the effects of the alcohol.

"Well, no more listening for you. I'll get us a couple of beers, and you can tell me what's on your mind." Ben was definitely on a roll – any other time he'd be claiming a need to be at home by now.

"You sure you don't want to catch up another time?" Jakob asked.

"Shit no. I'm enjoying this. And your crap can't be any worse than mine can it?" He grinned cheerily – maybe a little beerily – as he headed for the bar. Moments later he was back with a couple of beers, and a couple of shooters. "Might as well make a night of it. Those selfish fuckers can get along without me for the night," he said, knocking back his shooter. He watched as Jakob downed his shooter in one quick gulp, and said, "So what's going on?"

Jakob was getting quite drunk, although not as much as Ben, and his thoughts were becoming addled. But his lowered inhibitions meant that he was more inclined to give voice to his true feelings than if he were in better control of himself. For a moment, he didn't know where to start, then he blurted,

"I think I did something wrong," in a tone much more dramatic and impassioned than he'd used with Ellandra.

Ben guffawed a little, and then suppressed it. He'd heard this kind of start before. "Jesus, you're not talking about Errol Landers again are you?"

This was a reference to the kid who'd been chiefly responsible for bullying Jakob when they were at school together, the ringleader, mastermind and head torturer. Jakob had hated and feared Errol, but Errol had sought him out and tormented him at every opportunity. And there had been plenty of opportunities.

When the EMP had struck, Jakob's dad had locked the doors immediately, and announced that he would not be opening them for at least six months. When his boys protested – Jakob's mother was long gone from their lives by this time – his dad had said, "This is a game-changer, boys. An apocalypse, good and proper. Out there, people are dying. Pretty soon they'll be killing themselves and each other, and them that survive will have big problems. Winter will set in properly, and soon we'll be under snow. No-one can survive. Got to wait until the last one is dead, it's no good going out there and finding half-starved refugees – they'll be crazy, desperate and mean. When spring comes, we'll have a look outside and make a decision about what to do next."

His dad had refused to listen for radio signals, search for live television channels, or even switch on the cameras he'd set up outside. "Those cameras were exposed to the EMP, they're fried anyway," he reasoned. And as for seeking radio or television signals, he was brutally pragmatic. "Anyone that

81

can transmit will be looking for help. We can't afford to give it. We help one, we gotta help them all. That means sharing the misery, and then eventually dying with them anyway. You want that?" Ben and Jakob had shaken their heads, and retreated into their haven.

The three of them had lived in total isolation for seven long months, and in late May 2018, they had finally opened the doors. To Jakob's horror and disgust, they found the emaciated figure of Errol Landers living in a humpy just beyond the doors. How he'd survived that long was anybody's guess, but he was as near death as you can be without being a corpse. Frostbite had claimed most of his fingers and toes, his skin was almost crawling with sores and pustules that were weeping and suppurating, and his hair was a matted mess of straw clinging to a lollipop head on a withered, wasted skeleton with a distended belly. His dead eyes had sparkled briefly when he saw Ben, Jakob and their dad emerge from the shelter. Jakob's dad had handed him the shotgun he'd been carrying and said, "Put him out of his misery son."

Jakob had looked at the dying refugee with revulsion and loathing, and pulled the trigger slowly, looking Errol in the eye.

It was this experience that Ben was referring to when he mentioned Errol in the bar at Mickey's.

"No, it's got nothing to do with that," said Jakob with assurance. "Although in a funny way, I guess it does. Because although Errol has kind of haunted me for years and years, he doesn't any more. I can remember everything, but it's like those memories happened to someone else now. It's like I'm a camera, and the images are there on my hard drive but they don't affect me."

"Sounds to me like you're just getting old," said Ben. "And if it dulls those shitty memories, that's a good thing isn't it?"

"Well, yeah, it would be if it was just age, but it's not," said Jakob. "This hasn't crept up on me like age, it's come along and hit me like a truck. It's a new thing. I mean, really new. I didn't even realise it until you mentioned Errol just now, but since the thing happened, it's changed how I feel about everything."

"So what is this thing?" Ben was intrigued.

"That's just it – I don't know," said Jakob with deep frustration.

"Oh man, you are one fucked up individual," said Ben in a bemused tone, picking up his beer to have a long swallow.

"Yeah, thanks Ben, that's just the kind of help I need."

Ben put his glass down and looked at his brother, trying hard to appear sympathetic. The trouble was, he'd heard this kind of meaningless, self-absorbed drivel many times before. "Okay, Bro," he said. "It's cool. Just tell me what you know."

"You tell me what you know," said Jakob. "How did you know I wouldn't be at work on Thursday?"

"What are you talking about?"

"You called the station on Thursday and told them I wouldn't be in."

"No, I didn't."

"Yes, you did."

"Dude, I would know if I called and told your workplace you wouldn't be in. Who told you that I did?"

"Derren, my producer," said Jakob. Alarm bells were ringing in his head again.

"Did she say she spoke to me?" asked Ben.

"I didn't ask," admitted Jakob. "I'd assumed that you – or whoever it was pretending to be you, had just called the receptionist."

Ben furrowed his brow and took a long drink. "Bro, that is a mystery, it's true," he said. "So start at the beginning."

"There's not much to it," said Jakob. "On Wednesday a team of us went up to Colorado Springs for a shoot, and when we got back we came here to Mickey's. Lars and the girls went off to smoke some weed, I stayed here, and then I woke up and it was Friday. That's all I know."

"That's all you know?"

"Except that when I woke up, I was sure I'd done something wrong. Like something seriously wrong. Committed a crime. But I couldn't remember what it was, or where I'd done it, or how I got home, or anything else."

"That's weird," said Ben.

"Oh yeah. It gets weirder too – my clothes were all folded neatly, which I never do when I get that wasted, and for some reason I was sure I'd hurt my hands. Then later I find out that you've called the station to tell them I wouldn't be in, but now I find out that you didn't."

"You sure you weren't in the Tank?" asked Ben.

"Since when do the White Hats bring you home from the Tank while you're still asleep and put you to bed? And fold your clothes – after probably cleaning them?"

"Fuck man, what happened?"

"I don't know," said Jakob. "I asked Ellandra if she could get hold of the surveillance footage, and she went kind of strange about the whole thing, and told me to forget it."

"Forget it?" Ben was properly intrigued.

"Yeah." Jakob leaned closer to his brother. "She also told me that there are gaps in the surveillance."

"Gaps in the surveillance? Bullshit. Everything gets recorded. Everything."

"That's what they want you to think Ben. But it turns out, as long as you *think* you're being watched, that's as good as being watched."

Ben drank off the rest of his beer, stood up and went to the bar without a word. He looked troubled; so it was no surprise to Jakob that he returned with two more shooters along with fresh beers for both of them in his big, bear hands. They skolled the shooters immediately, without saying anything, and then started on their beers in further pensive silence.

Eventually Ben asked, "And Ellandra wouldn't help?"

"No, she kind of flipped out about it, then clammed up," said Jakob. "She was really serious about me forgetting it.".

They both fell silent again, each lost in their own thoughts. After a long time in which nothing was said, Ben hunched forward and spoke in a hoarse, conspiratorial whisper. "You know what we gotta do," he said.

"What?" Jakob was curious.

"We commit a crime, and we see what happens," said Ben with a wicked grin.

Jakob was shocked; this was an idea worthy of his own warped mind, but not one he expected from his staunch, stoic, conservative older brother.

"Are you fucking crazy?" he said. "That is the dumbest idea I ever…" He stopped mid-sentence and chuckled. "I get it, you're yanking my chain, aren't you," he said with a forced grin.

"Bro, I'm deadly serious," said Ben. His eyes were bleary now, and his speech slurred. He didn't have the same tolerance for booze that Jakob had.

"We can't do that," rasped Jakob, resorting to the same kind of hoarse whisper Ben had used to broach the idea.

"Why the fuck not?" asked Ben. He was getting bolshy now too. "What's the worst that can happen?"

"Dude, we could be arrested. It does happen you know."

"Bullshit. For a start, I'll do all the dirty work," he said with a wink, "while you watch what happens. The White Hats will probably pack me off to the Tank for a night to sleep it off, give me a plate of bacon and eggs in the morning, and send me home. No-one ever goes to jail in this town."

"You don't know that," hissed Jakob.

"I'm willing to bet on it," said Ben. He got up from his stool, standing unsteadily but resolutely with his hands on his hips. "Come on, let's do it man," he said.

"You're fucking crazy," said Jakob. "I won't let you."

"Dude," said Ben, "you can come and watch and see what happens, so you know, or you can stay here and never know. You said yourself, there are gaps in the surveillance, and Ellandra wouldn't help you get hold of it anyway. So the only way to know what happened to you the other night is to go out and commit a crime, and see what happens. If I finish up at home in bed with my clothes washed and folded, we'll know something's up. If I finish up getting a nice fresh breakfast in the Tank, we'll know that you're full of shit, you just slept for a day and a half and you can't admit you were that fucked up. Don't worry, I won't hurt anyone," he said reassuringly. He stomped heavily out of the bar, with Jakob trailing nervously behind.

9.

Out on the street, Ben strode purposefully, while Jakob tagged along nervously. It was evident that Ben was in a rebellious kind of mood, and ready to prove his own individuality to himself by doing something stupid. He was inundated by the demands of family life and his long-held, unchanging job, and he wanted to assert his self-identity. Jakob hoped to talk him out of it.

Ben stopped near a corner. Around them were houses and small, local shops that had been closed for hours. It was dark and the illumination from sparse streetlights was minimal, but it was easy enough to see the similarities, and the differences, between the closely packed semi-detached dwellings. They all shared a common design, each with a front yard no more than a metre or two wide, behind short brickwork fences with paving stone pathways down the centre of the block, the front door in the middle and two windows either side of it. But the bricks making up every house were different colours and textures. The windows were never quite the same size or depth as those next door. While the tiles on the roofs looked almost identical in the dim lamplight, they were really particoloured and laid in random patterns.

As with every block in New Elysium, there was a pair of shops or business premises that broke the monotony every twenty or thirty metres or so, with their wide windows facing directly onto the street, but these, too, were less than perfect matches thanks to the recycled materials from which they were all built.

Straight ahead of Ben, on the corner, a pylon loomed; a four metre tower with an array of cameras arranged around its girth so that every angle was covered twice – a double-helix of observation and examination. At the top of the pylon, the weak streetlight shed a small halo of light that the cameras did not need; they shot in infra-red as well as visible light.

Next to the camera pylon was a litter receptacle; a rectangular steel structure with four metal boxes lined up inside it, one each for organic waste and paper waste, one for glass and plastic, and a fourth for metal objects. Ben picked a couple of glass bottles out of the glass recycling bin, and threw them, one after the other, at the camera tree. Neither connected, but both smashed loudly on the road behind the pylon.

"Jesus!" cried Jakob. "What the fuck are you doing?"

"Ha ha, chill, Bro," said Ben drunkenly. "This is fun." He reached into the recycling bin again, hauled out two more bottles, and hurled them at the camera pylon. This time his aim was straighter, and both tore chunks of electronic equipment off the pylon. Shattered glass and chunks of plastic showered the road from the bottles and cameras. Ben laughed.

"Ben, just stop!" said Jakob. There was urgency in his voice, and alarm in his eyes.

"Dude, go hide somewhere and see what happens next,"

said Ben. He pulled the entire metal container out of the bin, staggered up the street with it, and heaved it through the plate glass window of a general store. The boom and chatter of splintering glass echoed down the quiet, dark street, creating a hideous racket that frightened Jakob even more. He jumped over a low fence and crouched behind it, fearfully watching his now rampaging brother as he returned to the trash basket and pulled out another container, this one full of rotten food and other organic matter. The lights in the shop went on, and the shop owner, pyjama-clad and dishevelled, came out of the door.

"Hey, what do you think you're doing?" he asked Ben, as the latter advanced toward the broken window and started pouring putrid waste all over the devastated display of foods and household goods. Ben, still holding the metal box, didn't answer the shopkeeper. Instead he turned slowly, almost serenely, and swiped the shopkeeper across the face with the corner of the box, making a heavy thud. The shopkeeper went down in a crumpled, insensible heap, and Ben threw the weapon through the broken shop window.

"Ben!" screamed Jakob, but it was too late. Electro-vans were converging from both ends of the street, and in seconds, as Jakob cowered behind the tiny fence less than twenty paces from the action, four White Hats leapt out, smothered Ben in a restraining smock, and shoved him into the back of one of the vehicles without a sound. An instant later, the vehicle holding Ben was off down the street, while the two White Hats from the second van attended to the wounded and bleeding shopkeeper. They helped him up and walked him inside the wreck and ruin that had been his shop, and Jakob took the opportunity to jump back over the little fence and scurry off down the street like a startled jackrabbit.

For the next three hours, he wandered aimlessly, wondering what might be happening to his brother, and how he would tell Kohl, his sister-in-law. Almost inadvertently, he found himself outside the wide grey expanse of the Tank, the New Elysium Justice and Police Service Centre. Tired, confused and concerned, he sat on a bench opposite the Centre, and awaited the dawn. He hoped that in an hour or two a well-fed, well-rested Ben would emerge from the Tank, and they could go home.

As the sun rose, to pass the time and keep his mind off what might be happening to his brother, Jakob watched the large group of local people, all wearing standard issue exercise gear, gather and line up in rigidly straight ranks in the park next to the Centre. In short order they were all bobbing, weaving and bouncing in rhythmically disciplined unison, to the barked instructions of the session leader. It occurred to Jakob that the whole scenario had more the appearance of a military parade ground than a local park, but then again he was probably just being overly judgemental.

By ten am, half an hour after six sorry and ragged looking individuals who had obviously been guests of the Tank for the night had shuffled out and proceeded down the street, blinking and shaking their heads, it was clear that Ben was not going to come out of the building. Unsure what to do next, Jakob caught an electro-bus home, and fell into an exhausted sleep.

10.

The jangling of the telephone pulled Jakob out of a deep but disturbed sleep. He had been dreaming that he was a newborn, trying to make sense of his world. It was as if his eyes had opened for the first time, and he was so brand new he couldn't even move, and then he realised he was strapped into the bed, only it wasn't a bed, it was more of an operating table. The noise of the phone came like an alarm in his dream, screaming with piercing urgency from one of the machines ranged around the table and startling the faceless white-coated people around him. Slowly the dream faded and he was lying on his own bed and the phone was ringing.

He lurched out of bed and answered it, his vision blurred and his voice thick. "Hello."

"Jakob. It's Kohl." Ben's wife sounded tense, but there seemed also to be a sense of relief that he was at home and answering the phone. "Thank god you're there. What happened last night?"

"He. I. Um, is he there with you?" Jakob asked.

"No, he's in hospital," said Kohl.

"In hospital?" Jakob was confused, and suddenly terrified. "What happened?"

"I was hoping you'd be able to tell me," said Kohl in a small, plaintive tone. He could almost picture her fine, narrow features drawn tight by stress and worry. "All I know is I got a call saying that Ben suffered from acute food poisoning, that he is in hospital, and they'll bring him home tomorrow."

Food poisoning? That made no sense at all. "Which hospital?" he asked.

"They wouldn't say," replied Kohl. "They said he can't have any visitors, but that he'll be fine. What happened?"

Jakob hesitated for a millisecond, then answered as evenly as he could. He didn't want to lie to Kohl, but how could he tell her the truth, that her husband had gone on a violent rampage, destroying a general store and seriously injuring the owner? If Ben wanted to tell her the truth, he could, but Jakob wasn't going to do it. Besides, this bogus food poisoning tale was a wrinkle that he didn't have time to work out right now.

"We had a few beers," he said, "probably a few too many, and then I left him at Mickey's. He, um, he said he was going to have a snack before he left, maybe he got a bad hot dog or something? You sure he's going to be alright?"

"As far as I know," Kohl said miserably. "Nothing else happened?"

"Why do you ask?" he said, suspicion colouring his question. "What have you heard?"

"Nothing," she said. "It's just not like him to do that. And it's definitely not like him to get sick. He can eat anything."

"He had a lot to drink, Kohl. I think he just needed some time out," said Jakob. "I think he counted on Ben Junior playing football more than he realised."

"Oh."

"Yeah, he's struggling because he doesn't know how to tell Little Ben that it's okay if he doesn't play football. In fact, he doesn't even know how he'll cope if Little Ben does stop playing. So try and go easy on him," said Jakob. "Just because he doesn't look stressed, doesn't mean he isn't. I think he's having kind of an anxious time right now."

"Oh," repeated Kohl, sounding a little dispirited. "Okay, thanks." She hesitated a moment. "You sure you're okay?"

"I'm fine," he said in as cheerful a voice as he could muster. "You know me, I can drink your old man under the table any day."

"Yeah, I suppose you can. Alright, sorry to have bothered you."

"No problems Kohl, any time. You take care."

"Yeah, you too Jakob, bye."

"Bye."

He hung up the phone and stared at the patch of carpet under his feet. Food poisoning? He'd been drunk, but his memory was clear. He'd watched Ben vandalise the shop and assault the owner, and the White Hats had taken him away. It had all happened so close to him he could still smell the garbage and the faint body odour of the White Hat closest to him. How had that become a case of food poisoning? He wondered if the White Hats had beaten Ben, or whether Ben had shown some resistance in the back of the van and been given a taste of his own medicine. But that didn't make sense, because if they'd injured Ben, the authorities wouldn't have concocted a story about food poisoning.

Not knowing what else to do, Jakob dressed and left the

house, taking an aimless stroll through the cold, regimented streets.

The weather was getting colder every day, it seemed, and flurries of snow were becoming more frequent. This kept a lot of people at home, apart from the surprisingly many who came out for the calisthenics sessions in their local parks, or who, on a Sunday like this, might walk to the local café for a cooked breakfast. It was a quiet, orderly and clean environment; nothing was out of place, there was no rubbish in the gutters, no graffiti on the public installations, and nothing that broke or became damaged was left that way for long.

Without intending to, Jakob found his steps taking him down the same street where Ben had gone wild the night before. The scene of the crime was spotlessly clean, as though nothing had happened there. The window was repaired, the waste and recycling bins back in their places and empty, the camera pylon undamaged and looking like every other camera pylon he had ever seen. The absolute normality of it all shocked Jakob, and frightened him nearly as much as the violence he'd witnessed the previous night.

He walked into the shop, which was open, to see if the shopkeeper was there. The pretext for walking in was to buy a bottle of water, so he made straight for the display fridge and picked up a bottle of Colorado Cool Spring Water. He noticed that the interior of the store smelled faintly of garbage.

He was almost afraid to face the shopkeeper, so he kept his eyes on the floor as he approached the counter, and only looked up at the last moment. He was both disturbed and relieved to look up at last and see that the man who'd been bashed with a metal bin only hours earlier. His head was swathed in a thick white bandage, his eye was swollen and black and he had a graze on his cheek that oozed a trace of blood. His lip was cut and puffed up, and his right hand was bandaged as well. He looked a mess, but for some reason Jakob felt much better in seeing him that way.

"Ouch, what happened to you?' said Jakob as casually as he could.

"Out of control electro-van smashed into the front of the store," said the shopkeeper. "Came around to collect the trash cans at the front, and ended up coming in through the window. Terrible mess, and I happened to be in the middle of it," he finished with a weak smile.

Jakob couldn't hide his perplexed expression. "So you didn't have any, ah, trouble?" he asked.

"What do you mean? Who are you?" said the man with a sharp edge of suspicion on his voice.

Jakob shrugged nonchalantly, but his eyes were nervously darting around the store. "Never mind," he said, laying down his money and picking up the bottle. "Keep the change."

"There is no trouble in New Elysium," said the shopkeeper. "And we aim to keep it that way." He leaned forward on the counter and stared hard at Jakob. "Who are you?" he repeated.

"Hey, forget it," said Jakob. "Just forget it." He hurried from the store and strode as quickly as he could down the street without breaking into a run, keeping his head down and avoiding getting too close to the camera pylons. He took the most direct route home.

11.

The rest of the day, Jakob was afraid to venture out of his house. He was upset and bewildered, and wondered seriously if he was losing his mind. Was it all hallucination? Was he seeing things that weren't there? Had his mind been invaded by the phantom memory of something he wasn't even sure had actually happened – something he couldn't describe or process, – and had it turned him into some sort of psycho? It seemed distressingly possible. And yet, there were some facts he could count on. He had definitely been there and seen what had happened when Ben went crazy outside the store. That the shop owner had seen fit to cover it up was odd and unnerving, but didn't change what had occurred. And he could see why the shop owner would do that; the urge to keep the peace, not to disturb the harmony and goodwill of the community was strong in every citizen of New Elysium. They all knew that happiness was a fragile and possibly fleeting feature of a short, volatile existence, and they would do almost anything to protect it, even if that meant ignoring certain aspects of their lives.

But how had Ben finished up in hospital? After his own mysterious event, real or imagined, he had woken up in his own bed at home. Maybe that was impossible in Ben's case – he did have a wife and kids at home. So the hospital story was a cover, then? But for what? And who was doing the covering up? It was all so maddeningly difficult to grasp, and he realised he was now making up weird conspiracy theories to fill in the gaping holes in his own knowledge.

The only thing for it would be to talk to Ben and get his side of it. That would at least provide some answers as to where the White Hats had taken him, what they had said and possibly done to him, and how the food poisoning story fitted in, if it did at all.

Late in the afternoon, exhausted by the constant conjecture and fantastic possibilities floating through his now completely addled mind, Jakob took himself off to Mickey's. There he sat in the darkness, staring sightlessly at the television and nursing a single beer that tasted awful and made him feel vaguely ill.

12.

Monday was a long, hard day. The crew was out driving around gathering stories and interviews for the following week's show, which was the usual agglomeration of local celebrities swapping vapid anecdotes with Fleur, visits to various shops for thinly disguised PR puff pieces masquerading as stories, and collecting stock shots of wide, clean, well-organised streets, spotlessly maintained parks, and sparkling new buildings to house the city's ever-growing bureaucracy.

Jakob found it difficult to concentrate all day, fixating as he was on what was going on with Ben, whether he had come home safely, or if some other mishap had waylaid him. Consequently, he was irritable, gruff and unduly hard on the equipment. More than once Derren had to tell him to chill out, and Lars even suggested a mid-afternoon joint, "Just to calm you down man, you seem stressed."

Unable to tell his team-mates anything, and trying to keep a lid on his anxiety and – he had to admit it – growing paranoia, Jakob spent the latter part of the day keeping up a falsely positive attitude, which only served to irritate him even further. He couldn't wait to get away from his work-mates, and even declined the offer of a drink at Mickey's when it was all over.

He caught the electro-bus straight home from the television station after having packed away his battered camera gear, and locked the door. He went straight to the telephone and called Ben. But Ben Junior answered.

"Hi Little Ben, it's Uncle Jakob," he said.

"Oh hey, Uncle J," replied the boy. His voice reeked of teenage apathy.

"Is your dad home, dude?" said Jakob.

"Ugh," Ben Junior grunted at the use of the word 'dude'; to his ears it was a relic of another time. He and his friends called each other 'flap', for some reason nobody could quite fathom. "Yeah sure, I'll get him," he said.

A moment later, Ben was on the phone. Jakob was apprehensive; would his brother be angry with him for getting him into that situation? Would he be unwilling to talk to Jakob lest the White Hats were listening in? Would he still be suffering from food poisoning and therefore unable to talk?

"Hey, Bro," came Ben's voice with its usual deep bass boom, sounding cheerful. "How you doin'?"

"Uh, yeah good thanks, Benno," said Jakob a little uncertainly. "How are you feeling?"

"Great," came the reply. "I could have gone to work today but Kohl insisted I stay home. So what the hell happened?" he asked. "Did you get sick too?"

"Um, no, I'm fine," said Jakob. "What do you remember?"

"Nothing much, to be honest, Bro. I seem to remember having a good long bitch to you, and taking down a couple of shots, but that's about it. I can't even remember what it was I ate that made me sick."

"You don't remember leaving Mickey's?" asked Jakob.

"Nope. But that's not surprising given that I was out cold at that point. They told me at the hospital that I'd collapsed in the bar after you left," Ben was matter of fact.

"You collapsed after I left?" Jakob was perturbed, even a little nervous. "Are you sure? They told you that?"

"Well, they said that I was alone in the bar," said Ben. "I gathered that you must have left. Shit Bro, we must've had a fair bit of booze," he laughed. "I'm still not sure it wasn't alcohol poisoning. I know you can handle it, but it's been years since I put away that much."

Jakob attempted a conspiratorial laugh. "Hah-hah-ha, you were pretty hammered. I was fine. I strolled to the bus stop and rode on home like it was nothing."

"Man, you are a machine!" laughed Ben. "Anyway, I better go, dude. Kohl's made a huge dinner, and I'm so hungry, I could eat a stuffed cat. It's like I've never eaten before."

Jakob let out another little cackle. "Okay Bro. I'm glad you're okay."

"You too, Bro, cheers."

Jakob was more confused than ever. His brother seemed to have no memory of the events of Saturday night at all. He sounded fine, happy – more so than he had just two nights ago. The deep, uneasy feeling that Jakob had been trying to suppress all day surfaced again.

Something was going on, and whatever it was, it was peculiar, even sinister, but like his own phantom memories, the truth was too hard to grasp. No idea or scenario that he could come up with fit what had happened in any meaningful way.

He sunk his head into his hands and massaged his temples with his thumbs.

Almost immediately he was jolted out of his despondent reverie by a loud knock at the door. He'd jumped out of his chair and was half way across the room and into the hallway before he even realised what was happening. He guessed – well, hoped actually – that it would be Lars, ever the dope fiend, not taking no for an answer and bringing some weed around. He had to admit, he was ready to accept it, too. His escalating paranoia, compounded by this maddening mystery that had now enveloped his brother as well, was getting too much.

He opened the door, sardonic grin at the ready, only to have it freeze into a grimace in an instant. There was a White Hat standing at the door. He was not actually wearing his white hat, but the shirt – sans tie – was unmistakable, as were the trousers and boots. An off-duty White Hat. His face was round and his fading, dark-brown hair tousled and a little bit curled, and his rosy cheeks were highlighted by the broad smile that played on his plump red lips. He was about the same size as Jakob, but his frenetic energy, which almost enveloped Jakob himself, made him seem much bigger. Even before he was in it, he filled the room.

"Jakob, is it?" he said jovially, pushing his hand out and gripping Jakob's firmly. Jakob just stood looking at him, vaguely aware that his frozen countenance and frightened eyes possibly made him appear a trifle suspect. He looked at the White Hat's hand as he shook it back, not quite as vigorously.

"Dave," said the White Hat. "Dave Bellville. Your new next door neighbour."

"Huh?" said Jakob.

Dave winked and subtly but indisputably pushed his way into the house, bringing a six-pack of beers out from under his left arm and presenting them to Jakob. "It's the accent," he said with a sunny grin. "Bloody Australian mate. Half the time you Yanks don't know what language I'm speakin', but rest assured, it's the King's English. Beer?"

Jakob stood aside to let Dave into the house, accepting the six-pack and following him into the lounge room. As he entered the room, Dave stopped and turned around, reaching for one of the beers in the six-pack and wrenching it out, twisting the top off it in one swift motion, and putting the neck to his mouth. He swallowed at it greedily. Jakob felt a little sick. As if he'd been doing it all his life, Dave strolled over to the couch and sat down, making himself look and feel at home in less time than it took for Jakob to cross the room and head toward the kitchen.

"Grab yourself one, put the rest in the fridge, and come sit down mate," said Dave in his affable, broad-vowelled accent. Jakob did as he was told as slowly as he could without seeming to dawdle unnecessarily. His mind was struggling to catch up with events, and his heart was still pounding wildly, as it had done the moment he'd caught sight of the uniform. It didn't matter that Dave was clearly off-duty and at least partially out of uniform, nor that he was so outwardly friendly. Jakob still suspected that his business wasn't all about beer and chatting.

As he turned away from the fridge, beer in hand as instructed, Jakob put on as friendly a smile as he could with such short notice and in such circumstances. He knew he had to make a good impression on Dave, but wasn't really feeling up to the task.

Luckily, Dave didn't seem to notice. He was irrepressibly bright and upbeat, and his manner was calculated to put Jakob at ease. This worked after a while, but it was a shaky start – Jakob got the impression that Dave knew much more about him than he let on, and his conversation seemed designed to let Jakob know this, and to probe for further details. But at the same time, he was disarmingly friendly, funny, self-effacing and apparently honest, so it was hard not to like him.

"So I'm your new neighbour, Jake," began Dave, repeating his prior declaration, as if to reinforce the permanence of their association. "I moved in yesterday – I'm surprised you didn't hear me. I came by for a beer about sunset but you weren't here. I was spewin' because I'd been flat out all day and I was tonguing for a bloody beer. Where were ya, ya mug?" he asked in a playful, mock distressed tone. "Just hanging out at Mickey's, with your brother or something?"

The reference to Ben was alarming, as was the mention of Mickey's. Jakob was sure it was a none-too-subtle ploy to let him know that Dave was across his movements and habits. How much did his new neighbour know, really? He had to play it cool.

"Just a quiet drink last night, yep. I had a few drinks with my brother on Saturday night, and you know, he has a family, so we don't get together often."

"Oh, he does, does he?" said Dave absently as he pulled on his beer. "Lucky bugger, having a shag on tap like that."

Jakob looked at him dumbly; Dave giggled and said, "Mate I'm sorry, I can't help it. It's a nervous habit when I meet new people. I suddenly become more of an Aussie than Crocodile fuckin' Dundee, not that you'd know who he is. I yabber on like a fuckin' idiot and I know it, and half the time you poor bastards can't understand me. I can't shake it. You won't hold it against me will ya?" His delivery was rapid, his words indistinct and unfamiliar in any case; Jakob wasn't sure what he was saying.

Jakob shook his head. "No, I guess not," he said. He could feel Dave's eyes on him all the time, and he was not really comfortable with the Australian's loud, bumptious persona, but he also found himself warming to him. Anyone that much a caricature couldn't be all that threatening, could they?

"So what happened to Leon and Sam?" Jakob asked. They were the young couple who'd lived next door to him for the last two years, since he'd been assigned his place in the semi-detached row.

"Who? I dunno mate, no idea. I moved into old Edgar's place, on your right. You thinking of the other side?"

"Ah, yes I guess I was," said Jakob. "I just naturally assumed Sam and Leon would have been the ones to move on. They've been talking about starting a family so I assumed they'd been assigned a bigger place."

"Nup. Edgar's not terribly well," said Dave in a suddenly serious voice. "Got the C. Still a lot of nasty shit floating around in the air around here, you know how it is."

Jakob did indeed know how it was. Although their home was in what they thought of as a clean corridor, the New Elysiumites were still subject to radioactive particles being swept in, usually from the east, on odd breezes and other weather events. It was an ongoing hazard.

"That's a shame," he said.

"Yeah, it is," agreed Dave.

"But on the other hand, it gets me out of the bloody high-rise I've been living in in the centre of town for the last five years. And it gets you a fun-loving new neighbour – me!" Dave leaned over and shoved his near-empty beer at Jakob, who took the hint and clinked his own bottle against it.

Although it had been Jakob's intention not to drink at all that night, Dave insisted that they have at least one more, then one more, and then they started on Jakob's supply. Most of the time Dave talked and Jakob listened, although he asked a few polite questions, and found himself answering a few questions as well.

"So I gather you're in TV, Jake?" said Dave, several beers into the conversation.

"Um, yeah," replied Jakob. Dave seemed to know a lot about him. "How did you know?"

"Don't fret mate," said Dave. "And don't tell anybody, 'cause I'll get in all sorts of trouble, but I had a quick look through the system when they assigned me my new place, to see who my neighbours would be. Sorry, mate, but I just couldn't help it. Glad I did, too, really. Imagine if I'd rocked up to Helga's on the other side of my place with a six-pack?

Jesus, I'd be lucky to get out of there alive." He laughed a hearty, sincere sounding laugh, and Jakob joined him. Helga did have a reputation as something of a man-eater. The entire block was made up of housing for singles and young couples, and she'd seduced most of the men, and some of the women. He was relieved to hear that Dave was driven by mere human curiosity rather than official business, too, so there was some relief in his laugh.

"So ... television eh?" prompted Dave. "Pretty cool."

"Well I suppose," said Jakob. "But it's not as glamorous as you're probably thinking. I'm just a camera operator."

"Just a camera operator?" repeated Dave theatrically. "Only the most important bloke in the game. If you don't get it right, the whole thing's fucked, eh?"

"It's not that difficult," said Jakob. "A trained monkey could do it."

"But a trained monkey doesn't do it, you do. Don't ever sell yourself short, Jake. You're an important man."

Jakob was humbled and embarrassed by the White Hat's obvious amity and consideration. He could tell Dave wasn't just putting it on, that he truly did feel that way.

"I'm just a nobody," he said.

"Bullshit!" said Dave, suddenly sitting upright, then leaning forward to look pointedly at his host. "You know what? Technically, society can get along without you. You disappear, society stays here and rambles along, and nobody's any the wiser. But without the unimportant Jakobs of the world, where exactly is society, Jake? In the shithole. You may not be important, but you're essential. Don't ever forget that."

Jakob said, "Uh huh," in bemused agreement, and he had the feeling that Dave was trying to tell him something, but he didn't know what.

"If something happened and you disappeared, Jake," said Dave in a brotherly, slightly alcohol affected tone, "that would be terrible for society. Because Sam and Leon next door, and Helga, and that punk kid behind the bar at Mickey's, and your workmates at the TV station, and your brother Ben, and a whole lot of people you never think about, they need a Jakob in their lives. They expect a Jakob to be there, and if a Jakob's not there, then there's a big motherfuckin' Jakob-sized hole there and they want to know why. It becomes problematic and distressing for them, especially if you disappear under some sort of dark circumstances. They start to ask questions, and they start to examine their own place in society, and it all starts to come apart. You see?"

Jakob nodded, but he didn't see anything at all. He vaguely wondered whether Dave was speaking English.

"But don't ever let that fool you into thinking you can do whatever you want, Jake," said Dave. He waved a finger in Jakob's face. "Because you can't. Everyone is replaceable, no-one is indispensable."

"I'm not sure I follow you Dave," said Jakob.

Dave straightened up in his seat, shook his bushy head, and appeared to check himself. "You're right," he said. "It makes no sense. Forget I said it. How about another beer?"

When Jakob returned with the beers, they talked about Dave's childhood in Australia, about the family he hadn't seen in two decades, and about his decision to stay in Colorado after the EMP.

"I was a young private on exchange from the Australian army back in '17, learning some deep dark Yankee secrets at Cheyenne Mountain. By the time I was able to get out of here, I'd decided I wanted to stay and help you lot build a new society. Not every day a bloke gets to do that, eh?"

"No, I guess not," agreed Jakob. "So how old were you then?"

"Twenty, mate," said Dave in the gravest tone Jakob had yet heard him use. "Twenty in twenty-seventeen. Who'da thought those'd be the numbers that ended up ruling me life?" he mused, almost to himself. He shook his head and chuckled. "Shit Jake, don't ever steal me credit card mate, I think I've just given ya me fuckin' pin number."

Jakob laughed, and swigged on his beer. It was getting harder and harder not to like the Australian.

"But I really believe in what we're building here," Dave went on. "Oh, shit, it's not perfect. It's a bit too regimented and pre-arranged for my liking – and this from a bloke who spent his life in the fuckin' military – it's too clean and predictable, although there are parts of it that are hidden and downright fuckin' shady. But what I love about this place is the idea. The belief that you can build a civilisation that's actually civilised, where people respect and get along with each other, that's founded on real principles – sustainability, cooperation, humanity. Of course," he interrupted himself, "we're a bloody long way away from that. Oh, we've got some mighty hurdles to jump before that's the case. But we're willing to have a crack, and that's something we should all admire. Don't ya reckon?"

Jakob was too drunk to follow Dave's thread well enough to unravel its meaning. He didn't even know if there was a meaning, or if Dave was just spinning out drunk-talk. He grunted and nodded.

"You know, you're alright Jake," said Dave. He was being genuine. "I hope nothing happens to you. You could go on this way for a bloody long time."

"Um, thanks Dave," said Jakob, creasing his mouth into a smile that furrowed his brow. "You're alright too," he said, and waved his beer at his new friend. They clinked again.

Dave quickly skolled the rest of his drink, and abruptly stood up. He held out his hand and said, "I really ought to be going, mate. I've taken up enough of your valuable time, and drank way too much of your precious amber fluid. It was a pleasure to meet you, and I hope I see more of ya." As Jakob shook his hand, Dave said, "In a social, not a professional sense, of course," and winked.

After Dave had gone and the place was quiet again, Jakob tried to determine if there was some hidden meaning in his visit and his conversation, and if there was, to decipher it. But his mind was clouded with alcohol, and he was tired, and nothing that he could come up with made any sense. He told himself he just needed to move on and forget about the weirdness of the last few days. Dave's arrival probably wasn't connected to the business with Ben, or his own mysterious loss of a day and a half, he told himself; it was all just a massive coincidence. So he could just forget the whole thing.

And if Dave's arrival *was* connected with those unsettling events, then all the more reason to forget it, because it meant that he was definitely on some sort of official radar. Either way, he needed to keep his head down and stop asking questions, even of himself. Just go to work, hang out at Mickey's, and try not to be such a downer on his workmates and family. That was his resolution, and would be his new mantra.

13.

It didn't work. He discovered that the power of positive thinking wanes after about an hour and a half of intense concentration, and descended slowly into a maelstrom of depression
and unhappiness. He didn't sleep well, so he was too tired
to get up in the mornings. While he was reluctantly making
breakfast, he would have an unshakeable feeling of dread –
a physical feeling as well as a psychological one, manifested
by a knot in his stomach and a tightness in his chest, as if
his whole body was tensed up, waiting for a blow that never
came. At the same time, his mind kept saying to him, over
and over again, "oh fuck, oh fuck, oh fuck," or, for variety's
sake "fuck this, fuck this, fuck this." It pushed out other more
reasonable thoughts, and made him grimmer and more tired.
By the time he arrived at the station each day he was already
shattered and in no mood for talking, let alone ready for the
kind of inane banter that Lars used to get himself through
the day, or Toney's sarcasm-laced solicitousness.

"You okay there, Jakob?" she'd say. "Or should I get you
a chair? Perhaps a cup of soup and a blanket for your legs?
Smiling is way too much work, right?" It didn't help his mood,
and at times he wanted to throttle her, even though she was
right; he was being a pain in the ass, making the job more
difficult for everyone and bringing them all down.

Strangely, though, being at work was the best thing for him. He had to step outside of himself to work, and when he did, the fear in his guts subsided and he spent less time awaiting that imminent blow, so he was more able to deal with people and problems. Some days, he was positively cheerful by the time he got home, more tolerant and more tolerable. His workmates, particularly Derren, who was endlessly patient with him, and Lars, who spent a lot of time trying, mostly with limited or no success, to lift him out of his funk, really were helpful. But he rarely told them that. He was too tired, too broken down and insular to acknowledge what they were doing for him.

The problem was that he couldn't rid himself of the idea that he had done something wrong. He still didn't know what it was – had no idea at all really – yet he was sure he had done it, and that he would have to pay for it sometime or other. His dreams were vague and unsettling, and he could never remember any details from them anyway, only the anxiety and foreboding that they induced. But he was sure that if he could read them he would learn just what it was he had done.

It didn't help, either, that he continually ran into Dave. The White Hat seemed always to be between shifts, looking casually chilled and chirpily fit and healthy, always enquiring after Jakob's wellbeing, and maddeningly oblique about the source of his curiosity. One of the most tiresome, grating and in many ways terrorising things about Dave was that whenever he spotted Jakob – and he was an expert at doing so, always just happening to be where Jakob was – he always said, "G'day Jake, keeping out of trouble?"

Jakob hated being called Jake, and the pointed nature of the question always seemed to have a purpose that he couldn't divine. At one stage, when they were having some of their many drinks together – Dave would never take no for an answer – Jakob asked why he always greeted him the same way. Dave explained that it was just an old Australian expression, and Jakob shouldn't take it seriously, but Jakob couldn't buy it. It just happened far too often, far too jovially, far too carelessly for it to be just a funny habit.

Then there was the fact that Dave wanted to know in detail everything that Jakob had done, everywhere he had been and everyone he had talked to during his working day, or since they had last seen each other. He was so friendly, so genuinely interested that Jakob couldn't be sure that it was professional interest, and yet he couldn't convince himself that it was not. The fact that Dave talked a lot about himself, and where he had been and what he had done during the day – a White Hat's life was surprisingly boring, and his anecdotes involved a lot of driving around, helping people find various parks, picking up stray bits of litter, and spending quite a lot of unexplained time at the Energy Directorate – helped to persuade Jakob that Dave was just naturally curious, and not taking any real notice of the answers. But he could never be sure.

So, life went on. There were of course bright spots. Several weeks after the incident with Ben, Kohl called Jakob one evening and invited him over for dinner on the following weekend. She must have detected the surprise in Jakob's voice – although they had always been on friendly terms, she had never invited him over for dinner before – because Kohl felt obliged to explain the invitation.

"Well, it's Christmas next week, and we really want to celebrate with you, but also because I just wanted to thank you," she said brightly. Christmas? How had that escaped him? He'd been so wrapped up in his insular world of un-happiness that he hadn't even noticed the profusion of dec-orations, the explosion of coloured lights and the unusually festive mood that pervaded the city.

"I don't know what you said to Ben that night you went out together," Kohl continued, "but whatever it was, it worked. He's been like a different man. He's much more understand-ing of Little Ben's decision not to play football, he spends a lot more time listening to us and talking to us. It's been wonderful."

"I'm sure it wasn't anything I said," offered Jakob humbly.

"Well it sure wasn't the food poisoning," said Kohl with a laugh. Jakob laughed too. But after he'd hung up the phone, he wondered what had wrought the change in his brother. It was vaguely conceivable that Jakob's ability to simply listen and offer a few token words of advice had had some sort of cathartic effect on his brother. But it was more probable that he'd gained an insight into Jakob's sad existence and realised just what a treasure he had in his family. Then again, it was quite possibly something else, which actually was related to the mysterious food poisoning. He just could not imagine what it was.

Unfortunately, as much as he looked forward to the din-ner, the call stirred up the issue of what had happened that night again, and for the next few days Jakob slept even more fitfully than usual, and was grouchier than usual at work. So much so that on the Friday night at the end of their working week, Lars and Derren would not allow him to slink off home without a Friday night drink. They staged what they called "an intervention."

"You're not getting out of it Jakob," said Lars imperiously. "It's Friday night a week before Christmas and you're coming to Mickey's to have a couple gallons of beer, then you're coming to my place to smoke some weed."

Derren put her hands on her hips and nodded, lips pursed, while Toney kept her arms folded and said nothing, but looked, for her, quite sympathetic. Fleur had, of course, disappeared immediately they'd finished their last assignment for the day. Jakob relented, and they went to Mickey's and had a raucous good time. He appreciated his friends' effort to pull him out of his slump, and he made a genuine effort to lift himself. He didn't talk about what was troubling him, and nobody asked anyway. Nobody brought up any topics of even the remotest seriousness all night, which was a blessing. Except of course when Lars predictably ranted about Fleur not joining them, which gave his three companions an opportunity to mercilessly bait him, making rude humour out of his infatuation. Jakob joined in, and found lampooning his friend regarding his ludicrous crush on the young girl distinctly liberating. He discovered that it was okay to mock emotions rather than give into them, or treat them as seriously as he had lately. At least, as long as those emotions belonged to somebody else.

The only dark spot was when, soon after they'd arrived, Jakob went to the bar to buy a round and found, almost inevitably, Dave enjoying a beer.

"G'day Jake, keeping out of trouble?" Jakob refused to take the bait. He grinned and winked at the garrulous Australian.

"Not tonight, Dave. It's Friday night!"

Dave chuckled and raised his glass to him. "Good on ya mate, that's the spirit," he said. "But don't overdo it eh? Hate to have to haul you away."

"No chance," said Jakob, surprised at his resilience to what he would normally have seen as a veiled threat.

"I'll be looking out for you, Dave," he said as he turned to walk back to the table he was sharing with his workmates, four brews in hand.

Later, Jakob and Lars walked the short distance to Lars' place, without Derren and Toney, and sat down to smoke some weed as Lars had prescribed. Jakob only had a few tokes, because it had been quite a few weeks since he'd smoked, but he was gratified to find that almost instantly that floating, buzzing sense of calm and carelessness coursed through his veins and settled him deeper into his chair. Relief flooded through him, and it felt warm and welcome. The light seemed to have dimmed just a little, sounds were softer, and trouble was far, far away. He and Lars joked and talked shit, to the point where more than once each was carrying on a different conversation to the other, but it didn't matter. Lars ordered a pizza, and they ate greedily and messily, guzzling more beer as they did so. Jakob escaped himself more truly than he had for weeks, or even longer.

He stumbled home, drunk, stoned and happy, sometime after midnight, weaving in dancelike abandon down the streets, lost in his own inner music and immune to the cold, taking care only to act as straight and sober as possible on the electro-bus. Most of the other passengers, and there were quite a few of them, were in a similar state, and as long as he behaved he would be left alone. When at last he arrived home he was startled but not surprised to see Dave, rugged up against the chill, sitting on his tiny porch with a beer in his hand.

"Night cap, mate?" he called out as Jakob approached.

"I think I'm done, thanks Dave," said Jakob woozily. He stepped onto Dave's porch and held out his hand, a broad silly grin on his cold-ruddied face. "But Merry Christmas, mate!"

Dave shook his hand and cackled. "Mate, you're rat-faced. Look at them eyes, like piss-holes in the snow. Fuckin' good onya!" he said, cheerily and sincerely. "You better take yourself off to bed before ya face plant."

Jakob saluted his neighbour, said, "Roger that", then toddled off merrily to his own front door. He was face down on his bed within a couple of minutes, and had the deepest, most rewarding sleep he'd had in ages. He woke up with a dry mouth and a mildly throbbing head, but the fear, the muted alarm that had dogged him for weeks was gone.

He dressed and went out to the co-op garden henhouse to collect a couple of eggs for breakfast, passing several of his neighbours along the way and greeting them cheerily.

Then he stopped in his own greenhouse to pick some herbs, nipped down to the bakery for a loaf of bread and some fresh milk, and retired to his kitchen, whistling as he put together his breakfast feast.

He spent the morning in his greenhouse, tending his tomatoes, cucumbers, lettuce and various other vegetables. It occurred to him that he could reinstate his dope crop if he had some seeds handy. He'd torn out and burned all his plants when he'd decided that he was going to give up, as a means of removing temptation. But it probably wouldn't hurt to have a couple of plants growing, just so he wouldn't have to beg Lars for a few buds every time he lapsed. He made a mental note to ask Lars for some seeds next time he saw him.

14.

Dinner that night started out well, even pleasantly surprising. When Jakob arrived, he was shocked to find Ellandra there.

"I hope neither of you mind," said Kohl. "But we hadn't seen either of you for so long, and I figured it's a good opportunity for the two of you to get together too. You're still friends, right?"

Ellandra had smiled warmly and said yes, she was fine with it. She even showed how friendly they were by kissing Jakob on the cheek, which he accepted happily, and reciprocated.

"I'm always pleased to see Ellandra," he said. His good humour had not deserted him all day, and although he was worried that Ellandra wasn't so thrilled to see him, he was excited to see her. She looked placidly beautiful as always, and he was determined to be a good guest. He really believed that he could get through a whole evening without falling into a slough.

The first part of the party went according to plan. The kids had been sent off to their part of the house, and the adults settled in the living room with champagne cocktails – Kohl's favourites – and canapés. The talk was all about Christmas and holidays and what Ben and Kohl were getting for the kids, and it was bubbly and flowing, without any awkward silences or any of Jakob's usual faux pas.

They moved on to a delicious dinner, a huge roast pork with all the trimmings, loads of vegetables and buckets of excellent wine, and more general chit-chat that was as enjoyable as it was inconsequential. They talked about local celebrities and public figures, plans for new communal facilities and amenities, and of course the kids, the kids, and the kids. It was only natural that Kohl and Ben would rave about their children, and neither Ellandra nor Jakob thought it insensitive that they did so, in spite of their own situation. So the whole meal went off in almost exuberant spirit. If he'd been asked, Jakob would probably have described himself as charming, and he was certain that he and Ellandra were getting on as well as they had for ages. Foolishly, he allowed this unexpected warmth to kindle a spark of hope that they might see more of each other.

Kohl stood up and began clearing away the dishes; Ben jumped up to help her. They left Ellandra and Jakob alone for a few minutes, and for the first time that night the conversation faltered. Jakob did not know what to say. His mind was at once blank and swirling with things he shouldn't say. Ellandra politely waited for him to say something, anything, but when it was obvious he was unable to form a coherent sentence, she said, "So how have you been?"

"Oh, okay," he replied, relieved that she had taken the burden of starting a discussion. "And you?"

"You know me," she said. "Very busy. Lots of winter public health issues, logistical problems, the usual. I guess you're on the downhill run to Christmas?"

"Yes," he nodded. "We're on our last few days of work. The show is on a break right now. Felicity is having her well-earned rest, and the crew is just shooting a few stories for news, and putting together a few items for next year. Are you doing anything over the holidays?"

"Just a few days off," Ellandra replied. "Although if we can get out, I may spend a day or two in the mountains with Tom Flynt."

"Tom Flynt?" he heard himself echoing. "The mountains?" He'd heard the rumours that there was an unofficial resort for important government people in the mountains. But Jakob was more focused on the name she had tossed into the statement with such insouciance.

"Surely you've heard that there is a small facility for government employees up near the old Cheyenne Mountain site," said Ellandra.

"Yes, yes of course," replied Jakob. "I'm sure it's lovely." He didn't want his façade to crumble as quickly or as completely as his happiness. "And you're going with Tom Flynt?" he asked in as disinterested a tone as he could under the circumstances, although of course the name had shocked him. It had been only a week or so since he'd been in Flynt's office, admiring his smirky confidence and envying his colossal achievement, and now he found that the man with everything was also likely in a relationship with his ex-wife.

"He's just a colleague." Ellandra was cool, and looked directly into Jakob's eyes as she said it, almost daring him to contest her coolness. He couldn't hold her gaze, and he felt the blood rushing to his face. He didn't know what to say.

Just at that moment Ben walked back into the room, sized up the situation accurately, and took action to avert real trouble.

"Jake," he said, making his brother jump almost out of his skin. "Come into the games room, Bro, and we'll have a cold brew to wash down the dinner."

Jakob couldn't get out of his chair fast enough. The two went into Ben's man cave, adorned with old photographs of him in his playing days, several of his old trophies, which he had insisted be stored in the survival unit, and various other bits of memorabilia including flags and trophies from the high school team he was coaching. There was a short timber bar, and Jakob took a seat on a stool while Ben grabbed a couple of beers from the fridge. He stayed behind the bar, standing, and leaned on it facing his brother.

"That looked a bit tense," he said.

"Ah, it's all good," replied Jakob. "Just that awkward moment when I find out my ex is dating someone else." He was trying to make light of it.

"Bummer," said Ben. "Still, you're not, um, fucked up about it are you?'

Jakob affected an unsuccessful toss of the head. "Shit no. We're done," he said.

"Sure you are." The facetiousness was written all over Ben's face as well as dripping off his tone.

"Honestly, I wouldn't give it another thought," said Jakob. "She can do whatever she wants. With whoever she wants."

"I'll take your word for it."

Desperate to change the subject, Jakob seized on the first

topic that came to mind – the one that was never far from the surface.

"So, that night you got food poisoning, you don't remember anything?" he said.

"Nope," said Ben. "I remember having a long talk with you about my problems. I remember having more beer than I've had in a long, long time. And I remember throwing a few unnecessary shots on top of all that. It's no wonder I was sick."

"So you don't remember the shop?"

"What shop?"

"We went to a closed shop and you, ah, opened it up," said Jakob cautiously.

"What do you mean?" Ben was nonplussed. "You told Kohl you'd left me in the bar. The people at the hospital told me that too. Nobody mentioned any shops."

"Listen, Ben," said Jakob in deadly seriousness. "I told you I thought I'd done something wrong, but I didn't know what it was. I told you that I'd lost almost thirty-six hours, and had woken up in my own bed, but I didn't know how I got there or where I'd been. You were that drunk, you decided that you'd go out and commit a crime, so I could watch and see how you were dealt with by the White Hats."

Ben's expression had veered from curiosity to concern to alarm as Jakob spoke. He obviously thought his brother was becoming unhinged.

"Dude, what the fuck are you talking about?" he said.

"I'm talking about you going berserk, smashing up a camera tree, and throwing a recycling can through a shop window and assaulting the owner," Jakob said. He was deadly earnest, and Ben could see it. But he shook his head.

"Well, that's just nuts," he said. "If I'd done that I'd be in jail right now. And so would you."

"I was hiding in somebody's garden," said Jakob. "I saw the White Hats take you away."

"Bullshit man," Ben replied. "It never happened. You must have been totally shitfaced to dream that up.

"I'm telling you it's the truth," said Jakob. "You disappeared for thirty-six hours, the same way I did. Only, because you've got a wife and kids, they couldn't just bring you home and drop you in bed. They had to do something else. So they made up that shit about you having food poisoning."

Ben was looking at Jakob with pity and sorrow. "Man, you are fucked up. That is some seriously paranoid shit. You need to see someone." He walked out from behind the bar, and headed back toward the dining room. "Come on, we're going to have a talk with Ellandra – maybe she can put you in touch with someone."

"Please, please don't say anything," pleaded Jakob, practically running after his big brother.

Ben stopped and turned around. "You're telling me I committed one of the worst – no probably *the* worst – crime this city has seen in twenty years, and that instead of being arrested, I was put in hospital with food poisoning? That makes no sense at all, Bro. It's scary how screwed up it is. And Ellandra can help you with it."

"No, please, I've already talked to her about it, and she made me promise to drop it. She'll be really pissed if you bring it up, and it will just make things worse between us. Give me a break Bro. Besides, she's going on Christmas holidays with some guy from her office. Can't we just let her have her break in peace?"

"Yeah, I don't know," said Ben. "Let's just play it by ear. But if I hear you start up with that crazy stuff again, I'm telling her the whole lot."

"Believe me, she knows," said Jakob.

They walked into the dining room, and immediately sensed that something had changed. Ellandra was sitting rigid in her chair, her jaw clenched, her eyes wide and dark, boring holes into Jakob as he entered the room.

"Kohl is just telling me you had food poisoning," she said icily, her gaze never leaving Jakob's face as she spoke.

"Oh yeah, it was nothing really," said Ben. "I'm over it now."

Ellandra continued to stare at Jakob. "And you were involved?" she asked.

He gulped – literally gulped and directed his gaze to the floor, intimidated by Ellandra's look – and nodded slowly.

Abruptly, Ellandra looked at her wristwatch, and stood up. "I really must be going," she said. A forced smile bent her mouth and without showing her straight white teeth, although from the shape of her jawline it was easy to see they were still clenched. "Thank you so much Kohl and Ben, it's been lovely. Jakob, you'll walk me out." It was not a request.

Quickly putting down the half-full beer he'd carried in from the games room, and making hurried goodbyes to his brother and Kohl, Jakob followed the rapidly striding Ellandra out the door, looking back to shrug before exiting the house.

Fifty rapid paces down the road, Ellandra halted her steely march and turned on Jakob.

"What the fuck is wrong with you?" she exploded. She didn't wait for an answer. "I told you to drop it, but you couldn't, could you? You had to involve your brother. And now…" her voice trailed off, and she put her face in her hands. "Oh Jesus," she said.

"What?" said Jakob, panicking.

"You've got no idea what you've done, have you?" she said. "You fucking could not leave it alone, and now you've done … this."

"What? What have I done?" he demanded.

"Just shut up Jakob. Shut the fuck up. And listen to me. You've caused more than enough damage. I don't know what went wrong with your programming, but you are one broken and fucked up individual. You need to stop this now. Go back to smoking dope. Drink yourself into a coma every night. I don't care. But for Christ's sake, drop this mad crusade of yours."

"What crusade? What are you talking about?" There was an edge of terror in his voice. Ellandra obviously knew something, but she wasn't sharing her knowledge, and that made it even more terrifying.

"You know. You know exactly what I'm talking about. Just drop it. Drop it!" she said. "And don't speak to me. Don't call me, don't come by my house. If you see me on the street, don't even wave to me. I won't wave back. You're a dangerous, stupid man, and if you don't watch yourself, you'll cause more trouble. Fuck!" she said again. "Just walk away. Walk away now." Turning on her heel, she walked away at a furious pace.

Jakob was near tears. He watched his ex-wife marching purposefully away from him, her head held erect and her back ramrod straight, and rubbed his eyes hard. Her words had struck a powerful fear into his heart. She obviously knew that the food poisoning story was a sham, that there was something much deeper going on, but whatever it was, she wasn't going to tell him. Whatever it was, it scared her and angered her beyond any emotion he'd ever seen from her, and that frightened him more than anything else. After all they had both seen, that this thing, whatever it was, should elicit such base horror and fury in her, meant that it was something truly awful in the fullest sense of the word – inspiring awe and extreme trepidation at the same time.

He walked home a cowed and beaten man. To the weight of his fear was added the burden of knowing that there was much more to this – including his ignorance about what he had done, what had happened to Ben, and how he could make it better. That Dave wasn't sitting on his tiny porch waiting for him when he got home was a massive relief. He let himself into his house as quietly as he could, undressed in the dark, and got into bed certain he wouldn't sleep. As it was, he drifted off soon after, emotionally exhausted. His dreams were confused, and when he awoke as bright sunlight flooded the room, shattering his fractured sleep, all he could think was to check his knuckles. Why weren't they damaged and hurting?

He spent the day in bed, on the couch, briefly in the kitchen fixing barely edible snacks, and then back in bed. Morose, tortured, deeply depressed and weighed down by an unnamed fear, he could hardly gather his thoughts, let alone deal with them. At one stage he gazed at his reflection in the mirror in the bathroom for a long time, not knowing who this man was and wondering why his life was so hard, until tears filled his dark eyes.

15.

He was tired and irritable again the next day at work. Perhaps even more so. The terror that Ellandra's reaction had caused in him had not abated, and her maddening refusal to explain what was really going on, what had made her so incredibly heated about it, ate at his mind. But he was also just plain tired, feeling more depressed than he had in a very long time. In the few moments when he wasn't obsessing about Ellandra and the connected mysteries of his own lost time and Ben's, he was wishing that he had a fat joint in front of him right there and then.

He wondered if having that little smoke with Lars on Friday had sparked a whole new episode of dependence in him, and quickly decided that it had. He knew that if he had a smoke that night it would make him feel much better about the shit-storm that had become his life, just as he knew that the little bit he had imbibed three nights earlier was probably behind the unexpected depth of his despair. It was in fact debatable which had a greater hold on him at that moment – the terror inspired in him by Ellandra, or the wretchedness of a cannabis-induced serotonin deficiency.

"Jakob, for god's sake pay attention." Derren's unusually pointed direction snapped him out of his melancholy funk. "It's Christmas, and this story on the year's most popular toys won't be on the news tonight if we don't get it shot in the next hour." Almost instantly she had reverted to her usual patient explanation, and the way she looked at Jakob told him she was more worried about him than pissed off. "Just a few more days and then you'll have six days off," she said. "Please help us out here."

"Sorry," he muttered. "Just a bit tired."

"Sure," said Derren. "Let's just do it and then we can all move on."

Lars and Toney were watching quietly, while the journalist fronting the story, who wasn't used to working with the Felicity Show team, looked confused. Why were they pampering this gloomy nerd? Lars sidled up to Jakob and said, "I've got a bag in my pocket. Make it through today and it's yours."

The idea that there was a smoke waiting for him at the end of the day abruptly and unaccountably brightened Jakob's mood. He was able to push aside the gnawing dread that had dogged him all day, and had a sudden surge of energy. The sooner they got all this done, the sooner he could sit and have a quiet spliff, and make his troubles go away. Or if not go away, at least become sufficiently muted that they wouldn't occupy all of his time, energy and strength. He found a really nice angle, framed up the journalist before the city's only large department store, and they recorded the story about a new range of electric motor skateboards that had been imported from Japan just in time for the Christmas sale without further interruption.

Through the day they put a number of stories in the can,

to be shown on the news over the following days, as well as a couple of items for the return of the Felicity Show. At long last the day was over, and Jakob was in the underground car park with Lars, next to the outside broadcast van.

"I'm guessing you enjoyed Friday night then," said Lars with a little jeer as he handed over a small plastic bag of bulbous marijuana heads.

"Hah, yeah I guess I did," replied Jakob. "I've got some shit going on, and it kind of helps," he continued.

Lars nodded vigorously. "We've all got shit going on JP," he said, using the nickname only he ever applied, and which Jakob hated almost as much as Jake.

Jakob arched his eyebrows. "You too?"

"This whole town is fucked up man," he said. "We all need something. Except of course for Fleur," he added bitterly.

"Ah," said Jakob. "Not spending any time with her over the break?"

"She's already on holidays dude," said Lars. "She just walked away without looking back, so I never even had a chance to ask her out. I think she's going up to the snow with some government big-knob."

"I feel your pain," Jakob said. "Ellandra's going up there too."

"Okay for some I suppose," said Lars. "Should we go and have a beer at Mickey's?"

Jakob hesitated, but agreed to a quick beer. All day he had been anxious to get home and smoke some of the green gold he had just put in his pocket. He could practically taste its sweetness rolling down his throat and filling his lungs, could feel the buzz it would send into his overworked, under-nourished brain. But now that he was sure it would happen, and well aware that having had a couple of brews beforehand would make it that much sweeter, he was actually happy to put it off for an hour or so. Besides, it looked as though Lars could use a friend, and some juvenile conversation about his crush on Fleur would be diverting, so the hour would pass easily.

The two walked up the ramp into the chilly evening, snow flurries swirling up and down the tidy, straight-lined streets and around the few people out collecting groceries, nipping into cafes and bars for an evening tipple, or just hurrying home from work. Jakob felt as good as he had for a couple of days.

They sat in Mickey's, and as expected Lars did most of the talking. He tried to disguise his infatuation with Fleur by feigning concern at her choice of companion for the Christmas holidays, but it was obvious he was just upset that she had a companion at all.

"I don't trust the guy," he said repeatedly. "Fleur is such an innocent child in so many ways. Sure she's a journalist and she's intelligent and asks questions and sees the world on that cynical journo tilt. But really, she has no experience in relationships. And this guy, this Garvin Wintz, he's just out for what he can get. He's much older than she is, and too smooth to be true. Just a sleaze, if you ask me."

"You're a lot older than Fleur too," said Jakob.

"But I'm different," said Lars. "I look out for her. I want to protect her and keep her safe from sleazeballs like Wintz.

With me it's more like a fatherly thing."

Jakob almost spat his mouthful of beer all over the table, but he managed to contain the explosion of laughter that erupted within him. He swallowed hard and peered at Lars in the semi-darkness of the bar, trying to determine whether there was even a hint of irony in what he'd said. There was none. He was about to call Lars' bluff, to denounce his 'fatherly' concern as thinly veiled lust for a woman much younger than he, but something stopped him; a thought that this interesting quirk in Lars' thinking might be useful to him.

"You ought to keep an eye on this Wintz fellow," he said with as much gravity as he could. "It's possible he doesn't have Fleur's best interests at heart, the way you do," he said.

"Not much I can do about it now," replied Lars in a quiet, gloomy mutter half spoken into his beer glass. "She's gone until next year."

"When she comes back to work, see how she is," said Jakob. "Check out whether she's happier than usual, or not as much, or if there's, I don't know, some sort of shadow on her. If this Wintz creep has mistreated her, you'll notice it. You know her better than anyone."

Lars perked up. "Good idea, Jakob," he said. "I do know her, you know. I know what she likes and what she doesn't – she hates the cold terribly, but she puts up with it because she loves to wear those tight, short outfits when she's on camera. She loves hot chocolate but she won't drink it because she's terrified it will make her fat, and that Derren will take on some sexy new young thing to replace her. She's just a kid, really. An adorable, smart and beautiful kid." He was off on

137

one of his meditations on Fleur's innumerable qualities, and Jakob listened indulgently. This could work out nicely for him.

An hour or so of Lars exalting their co-worker followed, after which Jakob had had enough beer and enough schmaltz, and was anxious to go home and smoke his weed. He hoped that Lars would not want to come along. It was his intention to get quietly, singularly stoned, contemplate the last couple of weeks, and hopefully drive all that angst out of his mind. Listening to Lars rattle on about Fleur, with occasional digressions onto other subjects that interested him even less than Fleur and her love life, was not on his agenda. Luckily, when he downed the dregs of what they had agreed would be their last beer and stood up, Lars made no move to follow.

"I think I'll have one more," he said.

"Fine," said Jakob a little too readily. "Say, do you think you could fix me up with a bigger bag of weed? This is good for a couple of days and I really appreciate it, but with Christmas coming up, I may need a stash."

"No problems, although you know you can buy some at the corner store, you cheapskate." said Lars, trying to regain his usual chirpiness. He really had been carried away by his reflections on Fleur, and he was missing her quite a lot, and trying not to.

"I just prefer yours," said Jakob, although he rebelled against paying for dope when it seemed there was so much about.

Laughing, Lars said, "I'll pick it in the next day or two and have it to you before we break for the holidays. But you know, you really should be growing your own, man."

"Yeah I will – if you can get me some seeds as well?"

Lars nodded.

"Thanks Lars, you're a good man. Fleur could do a lot worse," Jakob said.

"Ha, thanks Jakob. Take care man, and I'll see you tomorrow."

As Jakob was walking out, he noticed that Dave was sitting at the bar, and from the way he was sitting, half turned on his bar stool, Jakob could tell the White Hat had been watching his conversation with Lars. He waved, and Dave waved back with his usual energy and flashing smile. He stopped briefly at the door, holding it half open and letting the icy air in, and watched as Dave got up from his stool and walked over to join Lars. He could guess what their topic of conversation would be, and tried to defeat the paranoia rising in himself. At least if Dave was here asking questions about him, he said to himself, he could not be lurking at home to watch his comings and goings. Which would have been the cause of an irritating delay to his now urgent re-acquaintance with the luxurious stupor of fine greenhouse-grown pot.

It was bitterly cold out, so Jakob stepped into an enclosed electro-bus shelter and awaited the next service. Like the streets, the parks, the whole city's way of life, the electro-bus service was well organised and reliable, and it turned up right on time. No fare was payable, this was just one of many services provided free by the city, so in short order Jakob was at home, fishing out his oversized cigarette papers and chopping up a small mound of his weed.

The remainder of the evening played our exactly as Jakob had planned it. He sat in the cramped courtyard between his backyard and his greenhouse, and smoked his reefer slowly, watching the smoke curl and mingle with the frost on his breath, staring up at the vivid stars. The sky had become incredibly clear since the population had fallen so precipitously, filling with millions of dazzling points of lights in all colours, and he enjoyed looking up at the wandering planets and the fixed suns so far away that they appeared not to be moving.

Every now and then on night like these, if he was lucky, a meteorite would streak across the narrow stretch of ether visible to him, and he would wish for a better life without being specific about how it could or should be improved. But tonight was not one of those nights, and although he'd put on his thick jacket and scarf, it was too cold to sit outside too long. The clouds that had clogged the view for the last few days had cleared and left the way open for plummeting temperatures as well as wonderful viewing conditions, so soon after his joint was finished, he stood up slowly and went inside. He put some music on, switched off the lights and lay on his wide, soft couch. For a few moments he let his thoughts meander, touching on his troubles only briefly, lingering on his intractable and apparently hopeless love for Ellandra, and wondering what Dave might have asked Lars about him. But it didn't last long, that deliciously peripatetic introspection, because he fell into a deep and, for a long time dreamless, sleep.

He must have got off the couch to go to bed, because that

was where he woke up at the urging of his alarm early the next morning. He switched it off and lay back on his pillow, languishing in that brain thickness that followed a night on the dope, before finding both the motivation and the energy to leap out of bed and start preparing for the day.

He had no memory of his dreams but he felt less unhappy than usual, so he assumed they had been pleasant and restful. He fixed himself a large, healthy breakfast to make up for the previous night's almost complete lack of nutrition, and set off to work in unusually brilliant sunshine and jaunty hope.

16.

With the help of his stash and the upbeat mood of his colleagues, Jakob got through the final week before Christmas in excellent shape. The assignments were light and easy, the general air was festive and forgiving, and the sun shined on the city of New Elysium.

At nights, Jakob scurried home and got stuck into his weed immediately, zoning out while he cooked dinner and then sitting, bloated and drowsy with good humour, watching the television. His mind remained blissfully blank, he somehow avoided running into Dave Belleville at all, and not once did he wake up and look at his knuckles. Nor did he dwell on the mystery that had plagued him, the nature of his fractious and possibly defunct relationship with Ellandra, or any of the other million issues that usually kept him on edge. He was in that honeymoon period an addict experiences when he returns to his drug of choice and finds its effects even more welcome than he remembered, before it overtakes his life and begins to feed on and magnify his misery.

Over Christmas he stayed close to home, rarely venturing out. For a start, the sunny weather of the week leading up to the holiday disappeared and a foul blizzard blanketed New Elysium in snow and ice. For another thing, Ben hadn't invited him to join in their celebrations, so he had nowhere to go. He got up late, smoked early, and spent the dark days tinkering in his greenhouse getting a new crop of weed started. Or he went to the co-op greenhouse to put in some of his mandatory time allocation. If he was not engaged in agriculture or horticulture, producing or consuming, he spent the rest of his time staring at his TV, or, more frequently, into space, musing on irrelevancies. For several days he escaped everything that he believed was wrong with his life. He didn't wash much, didn't shave at all, and didn't care either way. Other than the greenhouses, he only went out to restock his meagre cupboard with processed foods and carbohydrates that he could eat when he had the munchies.

The only interruption to his glorious isolation came the day after Christmas, when Dave knocked on his door in the mid-morning. Jakob was just rolling his first joint for the day. He called out, "Hang on a second," scurried to hide his stash and accoutrements, then answered the door a few moments later, breathless. As expected, the big, woolly-headed White Hat greeted him with a beaming grin that suggested he wanted to come in.

"G'day neighbour," he boomed in his insufferably cheerful way. "Just called by to say Merry Christmas and Happy Boxing Day and check that you're okay. Haven't seen you for a couple of days."

Jakob smiled feebly as Dave peered deeply into his bleary, bloodshot eyes, then swung his head around, taking in the minor devastation that had accumulated over several days of sloth – empty and half empty beer bottles, grubby plates and food containers with encrusted cutlery hanging out of them, screwed up bits of paper and all the other detritus that accrues from doing nothing.

"Phew," whistled Dave. "Looks like somebody's been on a bender. You okay, mate?"

"I'm fine," said Jakob with quickly and poorly assumed vigour. "Just been relaxing," he added. "Sorry about the mess."

"You look pretty shot up there, mate," said Dave.

"No, really, I'm fine," said Jakob. "Just getting a bit lazy on the holidays."

"Well … okay," said Dave. "As long as you're keeping out of trouble."

"Oh, I am Dave, I am."

Dave grinned and shook his big boofy head. "Goodo," he said. "We won't worry too much about those funny little smells wafting over the fence then." He winked at his neighbour.

"Ah ha ha ha," Jakob giggled nervously, "I appreciate it." Although smoking dope wasn't technically illegal, Jakob was one of those generation who never got used to the idea that it was perfectly acceptable, and for whom the nefarious, secretive nature of its use only heightened the pleasure by adding an element of adrenaline.

"You know, if you're looking for someone to have a drink with, remember I'm right next door. I've got a few shifts over the holiday period – no rest for the wicked, eh – but I'll be around a bit here and there. We could even go to Mickey's one night if you're up for it."

"Thanks Dave, I appreciate it, I really do," said Jakob, although he had no intention of taking him up on the offer.

145

Dave looked around the room again, and said, "Well I can see you're not going to offer me a cup of tea, so I'll leave you to it."

"Oh, I'm so sorry," replied Jakob, red-cheeked. He moved to start shifting some of the rubble littering the room and the couch. "Sit down and I'll get you one."

"Don't fret, mate," said Dave airily. "I can see you've got other plans. Just wanted to say Merry Christmas anyway, and make sure you're alright. I worry about you Jakob, I really do."

"Thanks, Dave, I appreciate it." Jakob was aware that he seemed to be repeating himself, but he couldn't think of anything else to say.

"I'm not the only one either," said Dave. "Your mate Lars is a bit concerned, he tells me." His gaze was steady, his clear eyes probing, and his point unmistakable. Jakob understood. The White Hat was keeping close tabs on him. He nodded dumbly.

"I'm fine," he said. "Really, I'm fine."

Dave chortled sceptically. "Well as long as you say so, old friend," he said, "I'll leave you to it. Don't forget, I'm right next door," he added as he swept out the door.

Jakob retrieved his reefer makings, and sat down to roll his morning joint with lightly shaking hands.

17.

The Tuesday after Christmas, after wallowing in his smoky haze for six full days, Jakob had to go back to work. He was actually glad that he hadn't been given the entire period off between Christmas and New Year's Day, because even he had begun to get sick of being constantly stoned. In some ways, he'd begun to lose the ability to think at all, and while that was effective in relieving him of any need to address his problems, its efficiency had started to wear off, and a rivulet of despair had lately been trickling into such thoughts as he was capable of having. He recognised that he needed some stimulation, after all, and he was happy to be needed somewhere.

He was assigned to a news team that he didn't usually work with – the rest of his regular crew were all on holidays – so he attempted to knuckle down and just work. The theory was attractive, but the practice turned out differently. Little things that should not have affected him caused temper flares, biting acid remarks to his startled co-workers, and grinding disaffection. A boom mike inadvertently dropped into shot, a misplaced sandbag, a muffed take by the journalist, and a thousand other minor ruffles made him seethe and soured his expression, and he hated the long, dark, cold days.

At night he couldn't wait to get home and smoke away

his unhappiness, but even that stopped working the way he wanted it to. His mind kept returning to the many sides of the one matter he had successfully blocked for days; what had happened to him? Why was Ellandra so upset about Ben and what did she know? What was Dave Belleville's role in all this? Was he being watched? Investigated? Or was Dave really just a friendly busybody who couldn't help but interfere? And how could he find the answers to the questions that were now beginning to again repeat and reverberate in his mind?

Every night he smoked more and more, until he was so wasted his brain simply shut down and sent him into a practical coma. In the mornings he got up tired, less than refreshed and not really in the mood to deal with the people at work. But then, he needed to go to work so he didn't just sit and smoke all day, and he needed Lars to come back to work, if for no other reason than that his stash was dwindling much faster than he'd planned.

18.

At last the new year had begun. Jakob had spent New Year's Eve at home, adding copious quantities of beer and bourbon to his usual diet of pot and fresh air. The television was showing New Year's events around the world, and it was comforting to see places where normality had never been blown away as completely as it had in the Americas. Sydney, the first big city in the world to see the new year in, looked lively, warm and friendly. The people showed such abandon, it was charming and refreshing. They didn't try to hide their drunkenness or to mind their fellow revellers – they let it all hang out quite literally, and it was all so gloriously chaotic that in some ways Jakob wished he had been there.

Tokyo, Beijing, New Delhi, Tel Aviv, Paris, London; every major city that appeared on his screen was alive with colour, people and joy. It was messy, loud and lively. The streets outside his window were, as always quiet, clean and untroubled. New Year's Eve, like every other night in New Elysium, was subdued and controlled. Some might even say sterile. Sure, here and there party lights twinkled, music was respectfully turned up just a few notches, and people were even heard dutifully laughing. But as had been the case for the last fifteen years, the citizens of this disciplined, determined city were having a pleasant time, rather than an outrageously

149

good one. Fun was for other cities, in parts of the world that had not lost millions, and were not in the middle of an entire continent that was poisoned by radiation.

The television station was closed the day after New Year's Day, a Friday, so Jakob had burrowed into his couch and, rather more sparingly than had been the case at Christmas, smoked his way through the chilly days and nights. He was able to husband his weed resources well enough that by Sunday morning he still had enough for a couple of good sized joints, but he didn't want to blow them too early. He took a long walk around the streets of New Elysium. The roads that had been covered by snow overnight were all neatly ploughed and salted, the snow in arranged in tidy, identically level piles. The park pathways were all cleared too; there was no rubbish, no fallen leaves to mar the pristine whiteness or to deviate from the geometrical excellence of it all. It was as an Elysium should look – heavenly, hygienic, immaculate and brand new. On one or two occasions the sun managed to peep out from behind the thick clouds, and the scene became dazzling. It was so white it hurt the eyes, so pure it seemed impossible.

But it remained cold, so Jakob stopped at one of the near-deserted cafes on every second or third block to warm up and pass the time. He didn't speak except to order his drink or to excuse himself as he pushed past an occupied table, and nobody spoke to him. It was as though the blanket of snow had sucked the sound out of the people as well as the air; everywhere and everyone was hushed and serenely composed, unhurried and imperturbable.

Soon after the invisible noon – the clouds had closed in again and the snow had started to flurry – Jakob unaccountably found himself at Ellandra's door. This was unexpected, and certainly unplanned, but since he was there he decided he might as well knock on the door. Even if Ellandra should turn him away with more angry words, he would have seen her – made sure she was alright and let her know, if she still cared, that he was alright too.

She opened the door almost as soon as he knocked, as though she had been waiting for him. Her eyes were wide, her expression expectant and her smile welcoming – until she saw that it was Jakob.

Her eyes narrowed and the smile disappeared. "Oh, it's you," she said. "You're all I need." She walked away from the door, but she didn't close it, so Jakob took that as an invitation to follow her in. The house was clean and warm, no sign of any mess or disruption; it was perfect, like Ellandra. He followed her into the living room, and when she sat down on one of the plush armchairs, he took off his gloves, coat and scarf, draped them on the couch, then lowered himself into the armchair facing Ellandra.

Ellandra sighed. "What do you want?"

"Nothing. I don't know. I just happened to be passing..." he began.

"Oh for god's sake," she cut him off. "Just leave me alone will you?"

"Look," he found words he hadn't known he wanted to say coming out of his mouth. "Let's just have a truce, can we? No more talk of the past, no expectations of the future, just two people who know each other having a conversation. Wishing each other a happy new year."

She shook her head. "You still have no idea what you've done, do you?" she said.

He wanted to snap, "Because you haven't told me!" Instead he surprised himself by saying, "Don't talk about it. It's gone. I'm over it. A new man. Can't we just be friends?" The look on her face had not changed. "Acquaintances?" he said. "Associates? Two strangers who just happened to meet in your living room?"

Ellandra hesitated, but looked thoughtful. It was not in her nature to be dismissive, let alone as blatantly hostile as she had been to Jakob. Her defences broke down.

"Shit," she said. "You always get me, don't you?"

He grinned and nodded, sensing a breakthrough.

"I'm still unbelievably angry at you Jakob. You've done something terrible and I can't forget that," she said. "But I can't hold onto it forever. It's not your fault that you don't know what you've done, and who knows, you might live the rest of your life without doing it ever again. Besides, anger isn't good for me either."

"Let's just not talk about it," he said. "How was your Christmas? How was the trip to the mountains?"

"Hah, don't ask." Her laugh was humourless.

"Oh?" Jakob couldn't disguise the beat of pleasure and, in some measure, hope that her answer gave him. He hoped she didn't notice, but of course she did. She eyed him coolly.

"Typical military man really," she said. "All he wanted was to control me."

"That sucks," he said with an admirably straight face. "At least I never tried to do that."

"You were much more subtle," she said. "When you don't get your way, you're sullen and uncommunicative. You withdraw. But your intent is clear, even if your delivery is passive."

He was chastened, but persisted. "But this fellow, this Flynt, he was aggressive?" he asked.

Ellandra's beautiful, thick dark eyebrows arched.

"Yes he was," she said. "I already knew that he can be cruel, but I thought with me he would be different. He wasn't. He was in a terrible mood the whole time, away from his empire and without people to jump at his every word. He didn't want to go skiing or hiking in the mountains. Didn't want to enjoy the views or the energy. And didn't want me to either. I wasn't there as his friend or his partner, more like his trophy. Or in some ways his staff. He should have taken Garvin Wintz with him."

It was clear that she was aware of Jakob's motives in asking questions, but it was also obvious that she was in need of a friend. Or at least a friendly ear. Jakob tried to dial back his enthusiasm for her unhappiness.

"Shit, that's awful," he said. Just the idea of being up in the mountains again, free of the strictures of the city and all its straight lines and straight line thinkers, was liberating. He couldn't imagine what it would be like to actually be there, breathing it in and feeling its delicious openness.

"I'd love to go back up there," he said.

They had never been out of New Elysium together, even though Jakob had inherited his father's love of the open air and adventures in the wild and Ellandra had grown up skiing around the modest elevations of Boyne Mountain in Michigan. She'd fallen in love with the tall, rugged mountains of the Colorado Rockies as soon as she had been posted to Cheyenne Mountain. Early on in their romance they had spent long hours talking about their own adventures in the snow; accidents they had seen or had themselves, weather that had awed them, nights and days in the mountains, runs or places that were special to them. It had been a large part of their bond in those early days.

"You'd love it Jakob," she said. "Colonel Martin has built a wonderful facility up on Copper Mountain. He's had corps of engineers up there renovating and rebuilding ski lifts, chalets, and even refurbed the super-pipe at Main Vein. For a snowboarder like you, it's amazing."

"Sounds magic," said Jakob. It had been twenty years since he'd been on a snowboard, but he was sure it would all come back to him quickly and naturally. The things you learn when you're a child can stay with you forever, even if you let them lie dormant for decades.

They talked, like old times, about snow and mountains and exploring. In between stories, Ellandra fixed Jakob a coffee, and then lunch, and for the first time in a long time their conversation had that easy flow about it. It made them both content.

When the subject of mountaineering and its associated activities and attractions had run out of steam, Ellandra picked up the slack. "So, how was your Christmas?" she asked. "You look relaxed enough."

"Yeah I had a pretty quiet time of it really," he said. "Just stayed at home by myself I guess."

"Just smoking yourself into a glaze, then?"

Jakob was defensive. "No, not really. Well not that much anyway," he said.

She guffawed. "Oh come on Jakob, I can see it in your eyes. They're bloodshot, they have those rings around them that say you pass out every night and sleep the sleep of the dead, but wake up tired. Plus, your manner is so much less tense and you're less prone to take offence at anything and everything."

He looked wounded, and she laughed. "It doesn't bother me, if that's what you're thinking. You do whatever you want to do, it's no skin off my nose."

"I was lonely," he said, his eyes staring at the floor and the corners of his mouth turned down.

Ellandra laughed again, heartily this time, and longer than was necessary. "Really? That's your excuse? Who do you think you're talking to? I'd say – and this is just a guess – that you'd rather be at home alone with your pot than in a crowd without it. Am I right? Hmmm?" She was still smiling, and Jakob joined in her good humour. Blushing lightly, he suppressed a grin by pursing his lips.

"You got me," he said.

Triumphant, Ellandra gloated. "I knew it! You're so transparent."

"But I'm giving up again," he protested. "Tomorrow."

She was lost for a long moment in more laughter, and he couldn't help but join in. He knew how pathetic and completely unbelievable it sounded.

"It's true, you're much easier to get along with when you've been smoking," she said. "But when you're stoned, you're a pain in the ass. So let's make a deal. Get stoned whenever you want, but if you're planning on seeing me, don't come stoned, okay?"

This sounded like an excellent plan, and one that he could readily agree to. But he felt compelled to hold fast to his prior statement. "No really," he said. "I'm giving up tomorrow. For the new year."

"Whatever," she replied, not dismissively but still in good humour. "It's your life."

"Yep," he said. All this talk about weed had reminded him he still had two joints at home to get through, and that he had been with her for quite a while. But he was torn – he would happily stay if he was welcome. He clapped his hands on his knees and said, without getting up, "Anyway, I really should be going, and let you get on with the rest of your day."

"Yes, I suppose I should get on with my chores," said El-landra, standing up to see him out. Silently damning himself for having offered to leave, he stood and got up to put on his coat. Ellandra walked him to the door. She rested her hand on his shoulder, the gentlest of touches.

"Thanks Jakob," she said.

Surprised, he said, "No, thank you. For an excellent lunch, I mean," he said. "I really shouldn't have imposed."

"You're welcome," she said, and she meant it. "But next time you come over, shave first." He rubbed his hairy chin and affected to look chagrined. "Roger that," he said.

He stepped out into the late afternoon on a natural high. He'd been with Ellandra for hours, and they'd been able to chat easily, without any rancour or argument entering into it. She had even held out the possibility of it all happening again. It was all he could do to stop himself from skipping down the street. He took an electro-bus home, given that it would have taken him near enough to an hour to walk home, and he was anxious to celebrate his happy day with a smoke.

Later, as he smoked his second joint – he didn't really need it but he rationalised that it would be better if he rid himself of it there and then – he resolved to give up smoking weed for Ellandra's sake. He knew she thought him a better man if he didn't smoke, regardless of her assertions that it didn't affect her either way, so he thought he would surprise her by being clear, fresh, alert and clean shaven the next time they saw each other. This meant not seeing her for two weeks or so, because he would probably be grumpy for that long, but he theorised that not contacting her for a while would be a good thing anyway. "Let her miss me," he muttered to himself in his lazy, slurred stoner drawl.

19.

Shaving was a chore. There wasn't quite enough cereal in the pack to make breakfast, and he didn't have time to get out to the shop, or even into the greenhouse to pick something fresh to eat. The bread was stale and starting to grow mouldy, and the milk smelled funny. So it was a dark and stormy Jakob who stepped out of his house to get the electro-bus to work; hungry, woolly-headed and a minute behind time. He had to run to the stop to meet the bus just as it arrived, stumping along like an overstuffed teddy bear in his thick winter jacket, scarf and beanie.

The cold hurt his face, the crowd on the bus seemed pushy and hung over, and the prospect of a day behind the camera wasn't appealing. Jakob tried to think happy thoughts, but as soon as he could come up with one it would disappear and be replaced by a black thought. Everything seemed to have changed, and he should have been positive about himself, and Ellandra, and even their possible future together. And yet he was cranky, irascible and impatient. Already he had decided that if Lars was as good as his promise to bring some seeds and another handful of buds, he would smoke some weed that night, just to calm down. He could always give up tomorrow.

The day did not get a whole lot better, even when Lars

gave him a small bag of green goodness, including a handful of fat, mottled black and dark green seeds in the staff kitchen. Having made the decision to smoke that night, Jakob started chiding himself for being so weak. He would probably just be touchy and edgy again tomorrow, so why not give up now? Keep that stash for when it was really necessary? Stop being such a piss-ant.

That word, piss-ant. He'd heard that before, recently. It wasn't the sort of word he'd normally use himself, where had he picked it up? He looked at his knuckles and rubbed them thoughtfully. It all had something to do with a dream. Or was it a dream? Suddenly the feeling that he had done something terrible came flooding back to him. It picked up where it had left off, gnawing at his mind and chafing at his nerves. He was not a joy to work with.

By lunchtime Jakob resolved not to smoke the weed that he Lars had given him. But immediately after lunch, which tasted like ashes and cardboard, he changed his mind when a trivial misdemeanour by Toney made him steam with anger and seethe with impatience to get out of there.

By mid-afternoon he had committed to staying straight that night, whatever, only to change his mind again minutes later. And so it went all day, an endless inner debate about whether or not to smoke, whether he could be strong and break the hold that the weed had already reasserted over him, or whether he should just say fuck it all, and smoke himself into oblivion.

It was all so pointless though – he knew that now he had it in his pocket, now it was in his possession, he would be smoking that night. It would all happen on automatic. He would watch his fingers cutting it up and rolling it into a joint. He would taste the gum on the cigarette paper as he licked its fine edge, then feel the lumpy roundness of the butt-end on his lips as he put it in his mouth. He knew he would get stoned, then spend some time in the greenhouse, setting the new seeds to germinate so that he could grow his own crop and stop harassing Lars.

And still, intruding on these distressing thoughts and meditations on his own weakness came those other thoughts about that lost night, to further baffle and bewail him.

It was a tough day, again, and he was glad to get out of there. His home, his couch, that little bag burning a hole in his pocket: all beckoned, and he told himself over and over again that it was just for tonight, that tomorrow he would give up.

But he also knew that it was Monday night, and he knew his own history; if he smoked on Monday, inevitably he would smoke on Tuesday. Then Wednesday would seem interminable, a trial to get through before he could rush home and roll up another escape. And if by Thursday morning he had already clocked up three nights in a row stoned, well then he might as well just relax and go with it; the week was shot, and next week would be a good one for giving up.

He put on his coat, scarf and beanie, and was about to head out into the deep freeze that had gripped the city, when Lars caught him.

"Time for a quick one with me and Toney at Mickey's?"

Jakob couldn't say no. Lars had been very generous in

sharing his weed, and was the one on the crew most likely to reassure rather than berate Jakob when he acted like a bear with a sore head. So he nodded and they made their way to the bar.

20.

"Jeez, you were a bit fragile today Jakob, are you okay?" said Toney when they were settled in a dark corner with a beer.

"Yeah I'm fine," he said. "Just a little tired I guess."

"You're always tired." Toney was nothing if not persistent. "Don't you sleep at night?"

"I just have a lot on my mind," said Jakob. "Usually I sleep okay, but lately a few things have been getting to me."

"We noticed," she replied. "You need to try and lighten up a bit. Smoke some weed."

Nothing is calculated to rile a person who is in a dark place more than telling them to lighten up. And Jakob, despite the happy day he'd spent with Ellandra, or perhaps because of it, was in a dark place. It put him in two minds about smoking weed – again – and he knew which side would win.

"Can't we talk about something else?" he said as calmly and quietly as he could.

"So, how about Fleur and Garvin Wintz?" said Toney, happy to leave the subject of Jakob's moodiness alone, and even happier to try and slip a wedge into Lars' feelings for Fleur. Lars, who'd been tuning out of this same dreary conversation that they always had, snapped to attention. "What about them?" he said.

"Oh, she's smitten," said Toney. "She won't stop talking

about him. Seems he's quite the charmer."

"He's a snake," said Lars. "Some two-bit bureaucrat with a smart suit and a cushy job."

"He's assistant to the second most powerful person in New Elysium, Lars," said Jakob with a sly grin. "That's hardly some two-bit bureaucrat." He enjoyed watching Toney needle Lars like this. It took his mind off his own issues and reminded him that he wasn't the only one with what might be called romantic issues. He felt bad for Toney though, because in all the time they'd been working together she'd silently carried a torch for Lars, and he was the only one in the world who couldn't see it. Still, she was a trooper, Toney, even if she was occasionally a bit brutally honest. She liked to make it hurt, but she could also take it.

"They had an amazing time in the mountains at Christmas," she said. "Skiing, snowboarding, late night hot tubs, the whole shebang. Apparently he knows how to treat a lady."

"Yeah, well, he's scum as far as I'm concerned," said Lars.

Toney sighed. "When are you going to accept reality Lars?" she said. "You and Fleur just aren't going to happen."

"Whoa! Whoa, slow down there, Toney," said Lars, putting up his hands. "I never said I wanted to be with Fleur. I just care for her as a workmate, that's all."

Toney and Jakob both cackled and crowed over that one.

"One day you'll wake up and see what's been in front of you the whole time," said Toney. Lars looked taken aback, almost unnerved by that statement, but he recovered quickly.

"Here's to continued singledom," he said, lifting his glass and his disposition at the same time. He always was quick to put gloom and unhappiness behind him; Jakob wished he knew the trick.

"To continued singledom," said Toney, raising her glass and clinking it against Lars's now near-empty vessel. They both looked at Jakob, who lifted his glass, toasted with them, and finished off his beer.

Lars quickly slid off his high-backed stool to go and get another round. It occurred to Jakob that if he stayed late enough and drank enough he might not feel compelled to have a joint when he got home, so he was happy to see his friend darting off to the bar.

"Of course, singledom won't be a problem for our peerless leader much longer," said Toney.

"What do you mean?" asked Jakob, barely interested but satisfied with the conversation taking another benign turn. It would pass the time.

"She's been hooking up with Tom Flynt a lot lately," Toney said as Lars returned with the next round. "This is my last," she added as Lars put the beer in front of her.

Jakob tried to hide his delight at the news about Derren and Flynt. "Derren and Flynt eh?" he said. "That won't end well," he added with a broad smile.

"You seem cut up," said Lars.

"I'm just happy to see Derren hooking up," Jakob lied. "Sure, Flynt may be a complete asshole, but if Derren is amused by him, who am I to stop her?" He was practically giggling.

"Can't we talk about something other than each other's love lives?" said Lars. "You know – work, the weather, what's on TV tonight…?"

"Huh, sure," agreed Toney. A nod from Jakob signalled that they were all ready to talk about something else, but for several minutes nothing came up. They sat there dumbly, frequently sipping their beers and desperately trying to think of something to say.

"Man, I've got a really good strain of top notch weed growing at home," said Lars, latching onto possibly the one subject they could all share. They talked about the various types and strengths of weed they'd all smoked, about weird and wonderful nights and experiences they'd had when stoned, and laughed and wasted the evening away for another two rounds. At that point Toney announced that she definitely needed to go home, but Lars easily convinced Jakob to stay for yet another one. They were getting quite merry, but neither seemed in a hurry to go home.

After Toney's departure, Lars said to Jakob, "So are you back smoking dope or what? Feel like a joint in the park over the road?"

Jakob hesitated. It sounded awfully tempting. But then he shook his head. "No, I'm good thanks, "he said. "I think I'm going to try and give up again. I spent the day with Ellandra yesterday, so I think it will be worth staying off it, just in case we get together."

Lars nodded all the way through this, but he didn't look persuaded as to the depth of Jakob's commitment. "You sure that's a good idea?" he asked.

"Absolutely," said Jakob. "I know Ellandra prefers non-smoking me to stoner me, so I'll give it another shot."

"Doesn't that mean at least a couple of weeks of super-grouchy Jakob before just-grumpy Jakob settles in for the long haul? The last time you gave up was pretty hard for all of us, you know," said Lars.

"The truth is," said Jakob, "bastard Jakob is always fairly close to the surface. If I stick to any one course for more than a week or two, that side of me comes out regardless. If I don't smoke, I feel better and better for maybe ten days, but after that I start going downhill again. I get edgy and paranoid, and I start thinking about how much I wouldn't mind a smoke, and I get cross because I can't have any, and that just feeds my depression. Because that's what it is, you know. Then again, if I start smoking again, everything is great for a while, and I sleep well and I stop being such a hard-ass at work. But then after a fortnight of that, tops, it feels like the levels of pot in my system get toxic or something, and the madness comes on me again. I can't seem to escape it."

"Wow man." Lars shook his head. "Can't you find some sort of balance? You know, maybe smoke for a week, then take a week off or something?"

"Hah, I've tried," said Jakob. It felt like he was relieving himself of a burden. "But I know the way my mind works. Once I get back on it, my usage creeps up and up and up, until I'm smoking more and more and more, and all I want to do is smoke more. That makes me feel weak and foggy and disconnected, and I get easily pissed off any time I'm not stoned. So then I stop smoking, and for a while I come good, but then I start over-thinking everything. I get stuck in the same thought patterns, and I want to bust out and just forget everything, and I realise how weak-minded and pathetic that makes me, so I get angry at myself and at everyone else, and eventually I crack and get stoned, and begin the whole cycle again."

"Dude, you've got a problem," said Lars. He really was troubled by his friend's predicament. He was one of those tokers who could smoke or not, either way. If he did smoke, he enjoyed it. If he didn't smoke, he didn't miss it. And he bounced back from any disappointment or difficulty quickly regardless.

"I know," said Jakob. "It's like there are two people inside of me, and neither one will be happy until the other is completely out of their life. My gut feeling is that straight Jakob would be happy, if he could just get past that critical stage where boredom and unhappiness takes over and brings out stoner Jakob. I mean, if I could really cleanse stoner Jakob – the one I call the Sandman – out of my system, I'm sure I'd be better off. But then I would miss being stoned so much…" he tailed off.

"The Sandman?" said Lars with an edge of humour.

"Yeah, I know it's stupid but I really feel as if there is a whole other personality inside me, who just loves smoking dope, and that's all he wants to do. And when he gets the upper hand, that's all we do. We smoke, and think about the next time we'll be getting high."

"Sorry Jake, but that's pretty fucked up," said Lars. But then he realised he was sounding harsh, so he added, "I wish I could help man, I really do. But it sounds like this is something you have to do yourself." It was easy to sound caring if you didn't actually have to share any of the burden.

"Yeah, I know. It is." Jakob realised his drink was empty. "The sad thing is, the Sandman has a powerful voice when he wants to smoke. And sometimes he just takes over so I'm almost watching while he does what he wants." Jakob drank off the dregs in his glass. "Shall I get one more?" He definitely wasn't in the mood to go home and smoke now. In fact, this talk with Lars had given him new resolve to walk away from weed altogether, and he knew that if he was drunk, even the Sandman's voice would be subdued.

"Why not?" said Lars, relieved that this heavy, downer of a conversation would not continue, at least until Jakob got back. He was getting too drunk to make the right responses.

They must have been on their sixth, or was it seventh, round of beers, with the two that he brought back to the table. The table was a mess of empties. For a Monday night that was a lot, but Jakob was feeling good about it. He felt as though he'd unloaded a big secret. But he didn't really want to talk about it anymore. He began to wonder whether he'd said too much, and whether Lars might use the information against him at any stage. He didn't think so, but he had a habit of alienating people, and he hoped that that wouldn't happen with Lars.

On the way back to the table with the drinks, something happened that drove those thoughts clean out of his head. He saw Major Flynt's assistant, Garvin Wintz, walk in with a very beautiful young lady who could easily have been, but was not, Fleur. Wintz obviously had a type – tallish, lean, blonde girls, more athletic than skinny, who wore plenty of makeup but made it seem natural. Girls who were impressed by expensive imported clothing and the admiring looks from people of all ages and genders that Wintz usually prompted. This one was no exception. She was drop-dead gorgeous as far as Jakob was concerned, and from the way her head inclined toward her date, the smile that played on her lips and the light that danced in her eyes, she was very taken with Wintz.

Putting the beers on the table, Jakob grabbed Lars by the shoulder and leaned in to whisper conspiratorially, even though Wintz and the girl were on the other side of the room. "Hey. Don't swing around wildly, but just slowly turn around, have a look in the back corner near the door. Is that who I think it is?"

Intrigued but also amused by Jakob's mysterious manner, and feeling loose enough to play the game, Lars very slowly turned on his stool, and tried to focus on the other side of the room. The bar was the only well-lit part of the room and although it wasn't directly between him and the back corner, it was still hard to see through its light to what Jakob was talking about. When he finally figured it out, his eyes widened and his mouth opened. "Is that Wintz with Fleur?" he said.

"Yes, it's Wintz, no it's not Fleur," was Jakob's answer. Lars swung his head around to look at Jakob. His expression, one of surprise, indignant distaste and disapproval all rolled into one, was priceless.

A gleam came into Jakob's eye. "Looks like our friend Mr Wintz likes to spread the love around," he said in the crafty tone he used when he was plotting something.

"Surely he wouldn't have dumped Fleur for her?" said Lars. "Fleur's so much better looking than that girl. Probably a lot smarter too."

"Who said anything about him having dumped Fleur?" Jakob purred. "She'd be at home, getting her beauty sleep or putting cucumbers on her eyes or something because she has work tomorrow, so while she's indisposed, he's obviously using his time to pursue other interests."

"You mean he's cheating on her?" Lars was stunned. The idea that anyone could do that to Fleur was beyond his imagination.

"Well who's to say that Wintz and Fleur are even officially together?" Jakob shrugged. "Maybe they broke up. Maybe they never really got together. Maybe he's just entertaining his sister. Or his niece."

"Bullshit," said Lars. "He's cheating on her."

"Well it sure looks that way," agreed Jakob. "But maybe we should give him the benefit of a doubt."

"No, he's cheating on her, I'm sure of it." Lars had no idea how easily and expertly he was being led by Jakob.

"Let's not jump to conclusions. We don't know for certain that she's not his sister, or just a friend." Jakob turned his head to see what was happening over on Wintz's table, just in time to see him lean over and kiss the unidentified blonde.

"Oh, maybe not..." he said. Lars swung around in his seat, cursing himself for having his back to Wintz and the girl, and saw the end of the long, lingering kiss delivered by the smooth, well-groomed bureaucrat.

Lars was seething. "Man, that is disgusting!" he said. "Poor Fleur."

Jakob was eyeing Lars with intent. "It is. That poor girl, she has no idea of how badly she is being treated by him. I wonder how many others he's stringing along? Fleur could be just one of a number," he said.

Lars had his head in his hands and was rubbing his hair back and forth. He looked distraught. The booze had made him particularly emotional, but also confused. He was putty in Jakob's hands.

"Still, what are you going to do?" said Jakob, as if wondering how a force like Garvin Wintz could be countered.

"I have to tell Fleur," said Lars. He thrust his hands into his pocket and pulled out his phone. "I should call her now."

"You really think that's a good idea?" asked Jakob.

"Sure, why not? She has to know."

"Okay, so you call her at, what," he consulted his watch, "ten on a Monday night, drunk, from a bar, and you tell her Wintz is cheating on her. You think she'll say, gosh thanks Lars, you're my hero? Or do you think she'll believe you're trying to turn her against this man, who she quite possibly loves already, for your own purposes? Think about it Lars. She would not be thanking you, even if it turns out you're right."

"Of course," said Lars, putting his phone down on the table amidst the forest of empty glasses. "You're right, she wouldn't appreciate that kind of honesty right now. She might turn it back on me, when all I have is her best interests at heart. I'll tell her tomorrow."

Jakob frowned. He picked up his glass and had a long swallow, watching Lars carefully as he did so. Almost automatically, Lars followed suit, having a deep draught himself. "You sure about that Lars?" said Jakob. He was solicitous in his tone, duplicitous in his intent.

"Why not?" Lars was wary now. Jakob appeared to be giving him good advice.

"Well she won't believe you any more tomorrow than she does tonight, my friend. She knows how you feel about her, so anything you say will be taken out of context."

"You tell her then, she'll believe you."

Shaking his head, Jakob said, "No, I can't tell her. She'll just think I'm doing your dirty work. So she'll be angry at me, and despise you for being too weak to tell her about it yourself." His mind was moving remarkably quickly, and in very devious directions.

"But what can we do?" Lars was desperate for a solution.

"Well, you could go over there and confront him, I suppose," mused Jakob. Lars lifted his head. "But that probably wouldn't be such a good idea. He'd look at you like you're some kind of drunk idiot, you'd probably get kicked out – who knows, you may end up in the Tank for the night – and he'd tell Fleur all about this crazy workmate of hers who harassed him while he was having a quiet drink with an old friend."

Lars was flummoxed. He drank another long draught, then put his head in his hands again.

Suddenly, Jakob looked alarmed. "You're not ... you wouldn't? No, of course you wouldn't."

"Wouldn't what?" Lars cocked his head. He was listening – and walking directly into Jakob's trap.

"No, of course you wouldn't. Not you. You're not that sort of person," said Jakob.

"What? What are you talking about?" said Lars.

Jakob paused and peered into Lars' eyes with seeming concern and compassion. "You're not thinking of waiting for him outside, are you?"

"What? No." Lars was adamant. "Why would I do that?"

"You're right. Violence is never the answer," Jakob said.

"Violence? Who said anything about violence?"

"Oh, nobody, nobody," said Jakob with his palms up, all innocence. "It's just that, well, someone clearly needs to teach Wintz a lesson, and for a moment I thought you were going to be the one. Forget I mentioned it."

Lars was bemused, but now the suggestion had been raised, it took root in his booze-befuddled brain. "Teach him a lesson? How?" he wondered.

"Well I thought you might be planning to wait for Wintz outside, hit him from behind, hopefully knocking him out, and while he's down there maybe deliver a couple of kicks in the ribs for good measure, and then go on home. But you're right, it's a stupid idea."

That he might have the power to assault another human being had never entered Lars' fancy, but Jakob could almost see the workings of his mind as the thought tumbled over and over in there.

"I mean, you'd probably get away with it because, you know, there just aren't that many people around on a Monday night. But, no." Jakob shook his head again. "It would take a bit more gumption than you've got. And I mean that in the nicest possible way, Lars. You're a passive guy. A pacifist. You understand that hitting someone never solved anything, even if it would make you feel good."

"But he deserves it," said Lars. He looked across the room, where Wintz had a tight grip on the blonde's hand and was stroking the inside of her wrist while she giggled. His eyes narrowed and his mouth set. "I mean look at him. The smarmy bastard. I bet he does it all the time. Somebody really ought to teach him a lesson. And it would feel good."

Jakob's eyes followed Lars' gaze, and he nodded. "It's true," he said, "he looks like the sort who would keep on doing it until someone taught him a lesson. Still, it's not our call, is it?"

Lars sat up straight. "Maybe it is Jake," he said. Suddenly he sounded serious and sober. "If not us, who? If not now, when?" He was pretty much sold on the idea now.

A look of dismay and disquiet on his face, Jakob grabbed his friend by the arm. "Surely you can't be serious? How would you do it? Just wait outside, possibly with one of these glasses hidden in your coat," he picked up the heavy-bottomed glass nearest him, "and whack him over the head? There could be a lot of blood."

Lars examined the glass Jakob was holding. He picked one up himself, hefting its weight and considering the damage it could do. He slipped it quickly into the deep pocket of the overcoat he had hanging on the back of his seat. It disappeared completely in the dark folds. "Let's do it," he said.

There was a vicious, committed light in his eyes now.

Once again, Jakob put his hands up, palm-first, in a mild gesture of protest. "Whoa, buddy," he said earnestly. "I'm not that kind of guy. I've got nothing against Wintz. Even if he is a slimeball who's cheating on Fleur, I've never hit anyone ever before." In a flash, he knew he was lying but he didn't know how or why. He saw a bloodied face in the dark, and instinctively his left hand went to his right, where it rubbed the knuckle. It was a confusing, confounding moment. He wondered, suddenly, what he was trying to do to Lars. But he couldn't stop.

"All you have to do is distract the girl," said Lars. His look and his tone were almost lascivious, as though he could taste the power of victory over another man. "I'll do the rest. Somebody has to teach that asshole to behave properly."

"Are you sure, Lars?" said Jakob. "You know, you could get into trouble. Although at this time of night, I guess it would be easy enough to get away with it, if you're quick about it."

Lars was pumped, ready for action. Almost obligated to follow through now that the bloodlust had been awaked in him.

"Okay, you go wait outside in the laneway just down the road. I'll wait 'til they get up to leave," said Jakob in a low voice. "I'll stop the girl just inside the door, ask her the time, or when the next electro-bus is due or something. You follow Wintz once he gets out the door, and do whatever you have to do. Be fast, be sure, and get out of there."

At that moment, a heavy hand clamped on Jakob's

shoulder, scaring the absolute shit out of him. He jerked his head around to see the large, scruffy, grinning face of Dave Belleville inches from his own. His heart thumped so madly he thought it would fail.

"Look at you two, thick as thieves," boomed Dave in a jovial bawl. "What are you plotting?"

"Er, hi, Dave," said Jakob. His voice was shaky and he stuttered, and he was sure his eyes were dinner plates. "W-what are you doing here? We were just, um, having a beer."

The conspiratorial mood between Jakob and Lars was snapped, and the conspiracy itself evaporated in an instant. Lars appeared shocked, and Jakob was struggling to gain any composure at all. Dave Belleville was in his White Hat uniform, with only the official white pith helmet missing.

"Bottler," said Dave, even though neither of the pair of stunned, suddenly shame-faced individuals he was addressing knew that the term was Australian slang for 'good'. He pulled back the high-backed stool that Toney had been sitting on, and eased his bulk into it. "I reckon I'll join ya. But I'll only have a lemonade – I've got the White Hat electro-van out there because I've got an early start down at the Energy Directorate tomorrow." He didn't explain what he might be doing at the Energy Directorate, and neither Lars nor Jakob was disposed to ask.

"Let me get you a lemonade," said Jakob. "Lars and I were just going to have one more and then go, it's pretty late." He was babbling. "Right, Lars?" The latter nodded dumbly.

"I just knocked off, and I said to myself, 'Self, you should have a beer with Jakob,' so I went home but I could see your place was dark, and I figured you'd be here. So I said to myself, 'Self, I bet I know where naughty Jakob is, even though it's only Monday night, so why don't I go there and drive him home,' and here I am," said Dave. He looked very happy with himself, and if he'd caught any of Jakob and Lars' previous conversation, he wasn't letting on. As Jakob loped off to the bar, Dave looked at Lars and winked. "Don't worry Lars, I'll drive you home too mate," he said. "So long as you don't mind going in a White Hat van."

"That would be terrific, Dave, thank you," said Lars, starting to look relieved and trying to hide the light of guilt in his eyes. On the other side of the room, Garvin Wintz and his date got up and walked out of the bar, watched surreptitiously by both Jakob and Lars, and blithely ignored by Dave.

"Bit of a big one for a Monday night isn't it boys?" said Dave in a boisterous near-bellow when Jakob returned with the beers and the lemonade.

"Ha ha," laughed Jakob. "We only stopped in for one or two, but one thing led to another, you know."

"Oh, I know only too well," Dave said. "You get a taste for it, you forget what day or night it is, and all sorts of silly ideas come into your head."

Chagrined, stupefied into near-silence, Lars and Jakob sat drinking and trying not to look guilty as Dave rabbited on about nothing – sports contests, television shows, people he met, and anything else that crossed his mercurially peripatetic mind. He didn't seem to notice that Jakob and Lars were unusually quiet; he often had that effect on people, so it was nothing new for him.

In short order all three drinks were gone, and Dave gave the order to follow him outside. There they found an electro-van personnel carrier with a covered rear. Dave directed Lars into the rear section, which turned out to have a number of comfortable seats as well as a stretcher. Jakob sat in the front with Dave, looking nervous. Dave let out a hearty laugh.

"Don't worry, mate," he said. "I promise we'll go straight home, not to the processing station. Or the Tank," he added.

Dave drove straight to Lars' home without even asking the address, let Lars out, and even helped him down from the back of the van.

"You sure you're alright mate?" he said.

Lars looked a little unsteady on his feet, partly from the booze and partly from the vertiginous ride in the back – without any visual references to gauge which way he was moving, nor any warning of the sudden turns, stops and bursts of acceleration, he found the journey unsettling. This discomfort was not helped by the circumstances in which the journey had come about, or the vehicle in which it had been made. He was glad it was late when he finally got out, and hoped none of the neighbours were watching. As Dave got back into the van, Jakob hung his head out of the passenger's side window and slurred, "See you tomorrow."

The ten-minute drive home to the co-op where Dave and Jakob both lived was taken in relative silence. Dave could see that Jakob was half-asleep, and Jakob pretended to be more insensible than he actually was so he could avoid any questions, well-meaning advice, or unasked for pronouncements or judgements. Dave parked on the street outside his front door, and they both got out. As Jakob made for his own front door, Dave said, "You know, you really should look after yourself a bit Jake. You're the only one of you you've got."

"Thanks Dave, I appreciate it," mumbled Jakob, and he really did. The concern in his neighbour's voice was genuine.

Stumbling into the house and switched on a light, Jakob realised that he was too drunk to fix himself a meal, and thankfully too drunk even to contemplate a joint. But he was not too drunk to be horrified at what he had almost done. Had he really been so close to cajoling Lars into attacking Garvin Wintz? And for what purpose? So he could hide in the shadows and watch his friend being taken away by the White Hats, only to reappear a day or so later with no memory of the event? What had he been thinking? Could he really do that to a friend? A good friend who had done nothing but encourage and assist him at every turn. He put his head in his hands and wondered what sort of a person he had become. He didn't want to be that man any more.

He pulled the bag of weed that Lars had given him out of his pocket and looked at it. It was all the weed's fault, he decided. He said to himself, again, that he needed to give it up, and this little bag was the key – if he could just keep it without smoking it. If he put it in the cupboard but didn't smoke it, it could be his incentive, his emergency escape. Keeping it stashed, he would always know it was there in case things got so much on top of him that he really needed to get stoned, so he wouldn't be pining for it, or looking for it, or going to Lars and begging for it. It was available, and knowing that would help him test and strengthen his resolve.

There was enough to give him with a few days relief, but not enough to feed a renewed addiction. Yes, he told himself, he would get past this cycle of abstinence followed by gorging once and for all. He would win Ellandra back, and he would be a whole person again. If he had ever been.

21.

"Man, did we really go home in a White Hat van?"

They were in the staff kitchen, making a morning heart-starter. Lars was looking sunny and fresh, which was a good thing. Jakob had been a bit worried that his friend would have been spooked by how close he had come to committing a crime, and to perhaps ending up in the back of a White Hat van for real. Jakob laughed with him, shaking his head ruefully.

"I know, right," he said. "But that's my friend Dave. He shows up, he takes over, and he makes stuff like that happen. Still, his heart's in the right place."

"Yeah I've spoken to him a couple of times and he's a good man," said Lars.

"Probably a good thing he came along when he did." Jakob looked sideways at Lars as he made his double espresso. Seeing no obvious reaction, he added, "Otherwise I'd have a worse hangover than I do now."

"I feel kind of seedy too," said Lars, "but it was a good night. Except for that asshole Wintz." His face darkened slightly when he mentioned the enemy.

"What are you going to do about him?" said Jakob.

"Well, what can I do?" Lars was philosophical. "You're right that if I tell Fleur, she'll just be angry at me for interfering. So I guess I just have to keep my mouth shut." He dug an elbow into Jakob's rib, and said, "I guess we missed our chance, eh?"

Jakob covered up his surprise with a giggle. "I guess we did. Still, it was fun pretending," he said. "We would have kicked his ass."

"Oh yeah, we never would have gone through with it, of course," Lars said. His mouth was smiling, but his eyes were wary and watching Jakob's. "But if we had, his ass would have been totally kicked."

"Next time eh," said Jakob, moving away from the coffee machine so Lars could get in and make his.

"I just wish it hadn't taken so many beers to get through our little plan," joked Lars. "I'm feeling far too fragile for a Tuesday morning." Jakob nodded and looked lovingly at the coffee cup he was holding in both hands as though hugging it. Lars chortled.

Bustling in through the door, Derren looked from Lars' face to Jakob's and back again, accurately sizing up the situation in one glance.

"When you two are through comparing hangovers, can you load up the OB van? We have a big day ahead of us, picking up shots for tomorrow's interview. We need central city, co-op gardens, libraries, schools, local meets, everything that makes New Elysium the greatest and happiest city in the world."

The boys knew exactly what she was talking about. The following day at the taping of Felicity's show, a world-renowned director, the Australian documentary legend Stone

Carpenter, would appear to talk about his new project, an in depth examination of New Elysium. It was the most exciting thing to have happened on the show for a while, and Felicity planned to give Carpenter a solid briefing on what made New Elysium unique in the world, so she would need plenty of visual support material. It was clear to Jakob, if not everyone else, that as New Elysium's only weekly talk show host, and one of its very few bona fide civilian celebrities, Felicity was angling for a slot in the documentary. Perhaps even a speaking part.

The crew – minus Fleur, whose presence was not required – spent the day driving around the city, shooting everything that moved and many things that did not. Although there was an abundance of library footage of blooming greenhouses, happy co-op gardens full of willing hands creating luscious crops to share with their neighbours, crowded cafes, local 'meet markets' held weekly in meets across the city, orderly streets and geometrically perfect parks with identical play equipment played on by well-behaved, respectful and obedient children, well-disciplined school classrooms, and offices, factories and stores full of polite, welcoming, easy-going and docile New Elysiumites, Felicity wanted fresh images of everything. She wanted to present an up to date, upbeat, agreeable and attractive view of the city, which she firmly believed to be the greatest the world had ever seen. If all went to plan, and she appeared in the documentary and was lauded, this interview may even be the beginning of her ticket out of there. The world centre of show business had, since the swift and untimely demise of Hollywood in 2017, devolved to Sydney – Carpenter's home – and Felicity made no secret of wanting to make it big there, one day.

All day long they got hurried shots, coaxed people into trying to act naturally with a camera trained on them, zoomed, panned, locked off, then packed up, moved on and did it all again. The crew worked well and everyone, including Jakob, stayed positive and remarkably energetic throughout the long day. It was interesting and challenging to try and see New Elysium through his lens as it would appear to a first time visitor, and although the schedule was tight he worked quickly to find new angles on long-familiar targets, finding new inspiration at every location. It was as though he was seeing his own city through innocent eyes, and he really enjoyed the day.

They broke for a quick meal at a local delicatessen, but aside from that it was non-stop action for a full seven hours, with Derren forever hustling, hurrying, boosting and bossing in her gracious and affable way.

By the time they had finished unpacking the OB van and putting everything neatly away, it was late, dark and very cold. Toney suggested a quick drink at Mickey's but Jakob and even Lars demurred. "I think I need to go home and cook up a healthy meal," said Jakob.

"Yeah, I don't need to be going for one and having a hundred again," said Lars.

So they all went their separate ways, and within a quarter of an hour Jakob was stepping off the electro-bus at the stop near his home and striding quickly along the icy streets to the local store. There he picked up a piece of chicken, a fresh loaf of bread and a bottle of milk, and escaped into the sanctuary of his home without spotting, or being spotted by, Dave, who was no doubt lurking somewhere.

He collected a few fresh vegetables from his greenhouse, and spent a relaxing half an hour cutting the food and cooking his feast. He was in bed early, exhausted, without even thinking about having a beer or a joint. As he drifted off to sleep, he wondered if he could keep up such a blameless lifestyle, and decided that he could.

22.

In the dream, he was in a wooded area dripping with green vines and dark spaces, treading on a soft carpet of fallen leaves, twigs and moss. There was a timber house, with odd rooms poking out of it at odd angles from both storeys, and a wide rickety staircase just in front of him. He was with Lars, and he somehow knew that Lars was the physical manifestation of the Sandman that lived in his own mind. He didn't know why or how he knew that, but it was an unassailable truth. Lars kept on saying, "I just need somewhere to roll a joint," and Jakob kept nodding. He went into the house, and there were people lounging around in various rooms, people he did not know and whose presence he questioned but ultimately had to accept.

His immediate problem was that he needed badly to go to the bathroom. He didn't know if he could hold on much longer, and every time he found what looked like a toilet door it was locked. At last he found a vacant toilet, sitting strangely in the middle of a laundry area, with dirty clothes heaped in overflowing baskets, and a broken-down washing machine. He approached the toilet, and was disgusted to see that it was overflowing with brown liquid studded with floating turds. Mounds of used toilet paper crowded the bowl and were scattered on the floor around it.

He ran out and pushed past lazing people to find another toilet, but every time he did he encountered the same problem. He was desperate now, and finally, finding a bowl that could be described as acceptable, he sat down and squirted out a huge pile of horrid faeces. It filled the bowl; looking at it, he wondered if he had been responsible for all the other toilets cascading with foul brown muck. To his horror, he discovered that there was no toilet paper, and casting about for a substitute, picked up a dirty old t-shirt that was lying on the floor.

He woke up vaguely upset, and lay in the dark thinking about it for a while. Could it have been his mind telling him that he needed to stop smoking weed – that he needed literally to unload it from his life, and that he would face obstacles in doing it?

He was determined. In spite of the disturbing dream, by the time he got out of bed he was positive and enthusiastic about his future.

23.

"The New Elysium International Airport has been fully operational for over seven years," beamed Felicity, "but because of our isolation, the absence of other destinations nearby and our own lack of tourist infrastructure, most of the air traffic has been dedicated to cargo. Although a few lucky, wealthy or well-connected New Elysium citizens have waved farewell to it from the airport, we have welcomed precious few visitors to our city in the past. Is that all about to change? If it does, we'll probably be able to thank our next guest. He's an acclaimed documentary and feature film director from the new tinsel town, Sydney, Australia, and he's planning a documentary that will show the world just what a wonderful home we've made for ourselves here. Who knows, his work may even entice a few of his audience to visit us. Please put your hands together and give a rousing New Elysium welcome to Stone Carpenter." Raising her hands above her head, Felicity slapped her hands together noisily, and the small studio audience joined in energetically.

Taking lengthy strides, a lanky, limber figure in tight black jeans and pointy black boots, a subtly pink shirt and dark bronze leather jacket bounded across the stage. His long dark hair, highlighted in places with glimmers of grey, bounced as he skipped, then fell into place over his long, tanned face as he greeted Felicity with an air kiss. The hostess blushed prettily and sat down. Carpenter dropped casually onto the couch that had been placed next to her.

He turned to survey the audience, casting a seasoned, professional eye across them, as if he was scanning a huge auditorium filled with people, rather than the meagre crowd seated in the bleachers. His grey eyes crinkled with pleasure, and he exhaled. "Wow," he said with a smile.

Felicity could not take her eyes off him, and for a moment she appeared to forget that she was supposed to fill the silence that followed his breathy exclamation. Catching herself, she leaned forward and in an admiring tone said, "Wow indeed. It's a long way from Australia to New Elysium."

"It is," said Carpenter. "You guys aren't easy to get to."

"Let's hope it was worth the effort," said Felicity. "So tell me, just how did you get here?"

"Well Felicity, from Sydney it's a nine-hour flight to Honolulu in the Kingdom of Hawaii," he began. "Then there is a layover there for a day or two, then a long flight on a smaller jet to Monterrey, one of the few cities of any size and sophistication in Mexico. From there we took a charter flight to New Elysium, which as you know has no scheduled passenger flights in or out, and that took about five and a half hours. We arrived here early this morning, so you'll forgive me if I don't sparkle."

"You look so fresh," said Felicity. "It must have been those two days in Hawaii."

"It is very nice there," he said. "The Hawaiians seem to have done very well as an independent nation."

Felicity wasn't interested in hearing about any other place that might be doing well. This was supposed to be about New Elysium. "If you're tired, I won't ask you too many difficult questions," she said with a supportive smile, which Carpenter returned glowingly.

"So, you're here to scout locations for your documentary on New Elysium? How exciting – for us I mean."

"And very exciting for me too, Felicity," Carpenter said. "Your little city is something of a mystery to us in the outside world. You're the only city of any magnitude or, may I say it, accomplishment, in what used to be the continental United States, and yet you're virtually unknown to anyone. Here you are, tucked away in your little mountain country hideaway, fully self-sufficient, sustainable, I must confess quite beautiful and exquisitely planned, and yet practically unknown. When I return to make my documentary, I'll be coming here to change that. I want the world to know what a stunning example New Elysium should be to all of us."

"Oh, you're too kind," said Felicity. She was gushing and blushing all at the same time.

"Not at all." Carpenter was in earnest. "You must understand, the rest of the world hasn't changed much. There were adjustments of course, and economic problems, but in the main we just picked up where we left off, devouring the environment, being socially dysfunctional and antagonistic, and scrabbling around for scraps of success. We re-joined the rat race with barely a second thought. You, on the other hand, created a uniquely co-operative, sustainable and cohesive society from the very least of beginnings. That's something you should be proud of."

The audience burst into spontaneous applause, and Felicity acted as though the praise was meant for at her alone. She accepted it with a willing heart.

"And it's something I think you should share with the world," said Carpenter. He knew he was winning the audience, but it was also obvious that his passion was not a put-on.

"And that's what you're here to do," said Felicity. Her curls were positively bobbling with girlish glee.

"Yes, indeed. I want to see what makes New Elysium the city that it is. How do you have such a low crime rate? How do you ensure that all these co-operative gardens work, and that people don't quibble over who's growing what, or when? What's this incredible sustainable energy source that I keep hearing of, that nobody knows anything about in any detail? I've come on a fact finding mission, Felicity, because I think the world needs to see just what a brilliant model of collective responsibility and passionate participation you've created here. Once I understand it, I will make sure the rest of the world sees it."

"Well I think you're in for a real treat, Stone," Felicity said. "New Elysium is even lovelier and better organised than you may think. In fact, yesterday we had a crew go out and just quickly shoot a few little highlights of our town to share with you, and maybe give you some ideas. Although of course we wouldn't presume to tell you how to shoot your documentary," she added.

Stone Carpenter turned in his seat, craning around to

find a monitor to watch, looking genuinely interested. "I'd love to see it," he said.

Felicity jiggled her ringlets and gestured to the control box behind Jakob's camera. "Roll the vision," she said. As the images that the crew had shot the day before filled the monitors with scenes of New Elysium life, Felicity narrated for her guest and her viewers.

"Our city centre, as you can see, is built around a huge peoples' park," she said. "All of New Elysium is filled with parks like this. What you're seeing here, Stone, is a local meet. Every corner of every block – which we call co-ops – opens out into a wide public square called a meet, where markets are held, and people gather for all kinds of reasons. Every meet has its own row of hospitality and retail businesses, run by locals for the benefit of the co-op, that is, everyone who lives on the block, and wherever possible using produce from the co-op garden. Here we see a co-op garden, where everyone pitches in to grow almost everything that they need to eat, fresh and organic. Oh, see, this is North-West Boulevard. See how wide and airy it is? Rumour has it that Captain Flynt, who designed the city, got the idea from Napoleon the Third, who rebuilt Paris with wide boulevards in the nineteenth century so he could easily move troops around to quell any disturbances, tee hee."

"I'm sure there would never be any reason for troop movements in New Elysium," said Stone Carpenter, buying into the joke. "But it certainly makes for a lovely, open city," he said.

And so it went, through the five-minute edit of the footage that Jakob and his team had gathered the previous day, with Felicity acting as tour guide and Stone Carpenter her willing guest. As the short piece ended with a beautiful shot of the sun falling behind the imposing façade of City Hall, casting a molten lead glow on the polished glass surfaces, Stone Carpenter applauded loudly and the audience followed suit.

"That is magnificent," he cooed. "And beautifully shot. Who filmed it?"

Zeke, on camera two, immediately swung his lens onto a startled Jakob, who had been intent on his dual targets, Carpenter and Felicity, while the vision was playing, catching their reactions. Up in the control box, Derren instructed the vision switcher to put Jakob on screen.

"That would be our own camera operator, Jakob Petersson," said Felicity with a proprietorial air, indicating Jakob by waving her hand in his general direction. Unexpectedly, Stone Carpenter got up out of his chair and walked over to Jakob, holding out a hand for him to shake. Bashful but beaming with satisfaction, Jakob shook the famous director's hand gratefully while the audience clapped their appreciation.

Skipping back to his seat, Carpenter said to Felicity, "I wonder if you could spare Jakob for a day or two? I'd love to have him along as my guide while I scout the city, and pick up a few shots to show my team back in Oz."

A delighted look on her face, Felicity looked across to a vigorously nodding Jakob and then up to the control box, where she could just make out a thumbs up from Derren, and said, "Yes, of course, I'm sure Jakob would be thrilled to go along with you."

Zeke still had his camera trained on Jakob, so Derren ordered the focus to cut back to him. He said, "As long as I can take along the rest of my crew, Felicity."

Stone Carpenter laughed and nodded, and Felicity said, "Done!"

Throughout the rest of the taping Jakob was in a bit of a daze. To be asked to spend time with the famous Stone Carpenter was an honour, as well as being a welcome break from the routine of shooting tedious interviews with the low flying celebrities of New Elysium.

As Felicity threw to a commercial break with a happy, "We'll be right back with Stone Carpenter to talk about the international film scene in booming Sydney," Lars and Toney emerged from the shadows and clapped Jakob on the back. "Love your work JP," said Lars. "This is going to be fun!"

24.

There was no talk of post-work beers, even though everyone was in a celebratory mood. The three usual suspects, Jakob, Toney and Lars, were all keen to get home early and sober, sleep well and be up early and bright for a day with Stone Carpenter.

Jakob went home as soon as the program taping wrapped, and spent an energising hour in the main garden tending the winter rye grass crop, then cleaning up the tomato trellises in the hydroponic hothouse, checking the salad greens for bugs, and harvesting cucumbers and spinach, which he put into the community cool room. It was the first time in weeks that he'd spent any real time in the community garden, and although none of his neighbours ever said anything or put any pressure on him to contribute more, everyone knew who was carrying their weight and who was not. He enjoyed pottering about and said to himself that he really ought to come home early more often, and spend more time relaxing out there.

He was about to finish up when Dave Belleville burst in, stamping his feet and blustering about the cold. He'd dashed across the garden from his place in a t-shirt, track pants and socks, and he was obviously feeling the chill. He flapped his arms about, and only after a few seconds of this did he appear to notice Jakob. His face split into a broad toothy grin.

"Oh g'day Jake," he said. "Didn't see you there. Just popped in for a couple of tomatoes for a home-made pizza. What are you up to?"

"Just helping out, Dave," said Jakob pleasantly. He was pleased to see Dave while he was sober, for a change. He'd be able to field any of Dave's usual curly questions, and to see through his usual sly insinuations. "Say, thanks for giving Lars and me a lift home the other night," he said.

"Absolute pleasure, Jakey," said Dave, as he busied himself squeezing tomatoes on the vine, looking for a nice plump one. "Probably a good idea that I did eh? Can't have you two making a bloody nuisance of yourselves on the public transport, can we."

"We would have been fine, Dave." Jakob kept his amiable face on.

"I'm sure you would have mate," said Dave. "Even if you did look like you were plotting murder, all huddled up like that." He winked to show that he was joking, but once again Jakob was struck by Dave's incredible perceptiveness. He chose not to respond, on the basis that anything he said could possibly be taken the wrong way.

"So," said Dave. "Stone."

Jakob was immediately defensive. "No, I'm not stoned at all Dave," he snapped.

Dave giggled. "Not stoned, Jake. Stone," he said. "Carpenter, as in."

Blushing, Jakob studied the cucumber he was holding intently. "Oh, that."

"Yeah. I heard he was in town, and that he picked a certain

famous friend of mine to be his guide and shooting companion over the next few days."

"You don't miss much, do you Dave?" Jakob said.

Dave shrugged his burly shoulders. "Hey, it's my job," he said. "Big deal for you though eh?"

It was true, it was a big deal for Jakob, and he was immensely proud of it. He held further hopes that he would be invited to take part in filming the actual documentary. He didn't want to give too much away though, so he shrugged and kept examining vegetables with unwarranted intensity.

"Nah, good on you mate," said Dave, aware that Jakob was adopting a mask of humility he didn't actually feel.

At last Jakob turned away from the growing bed in front of him and looked squarely at Dave. "Thanks Dave, I appreciate it."

"Hey, you earned it buddy," Dave said, and he was being genuine. "Anyway," he said, plucking a tomato and tossing it lightly up and down in his hands. "Got what I came for. Catch ya later."

After Dave had left, Jakob tried not to let his mellow mood dissipate, but Dave's intimate knowledge of almost every aspect of his life was disturbing. His mind returned to the mystery of his lost hours, and he asked himself if Dave had anything to do with them. And if so, what? Even if the White Hat was not directly involved, why had he shown up that week? And what had happened to him, anyway? He shook his head and tried to concentrate on the gardening, but the moment was lost.

As he cooked his vegetable stir-fry, his spirits revived

a little. He was undeniably excited and positively nervous about the shoot with Stone Carpenter, and he hoped it would all go well. He ate heartily, watched television for just a short while, and took himself off to bed early for a good night's sleep.

It was not the most restful night he'd ever had; he was beset by dreams he couldn't remember and fears he couldn't name. But he rose in the early darkness hopeful of a good day. In spite of the disruptions, he'd had enough sleep that he wouldn't have that sour, sensitive edge to his outlook all day.

25.

The rest of his crew was in the office as early and were as eager as Jakob. They had the equipment neatly packed in the electro-van in near-record time. Consequently, they were reduced to sitting in the café downstairs at the city's only hotel, more of a small three-storey bed and breakfast really, while Stone Carpenter was upstairs getting ready. When he at last joined them, ten minutes late, he was breezy, cheery and dressed for a blizzard. "I can't take this bloody cold," he said with a rueful grin. "It's still summer in Sydney." As they went out to the van, a hotel employee lugging a huge crate followed them and stowed it in the van.

This done, and with formal introductions effected between Carpenter and Toney and Lars by Jakob, they all bundled into the vehicle and headed off for the day's shooting. Carpenter had a list of sites to visit and sights to see, starting with an exterior of the city from the east, so the early sun would be shining on the tall dark fortifications of the city walls. "I want to get far enough away so that we can see the whole of the east wall, and hopefully the mountains in the background," said Carpenter. "Is that do-able?"

"Too easy," answered Jakob, who was driving. He'd taken the position that, as the reason for this expedition, he was its captain. He was going to act the part as much as possible. In the back, Lars and Toney rolled their eyes at each other. Still, an over-enthusiastic Jakob was better than a dark, moody one.

As they drove away from the city centre along the wide, clean roadway of Grand Concourse East, Carpenter gave them his version of the history of the world since the EMP, much of which they hadn't really heard or paid any attention to. Like everyone else in New Elysium they had been almost exclusively focused on surviving for the first five or ten years, and then so isolated from the rest of the world that what was going on out there did not seem relevant. The Military Council had not seemed predisposed to keeping the populace informed about the state of the outside world either, and the media tended to concentrate on inconsequential matters like celebrities and movies, and reality television shows that reflected precisely nothing of reality.

"The EMP turned the world away from the path toward war," said Carpenter in what sounded more like a history book introduction than a casual conversation. It was as though he had rehearsed it several times during his long journey to the city. "It seems that the main driver of aggression had been the United States. Sorry," he apologised rhetorically, and kept speaking without waiting for acknowledgement. Everyone in the vehicle knew what he meant.

"All that talk about Russian aggression and Chinese perfidy, all that bluster about Iranian nuclear plots and South American havens of oppression, turned out to be pretty much a hundred percent propaganda," he said. "In fact, the people running the countries that had been most vehemently demonised by the right wingers running the United States in those days were the first to jump to its aid after the EMP hit. Of course, there wasn't much they could do since so much of the country was an irradiated wasteland, but China and Russia both accepted huge numbers of refugees, as well as thousands of overseas military personnel stranded in overseas bases. But the important thing is that when the United States disappeared off the map, almost all of the tension and antagonism in the world evaporated with it. It wasn't just that the USA was driving a lot of the belligerent talk, as well as dropping bombs and sending armies into quite a number of countries. It was also that we all, just about everyone in the world, realised that we're all vulnerable, and that we work best as a species when we work together. It was a wake-up call of a heavy, heavy order. Of course, the fact that most of the world's economies imploded helped. We had a global problem, or a series of them really, and it took a lot of cooperation and a long time to get through them."

They were outside the city now, driving directly at the fast-rising sun. Fields that in summer would be flaming with golden wheat and waving green with corn and other crops lay bare beneath the winter skies, awaiting the seeds that would bring them back to generous life.

"Europe was particularly hard hit," continued Carpenter. "Politically it had become a suburb of Washington, so in addition to dealing with economic disaster and fearful, agitated people, it was kind of rudderless. For a while it looked as though some strong-minded type would step up and become the dictator that the continent seemed to be craving, but eventually the European Community dissolved into its constituent states again, and government became what it should always have been; locally situated and determined. These days there's a much greater appreciation of the unique contribution that each individual country can make, and because they all mostly leave their neighbours alone to get on with their own jobs, relations are pretty good. In fact, I'd say that's the case for the rest of the world.

"The Asian economies all came through the problem fairly well, and we in the southern hemisphere were least affected of all in a physical sense – our fish are still edible, our skies clear and our political systems intact. Of course our economies suffered for a long time, and certainly we in Australia had to rebuild the manufacturing economy we'd off-shored in emulation of USA, but we're through that now, and the future looks good for us. And for someone like me in the film industry, my home is now the centre of the universe, so it worked out pretty well. Sorry," he apologised again. "That sounds a little insensitive."

"No, not at all," said Jakob. "It's really interesting to get another perspective. We'd almost forgotten about the rest of the world, to be honest."

"And we appreciate your candour, Stone," said Lars. "That's exactly the kind of narrative we would never get from Colonel Martin and the Military Council. They think we still need to be protected from the history of our own country. Or ex-country, as the case may be."

"Let's stop and see how that shot looks from here," suggested Jakob, pulling the van up to the side of the road.

They ended up driving a little further into the farmlands to get the widest possible shot, and Jakob did a long, slow pull-back from the distant mountains to the city, as well as several wider shots. From this distance and with the morning light falling on it the wall looked tall, straight and uniform, as though it were made of golden bricks. Up close, it was nothing of the sort. It was over a hundred and twenty metres thick at the bottom, rising to a tapered top over seventy metres above the surrounding plain; a giant, prickly caterpillar made of recycled concrete, rocks, bricks, steel and rubble scavenged from Colorado Springs, Pueblo and the other extinct towns around New Elysium. This giant rampart was capped by a parapet of concrete, wide enough to accommodate the small vehicles the White Hats drove around the city's perimeter once every couple of hours.

These establishing shots in the can, the crew got back into the van and headed back up the same road toward the city.

"Next stop, the Energy Directorate," said Carpenter, consulting his hand-written notes. "I'm curious about this famous but mysterious sustainable energy source of yours," he said. "What can you tell me?"

Jakob shrugged, and in the back Toney and Lars looked blank. "Not much, Stone," said Lars. "It's not something they talk about."

"What's it based on?" asked Carpenter. "Surely it isn't fossil fuel based, and I can't imagine it has anything to do with nuclear fission or even fusion. Is it geothermal? Solar? A combination? Or is there some other energy source that the rest of the world doesn't know about? It's all very intriguing."

"Sorry, I couldn't tell you any of that," said Jakob. "As Lars says, it's not something that the authorities ever talk about, and we Elysiumites don't ask a lot of questions."

"I can understand that," said Carpenter. "After all, your Military Council has created what appears to be a model society from virtually nothing, so why would you ask questions? Even my short time in your town has shown me that you are reticent, pliable people not given to making waves. I'm not sure your society is equipped to handle even gentle enquiries, let alone genuine questions. And that's not a criticism; you're just a product of your environment. But I'm an outsider, and it's my job to ask tough questions, so I intend to find out exactly what your secret is. If for no other reason than that if it's as wonderful an energy source as it seems to be, you really ought to share it with the rest of the world."

"You know, I never thought of it like that before," said Toney. It was hard to tell under the shaggy fringe that shaded her dark eyes, but she seemed to be chewing on this new idea quite meditatively. "We really have become very insular, haven't we," she said.

"You have," said Carpenter, "but that's to be expected. You're insulated. The nearest place of any consequence is a god-awful journey away from here, the way your city runs is like no other on earth, and almost nobody ever comes or goes from here. So don't feel bad."

He turned around to throw an encouraging smile to Toney, which she accepted with a happy, open smile. An observer might have wondered if there was something developing between them; it was obvious that Carpenter found her attractive, and she was clearly in awe of him.

The drive continued in silence as each of the van's occupants contemplated what had been said so far, what had remained unsaid, and what would happen next.

26.

The vehicle re-entered New Elysium via the gate they'd exited an hour or so before, and turned left onto South-East Boulevard a couple of kilometres short of the city centre. They had to drive all the way across the city to the far southwest corner to get to the Energy Directorate, and as they drove Stone Carpenter explained what he wanted from the location.

"This is just a reconnaissance mission," he began. "When I return with my own crew in a few months' time I hope to have pre-arranged an interview with the person in charge, but before then I want to see if I can get some clue as to what this wondrous energy source is, and what goes on in the generation area."

"The person in charge is actually Tom Flynt," said Jakob. "He not only designed the city, he's the brains behind the energy system as well."

Carpenter broke into a broad grin and shook his head admiringly. "He's a bit of a star that Flynt, isn't he," he said. "Still, that's a good thing, because I'll definitely be interviewing him when I return." He rubbed his hands together and looked very pleased with himself. "So we'll try to get inside today, but if not we can just pick up a couple of shots for reference. Somehow I doubt they'll let us in."

As they approached the vast, virtually unknown complex, their hope that they could simply arrive and be let in evaporated entirely. It looked more like a prison than an electricity station, with tall concrete walls that joined with the outer walls of the city so that its entire perimeter was encircled. The walls were topped by rolls and rolls of shred wire, and every hundred metres or so there was a tower populated by what appeared to be heavily armed White Hat guards. It was an absolute fortress. Nonetheless, they drove toward the gate near the north-eastern corner to at least ask the question.

The robust iron gate was actually a little below the surrounding ground level, as though the roadway dived under the wall, so they had to drive down a deep culvert to access it. The gate was recessed into the wall, and was unguarded – there was an intercom system and a keypad for authorised entrants to punch in their codes to enter. Jakob leaned out and pressed the button on the intercom, and when a curt "yes" came through the little speakers, Stone Carpenter leaned across him to conduct the conversation.

"G'day, Stone Carpenter from Australia here. You may have heard, I'm coming to New Elysium to make a movie and I'd very much like to bring my crew from your local television station, NETV, in for a bit of a look around. Just grab a couple of shots, maybe talk to a couple of people on the ground in there, you know, make you famous."

The voice behind the intercom was not fazed by Carpenter's warm, goofy Aussie introduction. In as few words as possible she said that she could not under any circumstances admit Mr Carpenter or his crew without the express permission of the Director, Major Flynt, who would assign them a guide if he were to allow them in at all. If they wished to apply for permission, they could do so at Major Flynt's office in the city.

Carpenter thanked the unseen sentry warmly, apologised for wasting her time, and finished with a "Cheers," but the look on his face was anything but cheery. If anything he looked suspicious, but not deterred. "Turn around, Jakob," he said darkly.

Jakob put the electro-van into reverse and went into a five-point turn in the narrow roadway, while his passengers remained quiet. Stone Carpenter looked around with intense concentration while Jakob spun the wheel backwards and forwards. As they drove up the short rise to ground level, Carpenter said, in a taut near-whisper, "There's a little track on the right at the top, take it."

Jakob obeyed, and they found themselves on a well-worn track that looked as though it was used by guards to check the perimeter at ground level. There was a cover of sparse bushes and scrub not much higher than a tall man's head covering the vacant land surrounding the installation, so they were soon all but invisible to anyone driving down the road to the gateway. Carpenter ordered Jakob to stop, and they all got out, right under the huge wall. Carpenter casually retrieved the heavy crate from the van. As he started to open it, the low whirr of an approaching electro-van broke the cold silence. Instinctively, they all ducked. "Go see what that is will you, Jakob," said Carpenter. His voice was steady and calm, as though they were out for a Sunday jaunt.

Sticking to the bushes closest to the wall and trying to remain invisible, Jakob crept the few metres back toward the roadway, parting a couple of scratchy, almost bare branches to peer down to the gate. He was startled to see a White Hat van, a personnel carrier like the one Dave had driven him and Lars home in – and even more so to see Dave lean out of the driver's seat and punch a six-digit passcode into the keypad on the wall. Jakob shrank back and watched through the sticks, feeling vulnerable. But the gate slid open and Dave drove through without even glancing his way. As soon as the van was inside, the gates rolled closed, and Jakob breathed for the first time in what seemed like several minutes.

Back at the van, he could see that Stone had unboxed a small quad-copter remote-controlled drone with a miniature camera attached to it, and he was setting up a remote viewer in the back of the van. Horrified and fascinated in equal measure, they watched the Australian put the thing together. In a few short minutes, he hit the button and the quad-copter rose to about three metres, making little more noise than the rushing of air from its four spinning blades. The monitor showed the four of them looking up at it in perfect clarity and definition. The drone kept rising, and the image of them got smaller and smaller as the field of view widened. In just a few seconds it was above the level of the wall top, and Carpenter piloted it inside the facility, with the camera pointing west.

The monitor showed, unexpectedly, that on the other side of the wall, really just a few metres from them, there was a huge open garden and growing area, mostly empty at this time of year but with some winter crops growing, and several corrals filled with cows and sheep, along with what may have been long, narrow chicken houses. There were also vast greenhouses and hothouses further south – it appeared that all together an area perhaps six hundred metres wide and fifteen hundred metres deep was given over to growing food. At the far end, where the east wall met the larger south wall of the city perimeter, there were three long, double storey buildings.

Carpenter put the bird into a further climb, and they could see that there were several large water tanks along the southern edge of the facility, a huge block of a building that was presumably the energy generation plant, and at the northwestern edge of the expanse, an array of enormous transformers that doubtless fed the electricity generated into the underground network of cables delivering it to the people of New Elysium.

The copter banked and started flying toward the generation station, dropping closer as it did so. There was a loud crack followed by the sound of an explosion within the walls that they could hear quite plainly, and the picture on the monitor went dead. The drone had been shot down.

At almost the same moment, several beefy White Hats emerged silently from the bushes and pointed semi-automatic weapons at the crew. Only Stone Carpenter had the temerity to grin like a naughty schoolboy.

Jakob had a vision of himself being seized by White Hats on a dark night, and he began to shake. It was as if he was in a different body, in a different time; a memory that somehow didn't exist and yet was there in front of him warped reality and made his head spin. He trembled and wondered if he was going to survive as the White Hats closed in on him. Then the vision passed and he was back outside the Energy Directorate with his friends and Stone Carpenter. The only thing that was the same was the presence of severe, menacing White Hats surrounding them, although in this instance they had not – yet – laid a hand on him.

"We might have picked the wrong spot to fly our little chopper, eh," said Stone Carpenter. Toney giggled nervously, but no-one else said anything for a few moments. Then one of the White Hats spoke up.

"This is a restricted area," she said.

"I didn't see a sign," said Carpenter.

"You don't need to see a sign," she replied. Her voice harsh, and her stare bored holes into his still smiling face. "This is an unpopulated industrial zone next to a dangerous electrical facility. You have no business being here, and you have no business flying drones over the space above it."

"It was the only way we could get a look," said Carpenter. He was cool but insistent, and the White Hats did not intimidate him. "Your lot wouldn't let us in for a tour, even though we asked nicely, so we figured we'd just have a quick squiz ourselves. No biggie."

"He's not from here," said Lars. "We probably should have warned him…" his voice trailed off. He looked concerned but not alarmed, as did Toney. Only Jakob appeared terrified. Rooted to the spot, his eyes were wide and his hands clenched and unclenched mechanically.

"Yes, you should have," said the White Hat. She wandered off a few feet and spoke into an intercom taped to her shoulder with her back to them. She nodded a couple of times, then turned around and walked back to where the tense group was standing.

"We're to escort you back into the city, where Major Flynt wishes to discuss this incident with you," she said. "Sergeant Ericsson, you will drive their electro-van, Dolan and Sharpe you will follow to ensure compliance," she ordered, before turning on her heel and stalking off, followed by the rest of the detachment.

White Hat Ericsson hustled the crew into the van, then waited while the other two picked up Carpenter's crate and remote control and took it to their vehicle, which had been left on the road outside the gate. Not much was said on the long, quiet drive back to the city. Carpenter seemed reluctant to speak in front of the White Hat, and Lars and Toney were subdued but calm. Jakob was not. He was terrified, and he kept passing his trembling hands backwards and forwards over his face. Sweat beaded on his upper lip and sometimes gleamed on his forehead. He was slow to respond to the few statements and questions put to him.

"What's the matter Jakob, you okay?" asked Lars a short way into the drive.

"Yeah you look really stressed," said Toney. "Relax, there isn't much they can do to us."

"Yeah I, um. Yeah I'm fine," said Jakob slowly in a dreamy, faraway voice. "It's just that I ... um. Never mind I'll be okay."

"Don't let it worry you Jakob," said Stone Carpenter easily.

"I'll take the rap, you lot will get sent home for the afternoon to contemplate your sins, and tomorrow we'll be back on the road. We've still got plenty of stuff to do."

"I'd be more worried about what Derren will say than Major Flynt," joked Lars unconvincingly.

27.

Garvin Wintz smirked knowingly when the three White Hats ushered Stone Carpenter and his guilty little team into the outer office, and without even saying anything got up and opened the door into Flynt's suite. As soon as they were inside Flynt dismissed the White Hats with a nod, leaving Carpenter, Lars, Toney and Jakob lined up with their backs to the door, looking out the huge windows. A bank of grey clouds was moving in swiftly from the mountains, and it looked as though it may begin to snow in a short while.

"Huh, looks like it would have been a crap day for shooting anyway," Stone Carpenter said to no-one in particular. "Maybe tomorrow."

"There will be no more work on this project," said Major Flynt in a short, decisive tone. There was none of the affable urbanity that he had showed on their last visit. His voice, his face and his stare were as cold and hard as frozen steel. He stopped in front of Stone Carpenter, callously invading the director's personal space and jutting his jaw even closer, so that they were eyeball to eyeball.

"You have grossly exceeded your authority and abused this city's hospitality, Mr Carpenter," he said. It was no surprise that he presumed to speak for the city. It was, after all, his creation.

"Your behaviour is an affront to the people who have worked so hard to get you here, and an insult to every citizen of New Elysium," the Major continued. "Accordingly I have no option but to terminate your visitor's permit and the city's agreement to appear in your little travelogue. Your hotel room is being cleared as we speak; your luggage will be delivered to you at the airport. I have ordered a flight to return you to Monterrey, from whence you can do as you wish. However, you will not under any circumstances return to New Elysium. Good day."

He turned his back on Carpenter and walked to his desk, leaned over and pressed a button on the intercom system.

"Garvin, Mr Carpenter is ready to go," he said. Immediately the door opened and two new White Hats appeared, ready to transport Stone Carpenter to the airport.

"What are you hiding, Flynt?" said a now red-faced Carpenter. "What goes on out there? Why does an electricity plant need bloody great gardens and feedlots?"

Flynt's nostrils flared almost imperceptibly, and he turned a frigid stare on the Australian as the two White Hats each took an arm to forcibly remove him from the office.

"New Elysium is no longer your concern, Mr Carpenter," he said. "Nor will it ever be again."

"I'll haunt you Flynt!" shouted Carpenter. "I've been stonewalled before you know. I didn't get to be the world's most awarded documentary maker by making puff pieces. You and your pissy little city won't come out of this well." The door slammed shut and they could hear muffled shouts as Carpenter kept raving all the way down the hall.

In an instant, Flynt's expression was softer, his tone more accommodating. He sat informally on the edge of his desk and looked at the three remaining before him.

"I understand," he said with placid indulgence. "You got caught up in the moment. You had a world famous director with you, and he led you astray." He shrugged. "We already know he supplied the drone, and that he tried to bully his way into the Directorate. It's easy to see how you were carried along. It was a bit silly of you to do what you did, but I know it was just a mistake of a kind that will never happen again. Am I right?" He smiled to show his sincerity. They nodded vigorously. The wave of relief that swept the room was almost palpable. Even Jakob, who'd been in a wretched state of dread ever since they'd been baled up at the Energy Directorate, began to relax a little.

"Of course, you won't speak of this to anyone," said the Major. "If anyone at the station asks, Mr Carpenter had to cut short his visit to attend a family emergency at home, and he will return at a later date. Is that clear?" Again a trio of heads nodded briskly.

"Excellent. You may go," said Flynt. "Please don't give me any cause to regret my leniency. Nobody is irreplaceable."

Jakob was first out the door, followed closely by Toney and Lars, and none of them looked back. As they closed the door, the Major smiled again, more warmly, to himself. He was fairly certain his point had been well made.

28.

The short drive back to the station was quiet. Lars and Toney joked very quietly about how they had fallen victim to exactly the kind of star-struck madness that the Major had referred to, while Jakob, driving, appeared lost in his own thoughts.

They had unpacked the electro-van and were about to go up to the production office when Jakob asked, "What do we tell Derren?"

"We tell her exactly what Flynt told us to say," said Lars. "We're not fucking around with this Jakob. And by we, I mean you." The look on his face said that he was worried Jakob would get them into real trouble.

"I just think she should know the truth," said Jakob. "She won't say anything."

"Nothing doing pal," said Toney. "You stick with the official version." She was almost angry, daring Jakob to present an opposing view so she could rip him apart. He ceded the point instantly; there was nothing he could say that would change their minds, and he wondered whether they might have been right anyway.

They went upstairs and dutifully trotted out the fabricated story to Derren, embellishing it with the plausible detail that Carpenter had taken the footage they'd shot in their time together. Derren gave them all the rest of the day off, which didn't elicit the joyful reaction she'd anticipated, and she was even more surprised when they each went their separate ways without even mentioning a few quiet ones at Mickey's. But she was too busy to dwell on it. She went back to work.

29.

If ever there was a night on which Jakob would have felt justified in getting out his stash and rolling a joint, this was it. What the drone had showed him of the Energy Directorate compound, the swift and terrifying reaction of the White Hats, and Tom Flynt's cold expulsion of Stone Carpenter swirled around his mind like mismatched pieces of a puzzle. What the hell could be going on in there? Why did the facility need feedlots, greenhouses and gardens? Why did the whole thing seem ominous to him, and somehow connected to his own missing day?

The dope was there in the hall cupboard, a few metres away. He could almost hear it calling him. Just one toke, or maybe two, and it would all go away. His plaguing questions would all dissolve in a blue haze and he'd be off to sleep, to unremembered dreams. It would be so easy.

But for some reason he resisted. He didn't want this to go away. It was important. He sat in his darkened room festering, forgetting to eat or do anything else until at last he had to go to the toilet. Then he dragged himself off to bed, anticipating a long, sleepless night, but instead a kind of emotional exhaustion overtook him and he fell quickly and deeply asleep.

30.

As he'd explained to Lars that night, there were three Jakob Peterssons; one who was depressed because he was smoking too much dope, one who was mildly psychotic because he wasn't smoking any dope, and one, mellow, pleasant, though not particularly engaged version, who had just the right amount of tetrahydrocannabinols in his system. This third Jakob never stayed around too long, so it was usually one of the other two who fronted up to work each day.

It was the second Jakob, the irritable, jumpy, snarly, uncooperative and occasionally furious one, that showed up for the next couple of weeks. He wasn't sleeping well, he wasn't enjoying the work or the company of his friends, and he didn't want to change. It was as though he was wallowing in this malaise, happy to be miserable and relishing the negative feedback his gloomy truculence elicited from his co-workers. Their repugnance at his behaviour reinforced his own lack of self-esteem and fortified the wall of self-pity he'd built around himself. And all the time, churning, burning questions tumbled around in the background of his mind, fuelling his unhappiness and giving it focus.

The Stone Carpenter business had made finding a solution to the mystery seem urgent, yet less achievable. He knew he was up against the power of the state, as such. It was obvious that there was something dark going on, and that it had affected him. And yet he had no way of finding out what it was, let alone if or how he could fix it. He felt as though he was the only person in all of New Elysium who had a problem, a lone questioner in a sea of acquiescence. So he retreated into ugly disaffection, alienating his friends with his biting hostility, tiresome cynicism and cantankerous carping. His only joy was time spent alone, often in his greenhouse but also in the community garden and hothouse, where he worked at odd hours to minimise the chances of running into anyone and having to engage in forced pleasantries.

The one shining light was the fact that Dave Belleville was not around. In fact, he was so absent that in his more paranoid moments Jakob wondered whether the White Hat was avoiding him, possibly wishing not to be seen with him after the Energy Directorate incursion. Often when he arrived home he could feel Dave's eyes on him from inside his house, which did nothing to assuage his mounting paranoia, but all the same he was glad not to have to interact with him. He was sure Dave would know all about the incursion, and he dreaded the thought of answering questions or being subject to Dave's penetrating gaze and knowing leer. So, as he did with everything else, he hustled, face down and collar up, everywhere he went, avoiding contact with everyone and anyone.

At night he wrestled with the questions besetting him. He even contemplated knocking on Dave's door and asking him straight out what was going on at the Directorate. But he knew that would be a foolish and possibly self-destructive move, and even he wasn't feeling that negative about himself. So he kept to himself and brooded, going out only to work, and being a pain in the ass of everyone there when he did.

Eventually, Lars and Toney, the two people who had to work most closely with him, had had enough. They forced him to go with them to Mickey's.

Lars pressed a bag of weed into his hands and begged him to go home and smoke it.

"You're giving everyone the shits JP," he said. "You make even the easiest jobs hard, and the hard jobs impossible. How do you think that makes me and Toney feel? Even Derren is ready to strangle you, and that's saying something."

Jakob stared at the coaster next to his drink on the table. "I know I've been a little bit difficult lately," he said. Both Toney and Lars guffawed; this was the funniest thing he'd said in weeks. "It's just that the business with Carpenter really threw me. I can't get it out of my head."

"You need to," said Toney. "If you don't, you could get us all in trouble. And you're not doing yourself any favours, moping around and making an asshole of yourself all the time."

"Yeah, just smoke the weed and go back to your normal depression for Christ's sake," said Lars.

"I can't." Jakob shook his head. "I don't want to smoke weed. I don't want to get better, unless it's by finding out what's really going on out at the Energy Directorate, and whether it has anything to do with that night."

"What night?" Lars was losing his patience.

"You know, that night back before Christmas, when something happened and I disappeared for twenty-four hours."

"You were shitfaced," said Lars. "You slept it off for a whole day, big deal."

"No, it's more than that," insisted Jakob. "Something happened."

"Well I'll tell you, something else that will happen if you don't straighten up and stop being a pill – you'll lose your job and all your friends," Toney said.

Jakob managed a weak smile. "I know it's been hard on you guys and I'm sorry, but I really can't help it. I'll try and get better."

"Just take the weed home and smoke it," repeated Lars.

"You know I've still got that other weed you gave me," Jakob said.

"Dude, smoke that as well. Get wasted. Out of your mind. Dribbling and drooling. It will do you good, and stop us from having to take to your head with a hatchet," said Lars. "Seriously."

"I'll see what I can do," replied Jakob. He drank off the rest of his beer and put the empty down carefully on the coaster. It was only his third. He got up from his stool, pocketing the weed Lars had given him as he did so. "I think I need to take a walk," he said.

"But it's early," said Toney. "Have another one with us."

"No, you two stay and have another, but I'll be off."

"We worry about you Jakob," said Toney. Her dark eyes were penetrating but also soft, like her slightly sad smile.

"Thanks," he said, meaning it. They were good friends, and he'd put them through the wringer since the Carpenter incident – which they seemed to have gotten over much more quickly and thoroughly than he had.

He walked out into the brisk, icy evening. It was still quite early, and he wasn't ready to go home and sit in silence and darkness, ruminating. His feet chose their own direction, and he allowed them to take the lead. A slight buzz from the beers invaded his brain, and kept it from its normal solitary slide into questions without answers. He watched the people walking around, the electro-vehicles humming busily up and down the wide streets and boulevards, and the warm light emanating from houses, cafes and bars. Ultimately, he knew exactly where his feet would take him. Maybe Ellandra could help him make sense of the whole mess – if she didn't immediately get angry and toss him out on the street with instructions never to darken her doorstep again. Although that was the most likely outcome, he told himself he had to try.

His fingers found the little bag of weed in his pocket. It felt bulky and a little bit mushy, and probably very sticky. It would certainly do the job Lars and Toney wanted it to, should he let it. But he didn't want to do that. He wanted to stay straight, because for a change he wanted answers rather than escape from questions. And he was convinced Ellandra was the key that would unlock those answers.

Approaching her house, his resolve faltered. Last time he'd brought the subject up, it had put a swift end to their growing rapport. Incandescent wasn't too strong a word to describe her anger. Hesitating just across the street from Ellandra's house, Jakob began debating with himself yet again. He recognised just how wretched he was being, but he couldn't help it. If Ellandra went berserk at him now, it might just send him over the edge. But then again she had had some weeks to think about it all, and she might just want to help him this time. Besides, anything would be better than this endless unhappy suspicion, conjecture and speculation. Regaining his resolve, he stepped off the kerb just in time to see Ellandra's front door open, and two people emerge – Ellandra and Tom Flynt, chatting gaily and then heading off down the street arm in arm. So much for the brevity of their relationship.

Suddenly Jakob hated Tom Flynt. Why was he involved in everything that was bad in Jakob's life? Why was Flynt's own life seemingly so charmed? Surely there were not that many differences between them. Confidence was the big one, as far as Jakob could see. Sure, Flynt may have a breathtaking vision and an artist's flair for bringing it to life, but Jakob reckoned he had those qualities too, it was just that they'd never been brought out. He'd never allowed them to see the light of day.

Turning to walk in the opposite direction to Ellandra and Flynt, Jakob trudged down the street, head down and spirits shattered. He thrust his hands deep in his pocket and once again found the buds that Lars had given him. It was almost as though he had no choice now, he would have to go home and smoke some weed, just to get the tragic image of his ex-wife and his nemesis together out of his head. If getting stoned also blotted out the other foul thoughts and piercing questions that beset him, so much the better. In fact, he might just stay blissfully blazed for the rest of his life. It would be nice to never think seriously again. And if he became disengaged, listless, apathetic and depressed, wouldn't that still be better than being torn and tormented?

An electro-bus came along just as he was passing the stop, and he got on. A short bus ride and he could escape it all, at least for the night. It sounded like a good plan.

Laying back on his couch, stoned and staring into nothingness, his thoughts went off on a journey of their own. Several weeks' worth of bottled up emotion and difficulty started working themselves out in a wild array of ideas and visions. Connections between his problems appeared and then, like dreams, evaporated before he could grasp them. Fancies collided with hopes, fantasies merged with desires, and reality vanished in a haze of unrealities. It was delicious and consuming, and he wondered why the hell he'd waited so long.

But then an idea struck him. A beautiful plan, brutal and audacious in its breadth, with the potential to unlock all his mysteries, crystallised in his mind. It was beyond anything he'd ever dreamed of attempting, but it seemed so right he couldn't ignore it. In that instant it took root, became implanted in his future. He would follow it through for good or ill, and it would sort him out, or more likely kill him. Either way, he would be free. He opened his eyes and accepted the challenge.

31.

Jakob woke up in his bed without remembering how he got there. He must have dragged himself in at some stage; his clothes were heaped on the floor and there was even a glass of water, untouched, on his bedside table. Then he remembered: the plan. It would demand more courage, ingenuity and commitment than he'd ever shown before. He was scared, but empowered. He would make it work. The alarm went off, and he jumped up out of bed full of energy and ready to go.

"Steady tiger," he told himself. The plan required careful thought and structure. If he went at it impulsively, it would come undone immediately and he would be in big trouble. He needed to think through the details and to go into it cool and prepared. No matter that his heart wanted to get started this very instant. His head knew that just wasn't feasible.

Containing his excitement and trepidation, he showered, dressed for work and made a vegetable omelette for breakfast. He was determined to make his day as normal as possible. All things being equal, he would put the plan into action that night. Cover of darkness was crucial.

32.

Lars cracked a huge, knowing grin the moment Jakob walked into the production office. "Ha ha, you smoked that bud didn't you," he said. "Look at you, you're a different man."

Jakob reddened and cast his eyes down, but spoke defensively. "Yes I had a toke last night, but that has nothing to do with the way I feel."

"Bullshit," said Lars. "I haven't seen you look so relaxed and well-rested in days – weeks even."

"Think what you like Lars," said Jakob. "I know why I feel the way I do."

"So do I my friend," persisted Lars. "But don't worry, I approve. Looks like we'll have a pleasant working day without Jakob the bear in the room. Coffee?"

He headed off to the staff kitchen without waiting for an answer. Jakob smiled to himself. They all thought he was so transparent, but none of them knew what was really going on. Well, they'd find out.

The day went well. It was an easy schedule of indoor interviews with various minor identities around town. On the drives from one location to the other Lars flirted with Fleur, Toney tried to keep them apart by inserting herself into the conversation or sitting between them, and Derren tried to keep the peace. Jakob did his job quietly, conscientiously and with good humour. There were no major flare-ups.

All the while, Jakob's mind was whirring with thoughts, ideas and strategies. The first part would be hard, but the second would require more courage and luck. After that he was into the unknown. He needed to be prepared, even if he didn't know what he was preparing himself for. It was tense and exciting. He just wanted to get started.

As soon as the van was unpacked and the gear stowed correctly, Jakob put his overcoat and scarf on, and headed for the door.

"Coming to Mickey's for a heart-starter?" said Lars hopefully when he saw Jakob's hurry.

"Not tonight thanks, things to do."

"The rest of your stash will still be there when you get home after a few beers," Lars said. "No need to rush."

"No smoking tonight for me thank you my good man." Jakob smiled. The "my good man" was a private joke between them.

"If you say so my friend," replied Lars, shaking his head gently. He didn't believe a word of it.

33.

All the way home on the electro-bus, Jakob was deep in thought. His fists were clenched and his stomach tight, but he was resolute. He was going to do it, and do it tonight. After he got off the bus he dropped in at the local bodega for a six-pack of beer. He would need them.

At home, Jakob noted that Dave's White Hat van was parked on the street. He was tempted to go straight to Dave's place and put the plan into action. But he needed a few more minutes.

He went inside and, without taking his coat or anything else off, sat down on his couch in the gloom. His mind was racing and his hand was shaking. Should he have just a small joint to calm his jangling nerves? The notion was tempting. Suddenly the clarity that had been upon him last night when the idea had presented itself was gone, and the enormity of what he was going to do weighed him down. Perhaps if he had a toke or two that clarity would return, and with it the determination that was now faltering.

But no, that wouldn't do. Smoking dope is the fastest route to procrastination, he told himself. If he rolled a joint now, he'd end up doing nothing. And if he did rouse himself to action, his thoughts would be clouded and his reactions sluggish. Everything would come apart. He sat for a few minutes, breathing slowly and bringing down his heart rate.

Then he stood. It had to be done, and done immediately. Should he wear his overcoat, and act as if he was still just on his way home? Or take it off and appear much more casual? Stop thinking, he told himself. He picked up the six-pack and strode out the door.

A few seconds later he was at Dave's front door, knocking without feeling his knuckles striking the timber. Dave answered the door in a pair of tracksuit pants and a singlet, initially looking gruff about being disturbed, but then delighted to see that it was his neighbour. Grinning madly, he pulled the door wide open.

"Jakob, you old bugger," he said. "And look at you, carrying a bloody six-pack. You're a sight for sore eyes. Come in mate, come in." He turned and started stomping back toward the lounge, where a television set could be heard blaring.

As he did so, Jakob reached into the six-pack and grabbed one of the bottles by the neck, took it in an upside down grip so that he was holding it like a club, and smashed it as hard as he could on the back of Dave's head. The White Hat stumbled forward, and a jet of blood spurted out of the gash.

Oh fuck, thought Jakob. If he stays upright, I'm fucked. He'll kill me. He lunged forward and hit him again. The Aussie crashed to the ground with a loud thud. There was blood everywhere, the noise that Dave had made hitting the floor was unexpectedly loud, and the front door was still wide open.

He watched himself close the door, then drag Dave into

240

the lounge room. He found Dave's police belt, unhooked the handcuffs, and, fumbling a bit, handcuffed the White Hat to the foot of his dining table. He took duct tape from his pocket and sealed Dave's mouth. He ran out and took some trellis wire from the greenhouse, and trussed up his prisoner's legs and elbows. Dave wouldn't be able to move.

While Jakob was mopping up some of the blood on his head, Dave came to. Jakob leapt away and threatened Dave with the bloodied beer bottle while the prisoner thrashed and twisted. But he couldn't move; the wire cut into his flesh, and soon he let his body go limp. His eyes starting out of his head with anger and confusion, Dave stared at his captor.

Jakob broke the long stand-off. "I'll take the tape off if you promise you won't scream. But one loud noise, and I will hit you again. I don't want to, and I'm sorry I had to do it already, but I will do it again. Do you understand?"

Dave nodded carefully, and Jakob gingerly leaned forward to rip off the tape. Stunned at the pain this produced, Dave dropped his chin on his chest and swallowed hard. His head, his singlet and pants were all soaked in blood. There was a dull fire in his eyes.

"Jesus, Jakob, what the fuck?" he said.

"I'm sorry Dave, I really am," Jakob said. "This is the only way."

"The only way to what? Kill me?"

"You're angry, and that's understandable, and you're kind of an innocent victim in this, but I have to know what happens at the Energy Directorate. I'm pretty sure it's connected to a day that I lost last year."

Dave snorted with contempt. "You're a fuckin' idiot, Jake," he said. "Even if you find the answer, you really think it will make you happy? It'll fuck you up. And then, at some stage, you'll have to let me go, and I'll fuck you up properly. You're on a one-way trip to shitsville, mate."

"You don't understand," said Jakob. "I can't live without knowing any more. I know there's something bad going on out there, and I have to know. You think I wanted to hurt you and tie you up? You're my friend. I actually like you, even though I'm reasonably certain you were sent here to watch me."

A rivulet of blood trickled from the top of Dave's head down his cheek, causing it to twitch. "Could you wipe that off mate?" asked Dave. "It's driving me nuts."

Still holding the towel he'd used to clean up Dave's head a little beforehand, Jakob dabbed at the stream of blood, then carefully turbaned the towel onto Dave's head to stem any further flows.

Dave's face softened, so he looked more understanding. "I get it," he said. "You're not yourself. Probably got a little weed psychosis going on. I'll tell you what, you let me go now, I tell my boss I fell over in the shower and we forget all about it. What do you say?"

Jakob hesitated for the briefest instant, then he smiled ironically.

"Ha ha, you won't catch me that way. I end up getting taken away, and I never find out what I need to know. And you need to understand Dave, I can't live without knowing. It's making me crazy."

"Finding out the truth won't help you in the slightest mate, I'm telling you. You'll end up exactly where you don't want to be, and you'll rue the day, every long day of your life."

"It can't be worse than not knowing."

It was Dave's turn to laugh ironically. "Oh, my boy you have no idea," he said. "You're a fuckin' idiot, you know that? Do you even have a plan?"

"Oh yes," assured Jakob. "I'm going to put on your uniform, and I'm going to take your van to the Energy Directorate and drive in the front door. Once inside I'm going to use your identity to go wherever I want, and get all the answers I need."

In spite of the throbbing headache pounding in his ears and the stress of having his arms tied together straight out behind him, Dave threw back his head and hooted with laughter.

"Just gonna drive on up to the front door, eh Jakey boy? The bloke that's afraid of his own shadow is gonna drive on up and smash down the front door. Oh, I'd like to see that. You're fucked at the first hurdle old son. You won't even make it past the gate."

A sneer appeared on Jakob's face. Dave's disdain gave him strength and fortitude. He put his face up close to Dave's and said, "Twenty twenty-seventeen," with a mocking leer.

This caused Dave's face to lighten up, and he even grinned a little. "So you know me passcode," he chuckled with a kind of reluctant admiration. "Who'd have thought an old stoner like you would remember a little detail like that?

Well good luck, mate, you'll need it. There's more to getting in and seeing what you want to than just a pin number. You have to be able to handle what you see."

Suddenly tiring of Dave's harangue, and with a rush of wanting to get on with the job, Jakob broke off a long piece of tape and stuck it over the prisoner's mouth, adding a second over the top of it for good measure.

He washed Dave's blood off his hands, face and neck – it really had splashed about – then rifled through his neighbour's wardrobe for a clean uniform. He dressed with care, putting on all the accoutrements of a White Hat: badge, nameplate, truncheon, walkie-talkie and the hat itself – actually more of a cream coloured pith helmet that looked like a pale split banana skin covering his head and most of his face. He looked good in Dave's mirror. The uniform fit quite well, and once again Jakob asked himself why Dave always seemed so much bigger than he did. The way he filled a room was impressive. Still, the uniform did give him an added presence. No-one would notice that the handcuffs were missing, surely?

"Just like the real thing," he whispered softly to himself. And he felt like the real thing. There was a giddy detachment to everything he did, but also the odd sense that he really had assumed the role of Dave Belleville. When he saw himself in the uniform, the last of his reservations dissolved. He really was going to do it.

Sauntering out of the bedroom, he paused in the living room. Dave stared at him with livid malevolence.

"Don't worry, 'mate'," Jakob said with what a patronising

twang, even though he really did feel sorry for the prisoner. "I'll be back to untie you once it's all done. I hope you know it's nothing personal." Dave answered with a muffled roar from under his masking tape gag.

34.

It was late evening by this time, and the streets around their co-op would usually be quiet, if not utterly deserted, but Jakob emerged from Dave's house cautiously. The last thing he needed was for one of the neighbours to recognise him, or to mistake him for Dave and try to strike up a conversation. Carefully locking the door – he'd already turned out the lights – he pushed Dave's White Hat down as far over his face as he could, and peered up and down the street. Not a soul.

He swiftly strode to his own place and retrieved a pen-sized video camera that had been charging all day, then jumped into the White Hat van. He was really doing this.

The drive to the Energy Directorate was eerie. It was so quiet in the unfamiliar vehicle, all the doubts that he'd been pushing to the back of his mind began to assail him again. He was already in deep trouble, why make it worse? Would Dave really just let him go if he went back there and untied him? What would be the consequences if he were to proceed and got caught along the way? Every vehicle that came toward him – and there were thankfully few – was potentially his downfall. The headlights peered into his face and seemed to probe his identity, unmasking the truth and laying bare his sin. And yet each went right by him without so much as a second look from the driver. Indeed, he should have realised that it was in the other drivers' interests not to draw his attention, lest the White Hat pull them over for an uncomfortable conversation.

And then the vast edifice of the Directorate was in front of him. The colossal, forbidding wall rose dark and menacing out of the night, with laser lights ringing the top and the dim glow of the guard towers providing regular relief from the blackness of the sky. Again he almost faltered. There had already been many turning points in this wild scheme, but this was the point of no return. If he was found out here, it would go very badly for him. But if he made it through, every step thereafter would take him deeper into criminality and enhance the intensity of the punishment he might receive.

It occurred to him that he had no real idea of what that punishment could possibly be. There was so little crime in New Elysium that such things as the penal regime were neither publicised nor easily accessible. His was conceivably the greatest crime ever committed in the city. Would they prefer the death penalty upon him? If they were to incarcerate him for life, where would they put him? Surely not in the watch house? Nor the Tank, to wallow around with the drunks. Would they have to build a prison just for him? The idea had a certain appeal, he had to admit. He would be famous – or more properly notorious. Even Ellandra would have to have a grudging respect for his courage then, if not for his intelligence.

Because this really was, when he came right down to it, a stupid thing to do. Dave was right, he would probably walk away without any answers, and if he did find any answers, he might not like what they were.

But then, it was already too late. The van went down the little dip under the soaring barrier, and he pulled up next to the keypad at the gate where he'd watched Dave Belleville enter on the day they'd been hauled before Flynt. He took a deep breath, opened the window and punched in 202017. There was an interlude of impenetrable silence, and without knowing it Jakob held his breath. A distant creak became a louder clank and a low bass rumbling – the gate began to slowly open. He was in!

He tried to remember, from the few seconds of vision that Stone Carpenter's drone copter had captured, the lay-out of the facility. The massive power generation building at the heart of the complex was his target, so it should be easy enough to find, but he needed to look as though he knew where he was going and what he was doing there. Given that it was night-time and there should be fewer personnel wandering around, he did not expect to encounter too many people, but when he did he needed to have his story straight. His delivery needed to be authoritative, his gaze straight and unwavering, and his purpose true. He hoped he was up to it.

The narrow, dimly lit road ran between the gardens and greenhouses that they'd wondered about before the drone copter had been shot down, and he knew that if he followed it in a straight line, he would run into the generation building at some stage. But it was hard to concentrate; the whole complex seemed to pulsate with a brooding energy.

At the first crossroads there was an obliging signpost

showing the way to greenhouses 1 – 6 to the south, and the administration block, which must have been down near the water tanks somewhere. There were also directions to the Egg Farm and Batteries 1 – 4, Cattle Yards and Piggery, Barracks 1 – 3, Transport Depot, Workshops, Kitchens, Mess and various other service buildings and amenities. The Generation and Distribution Centre was straight ahead. Jakob took all this in as he drove on at the regulation 10 miles per hour, taking care to keep within the rules and not excite any attention – not that there appeared to be anyone around to notice.

A few hundred yards on, he pulled up in a van bay outside the entry to the generation building. Drawing a long breath, he rehearsed his speech should anyone question his presence. It was a poor excuse for being there, but it was the best he could come up with, and he hoped that it would do. Success would depend heavily on the authority with which he delivered his spiel.

There were stairs leading up to a lit entryway, and he guessed that he should go in through there. He didn't know what to expect, or what he was looking for, but he knew that whatever it was, he would find it in this building.

The edifice itself gave away no clues – it was a vast, blank concrete block with no windows or decorative touches, impenetrable and uninviting. The door looked tiny in the enormous breadth of featureless grey concrete that stretched away into the darkness on either side. He switched the miniature camera on and slipped it into the band on his hat. He clenched his hand, and mounted the steps.

He'd expected another keypad, but instead he was surprised and disheartened to find instead an intercom pad.

"Shit." he breathed. But his resolve kicked in. This was his first opportunity to test his story. He pressed the button on the intercom, and a few seconds later a sleepy voice crackled through the little speaker.

"What?"

"Snap inspection," Jakob said. Even he found it unconvincing.

"On who's orders?" said the voice inside the box.

"Major Flynt's. Open up immediately." That came out with more authority, even a pleasing sense of arrogance.

The disembodied voice seemed more focused now. "State your name and rank," she said, following strict protocol.

"Sergeant Belleville," said out Jakob.

"Dave?" said the voice in the speaker. There was a hint of warm familiarity that chilled Jakob to the marrow.

"Floyd. Sergeant Floyd Belleville," replied Jakob. Shit! Why hadn't he thought of a better alternative first name? In fact, why had he chosen to use Belleville at all, for that matter? This was the sort of lazy thinking that could get him caught. "Major Flynt's personal aide with special responsibility for systems analysis and investigation," he rapped out, pleased with his recovery. "Open up now."

The door buzzed and clicked open. Dave's shoes clicked crisply on the hard linoleum floor inside. The long corridor ended in a wide set of double doors, glass at the top and timber at the bottom, with "Authorised Personnel Only" written across the glass. As if anyone not authorised would be in a place like this.

A few paces ahead of him on the right the sentry sat behind a sliding glass window. She was surrounded by a broad bank of monitors, which she pretended to be watching keenly, but saluted him as he approached. Smiling inwardly but maintaining his stoic outer visage, Jakob held up Dave's tablet, which he'd brought in with him, and used it to point to the main access doors.

"I have a lot to get through here," he said smartly, "I'll just go straight in, yes?"

The junior nodded dumbly. Her expression told him that she'd feel better the sooner he was out of her area. Presumably she could go back to napping. Pretending to make a note on the tablet screen, Jakob nodded back and walked purposefully toward the double doors. He was about five metres shy of the doors when the young White Hat slid open the glass window facing the corridor and stuck her head out.

"Sir," she called urgently.

Stopping mid-stride with an anguished look on his face, Jakob rearranged his features quickly into a patient smile and turned on his heel. "What?"

"You'll need a raincoat sir," said the girl in a timid, apologetic voice. "In the cloak room on your right."

Intent as he had been on the double doors, Jakob hadn't even noticed the cloakroom door almost beside him. He looked at it, looked back at the sentry and nodded, and said, "Of course." Long rows of clear plastic raincoats in various sizes hung on either side of the narrow cloakroom. Selecting one that looked as though it would fit, he put it on and buttoned it up, unsure of why he would need it but determined to look as though he knew what he was doing. By the door there was a box of sheaths for electronic tablets; he took one out and placed Dave's tablet in it, sealed it, and left the room. As he re-entered the corridor he glanced down toward the sentry box, but the White Hat had closed the sliding glass again, and was likely studying the inside of her eyelids, satisfied that the inspector would give her a positive report.

The wide double doors led to another short corridor with two solid doors at its end. He pushed them open, to reveal a huge open space, blinding white walls far into the distance, a ceiling high above him laced with what appeared to be reticulated water pipes and sprinkler outlets. The floor was porous white plastic. The vision that greeted him was so unexpected, so grotesque and incredible that it took several moments to process it.

A thick white round column in front of him rotated slowly on the spot – there were obviously gears or wheels of some sort where it disappeared below the floor, converting that rotation into energy. The impetus for the rotation was being provided by five lateral beams sticking out from the column, and on each of these beams were chained – yes, chained – people. Wet, hairy, ragged but powerful looking people, pushing their beams around and around and around, marching in dogged rhythm. It was like a sanitised version of an old movie about galley slaves, but instead of grimy, filthy conditions there was a spartan whiteness. Even the prisoners' soaking clothes were white. There were five people to a beam – that is, twenty-five people to a wheel – and there were six of these gigantic wheels spread throughout the immensity of the space around them.

Stunned, and unable to comprehend fully what was going on for a long while, Jakob stood rooted to the spot. The entire operation was being carried out in silence, but for the dull shuffling of feet on the floor, and somewhere a regular drip-drip-drip from an imperfectly sealed sprinkler. The people appeared not to notice Jakob or care about his presence. Their blank eyes stared straight ahead, their expressions remained grimly fixed, and their purpose clear. The cadence of their shuffle did not vary, nor did the strain on their faces lessen for even a second as they pushed the beam in front of them, step after step after step.

The horror of what he was seeing froze Jakob to his core. Who were all these people? Where did they come from? Could this truly be the source of New Elysium's legendary 'sustainable' energy? Actual slavery? Brutal and unending subjection to the cruelty, the desolation and savagery of forced labour. The callous barbarity of it shocked and frightened him. Who could do such a thing?

Almost blind with staggered disbelief, Jakob wandered about the eerily quiet room, watching the feet of the people chained to the massive wheels by their wrists, walking in abysmal unison. He saw the way they had to lean into the beam to push it around; he couldn't imagine how heavy it was, or grasp just how numbingly awful it must be to spend one's days and nights in this kind of desperate ruination. The detestable ignominy of it was almost too powerful for words.

At last, he began looking at the faces of those pushing the beams. The ragged, haggard but utterly expression-less faces, the seemingly dead eyes that appeared not to see what was right in front of them. They looked like ordinary people. Simple, standard middle-class people who somehow had found their way into hell, and were staring it in the face with fatalistic apathy. Where the hell had they come from?

Suddenly, a huge bearded mad with long shanks of draggled hair falling about his face, dripping with sweat and water, caught Jakob's eye. As one of the biggest and obvi-ously strongest men in the entire room, he was placed on the outermost edge of the beam he was pushing, carrying the most weight. He glared at Jakob for a second or two, his mind unwillingly clicked into gear by the sight of the White Hat uniform. But it was Jakob's face his gaze was boring into.

"You!" he screamed in a hoarse, guttural roar. Jakob was terrified, and then utterly crippled with dread and revul-sion when he realised he was looking into the eyes of his brother Ben. Struck completely dumb, he stared at the hulk-ing, fiercely contorted face he loved so well. How could this be?

"You!" repeated the apparition of his brother in that rum-bling roar. "You put me here!" The man who was, but could not be, Ben stopped and stood up straight and lifted a chained arm and pointed at Jakob accusingly. Instantly the person next to him, without looking up, lashed out with one hand, striking the man in his face and muttering, "Don't stop."

The Ben man bent to his task again, but he kept his head up and twisted it round to look at Jakob with those fiery, an-imal eyes as he kept on pushing. "You did this to me," he screamed again. He paused again and pointed his chained arm at Jakob. This caused the two people next to him to stumble, slowing the progress of the whole wheel, which elicited a chorus of moans and bawls from the whole gang of prisoners attached to it. Within a second or two, a scalding hot rain beat down from the sprinklers attached to the ceiling, a short, sharp burst that stung and burned Jakob's face, even though his white hat helmet and the raincoat he was wearing shielded him from most of it. The prisoners screamed and howled in pain and anger, and bent to their task urgently. Clearly this was an automatic mechanism to ensure that at no stage did the pace of the wheel's turning slacken; another layer of brutish abuse.

He had been rooted to the spot, but suddenly Jakob came alive again. He ran around the outside of the circle, catching up to the Ben man and then walking slowly backwards in front of him. The man looked up at him with hatred and disgust, his wan, drawn face a parody of the fleshy, well-padded and lightly ruddy colour of the real Ben.

"What do you mean? I did this to you?" Jakob said. Fear made his voice tremble.

"You know, Jakob," the man said, and his voice was filled with hate. "You got me along to Mickey's that night so you could talk me into committing a crime, just so you could see what happens. Well, congratulations asshole, this is the result. I hope you're proud of yourself."

Bewildered and distressed, Jakob shook his head. "What are you talking about? Ben did that himself, and he finished up in hospital with food poisoning. I don't know who you are, or how you come to look like Ben, or how you know me, but you've got it all wrong."

"You're the one that's wrong," said the man. Meanwhile, he kept pushing his beam, his feet keeping time with his fellow chain-gang members. He obviously wasn't going to risk another hot shower. Jakob kept up his unsteady backwards gait, his mind whirring with horrific visions of Ben trashing the camera pylon and beating the unfortunate shopkeeper.

"You know that was me with you that night at Mickey's," said the Ben man. "And that Ben who's at home with my wife and kids right now, he's a reprint, same as you."

Rationality deserted Jakob's mind. Reality was sent reeling into a far distant, dark hole. He was in a nightmare the depth of which threatened to close down his system entirely. His breath was coming in short gasps, adrenaline coursed through his veins in rushes of hot ice, and he shuddered violently.

"What are you talking about?" he shouted over the din in his ears.

"You're a fucking reprint, you idiot. A worthless copy of a real human. The real Jakob is asleep in the barracks, and in two hours he'll be here pushing a beam around in circles, making power so you can live your fake, fucked up life. The minute he beat up that old drunk, he was doomed, and you were destined to be. As if you didn't know."

Actual terror took hold of Jakob. He knew in his guts and in his heart that this was true. "But how could I know?" he wailed. Ben wasn't listening.

"If I could get out of this thing I'd fucking kill you in

a minute, you plastic shit," the Ben man said. The real Ben, Jakob told himself. "You did this to me out of idle curiosity, you shitbag. I don't know how you came to be impersonating a White Hat or how you came to be here, and I don't fucking care. You're probably here to check on the misery you made. But fuck you and your pathetic reprinted, second rate copy of a life. If the real Jakob was here now, he'd kill you as eagerly as I would."

"Wait," said Jakob. "Ben, I'm sorry. I had no idea. If I thought for a minute that this was how it would be, I would never have spoken to you about what happened to me."

Ben spat, looked directly ahead of him and kept pushing. None of his chain-mates paid any attention, apathetically but resolutely putting one foot in front of the other.

"I want to make this right," said Jakob. "I want to free you and the other Jakob and everyone else."

Ben croaked out a hideous, bitter and unbelieving laugh at this, and was joined by the man shackled to him by the links of a titanium chain manacled at their wrists and looped through special eyes jutting out of the beam they pushed. Both prisoners shook their heads as they laughed, and the one next to Ben dissolved into a coughing fit, plodding wretchedly along as his body was wracked by convulsions.

"Fuck off!" said Ben. "You try anything and they'll bring my family in here. And they'll bring you in here and I'll kill you with my bare hands. I fucking mean it deadshit, just fuck off and play cops somewhere else."

"At least tell me where the other Jakob is," said Jakob.

"You mean the real Jakob," said Ben.

"Whatever," agreed Jakob, not willing to argue the point. "Please just tell me where he is."

"I'm only going to tell you because he's not chained to a beam right now. He'll have his hands free so he can strangle you himself," said Ben. "Barracks 2, bed 19d. I hope you don't make it out of there alive."

Jakob stared at his brother, or rather this beaten, harrowing, furious, enchained version of his brother. His mind fled back to that night at Mickey's. He'd tried to talk Ben out of it, sure, but if he'd never asked his brother to meet with him, never spoken about his own crime and his need to know what had happened in its aftermath, this man would be at home right now with his wife and kids. Instead, some other Ben, a 'reprint', had taken his place, and the real Ben was here generating 'sustainable' energy for the unwitting citizens of New Elysium. It seemed like some sort of noxious joke, a putrid perversion of reality created by an evil dream.

Who could conceive of such a thing? And, having conceived of it, what sort of monster would put it into action? There must be hundreds of people who knew about this pitiless, torturous practice, and yet they said nothing, did nothing. With a chill Jakob remembered Ellandra saying to him, "I know the consequences of misbehaviour." So she was one of them. No wonder she'd been so angry. The Jakob she'd loved had been imprisoned and enslaved in the hideous system she herself was a part of and helped to operate.

Shaking his head as if to shock himself back to this surreal reality, Jakob stopped following Ben, who in any case was now acting as if their conversation had never taken place, and looked around. There were cameras strategically placed throughout the giant room, as was to be expected, and he questioned whether the lone sentry at the door was even now watching him and wondering why he was having what appeared to be such a personal, acrimonious discussion with one of the prisoners. He figured he'd better fall back on his role as snap inspector. Glancing at his tablet, pretending to make a note, he took a walk around the huge installation.

The people chained to the long, heavy beams paid no attention to him. In fact, most of them studiously ignored him, although if he turned quickly he would catch a glimpse of one or more tired, wary pairs of eyes watching him. There was virtually no sound but the shuffling of feet, and from below the floor the deep thrumming hum of the generators being turned by these human turbines.

He guessed that there was no reason for close supervision because the prisoners were all chained to the wheels they were pushing, and because if at any time the pace of their progress fell to a predetermined level, the scorching showers would automatically convince them to increase their speed.

At changeover time there must be quite a great deal of activity; he needed to ensure that he was long gone before then. His hand went instinctively up to the camera lodged in the band of his White Hat helmet. Hopefully it had not been damaged by the hot rain; it was designed to withstand water, and presumably the heat would not be a problem.

He approached a wheel and dropped his head so that the camera could get a good view of the people chained to it. He needed good vision of the conditions and the prisoners; it was obvious that in his final video the argument with Ben would have to be edited out. As he walked in slow counter-rotation to the slaves on the wheel, getting a good long shot of the draw, sallow faces and the dark sadness that radiated from them, he was startled to see a familiar face. Could it possibly be? No, it couldn't. But, peering closely into the man's downcast, bristled face he saw that yes, indeed it was. "Dave?" he said cautiously.

Dave Belleville lifted his eyes from the soles of the feet in front of him and glared at Jakob, cynical, incensed and uncomprehending. "Who the fuck are you?" he growled.

This Dave must have been in this place since before the Dave he knew had moved in next door; it was evident that he didn't know who Jakob was. So even White Hats could end up in this hell. For some reason this didn't reassure Jakob, and he quickly moved on. The awful weight of the place was beginning to crush him; he couldn't imagine what it would be like to live here, spending hour upon hour walking around in circles, pushing the same heavy beam with the same captives next to him, not speaking, not even thinking, but simply existing in torment – and knowing it would not end. He had to get out.

Without looking back at his brother, Jakob strode swiftly out of the enormous room, exiting the same way he had entered. He walked with feigned confidence back down the hall, stopping in the cloakroom to remove his raincoat, and to pause and gather his strength.

Continuing down the hall he briefly spoke to the sentry in a clipped, authoritative tone that, to his surprise, came across quite powerfully.

"That all appears in order," he said. "Put a call through to the barracks. Tell them to expect me in five minutes, I'll be inspecting, ah," he hesitated as though thinking of a random number, "let's say Barracks Two. I expect complete privacy – if the inmates see me with a known guard they will freeze up. I need candour and honesty from these prisoners."

"Yes sir," said the guard. She'd been trying to stay upright in her chair since Jakob had appeared in her sector, but had in reality been dozing. She hadn't seen a second of his 'inspection' in the generation room.

Holding his posture as erect as he could, Jakob left the building and got back into his van, sighing in relief. Already he felt a little disconnected from what he'd seen. Already it seemed less real, and less plausible. Who would believe an atrocity like this was even possible? He put a hand up and switched his camera off; the vision wouldn't lie, and could not be refuted. He would have the heads of those responsible for this.

35.

Barracks Two was in darkness except for the small office at the front of the long, ugly building. Inside, another lethargic young guard had been struggling to stay awake when his phone had rung and the sentry at the generation facility had told him an inspection was imminent.

"Don't worry, the inspector seems pretty cool," the White Hat on the other end of the phone had told him. "Just let him in and he'll probably leave you alone."

Jakob parked out the front and put his helmet on. The guard may have had more than a passing familiarity with the inmates housed in the building, and Jakob couldn't afford for him to make any connection between him and prisoner Petersson. As he approached the office, he jammed the hat tightly down over his face, aware that he looked faintly ridiculous but preferring absurdity to recognition. As with the previous sentry, he need not have bothered. The guard was not interested in appearing too nosy, or intruding in any way on the inspector's routine. It would be better for him if the inspector came and went without even noticing him.

"Belleville, snap inspection unit," said Jakob.

"Yes, sir," replied the guard. He handed Jakob an electronic passkey and said, "This will get you into any areas you wish to inspect sir." He also gave Jakob a large, heavy torch.

"You may need this too, sir," he said.

"I may interview one of the prisoners," said Jakob as casually as he could. "If I decide to do so, where can I take him?"

"There's an interview room at the very end of the barracks sir," said the young man. "We usually conduct interrogations in there. It's sound proof," he added.

"Well done." Jakob ventured a smile. "Keep up the good work."

"Yes sir," saluted the young man.

As soon as Jakob disappeared into the darkened barracks, the young White Hat slumped back into his chair. He hated dealing with disruptions like this, especially those involving things like inspections.

Steeling himself for what would come next – and who knew, it might end in the real Jakob making a screaming denunciation of his doppelganger – White Hat Jakob quietly entered the building and shone his torch along the long rows of sleeping internees. None stirred –mental and physical exhaustion sent them into deep, welcome slumber every night, and waking each day was a trauma.

There was a dank smell in the air, the product of unwashed bodies, the fetid fart-gas of a vegetable-heavy diet and the mouldy dampness seeping through the woodwork. Jakob couldn't imagine what this place would be like in the depths of winter, but he could see that the thin, threadbare blankets covering the sleeping people were barely up to the task of banishing the coolness of this late spring night.

Making a show of a silent, unobtrusive inspection in case the young guardsman was watching, Jakob shone his beam up into the ceiling rafters, studied the skirting boards and walked the entire length of the room with painful slowness, taking care not to shine a light on any face but peering everywhere else. The place was sad, despicably under-equipped, considering what the people who lived there were expected to do, and, to add insult to injury, woefully crowded. The prisoners were crammed into double bunks just a short width from each other, and there were four bunks in each row, with a total of thirty-two rows. So Jakob – the other, prisoner Jakob – was sharing his life with two hundred and fifty-five others. It depressed White Hat Jakob just to think about it.

He carried on past the last bunk and into the interrogation room, running his eye over every feature of the block, taking none of it in, his mind alive with fear and apprehension, and impatient to get to the next challenge in this mad mission. He expected to be caught at any time, and to be forced to end his own days in this grim dormitory or one like it, pushing a beam without hope of relief.

Having wasted enough time on his bogus inspection, Jakob slowly paced along the long ranks of beds, stopping now and then by one, as if randomly selecting one at which he might rouse a prisoner.

When he came to row 19, he scanned the beds quickly. The top bunk at the far left of the row was bed A, with bed B below it, so bed D would be the bottom of the bunk to the left of the narrow aisle that ran down the centre of the room – perfect. Jakob quickly flashed his torch over the face of the man sleeping in the bunk: it was him lying there. The face was thinner, harder, hairier, more muscular and more lined, but definitely his own, disembodied right in front of him. If the bounds of credibility had already been pushed that night, they were now at breaking point.

His mind retreated, he didn't want to know any more, it was all too much, and the consequences were too shocking to bear. But then a new thought entered the billowing cloud of fear, doubt and hesitation.

"None of this is my fault," he told himself. "He put himself here, I had nothing to do with it. I didn't ask to be born, or made, or whatever it was. In fact, I'm an innocent victim. It's not my fault I somehow remembered what had happened to him – to the other me – and that made me want, no, need to find out the truth. I can't help it if the truth is that he is a prisoner. But I can help him out of here. Surely he'll be grateful for that?"

It was grasping at straws, to be sure, but he needed any reassurance he could get. He was in too deep to just walk away. And he couldn't just abandon the other him, the real him, if he was being honest. Let the fallout be what it may, he was committed.

Leaning over, holding his breath, his right hand holding the torch pointed at the floor, his left hand darted across the empty space between them and clamped on the other fellow's mouth. The prisoner woke up instantly, his eyes flashing open urgently, his pupils wide with fear and visible even in the dim reflected light of the torch. Seeing the White Hat and uniform, he didn't struggle or make a noise, he just stared.

Adjusting the torch slightly so that more of the light fell on his face, Jakob whispered, "Can you see who I am?"

The other man's pupils, impossibly, widened again, and he nodded.

"Then you know I'm not here to hurt you," whispered Jakob. "I need you to come with me to the interview room at the back of the hut. When we get there, we'll talk. I'm here to help you. Do you understand?"

The other Jakob nodded again, and slowly, carefully, White Hat Jakob took his hand away from his mouth. As quietly but as quickly as they could, they made their way to the interview room. White Hat Jakob closed the door and locked it behind them, switching on the light. For a moment the two men stood blinking, regarding each other in the harsh brightness.

"What are you doing here?" said prisoner Jakob. He sounded suspicious, and weary.

"You don't seem very surprised to see me," said White Hat Jakob.

"Well, it's no surprise to me that you exist, if that's what you're thinking. I knew there was a reprint of me somewhere out there living my life. It's true, I never expected to meet you, but to be honest I'm too tired to care how you came to be here – I just want to know what you want so I can tell you to fuck off and go back to bed."

Jakob had intended for this to be a civil conversation, but already his hackles were up. The suggestion that he had somehow stolen the other fellow's life was galling.

"I'm not living your life, I'm living mine," he said.

"But it's not yours, it's mine," said prisoner Jakob. "I don't see any other Jakob Peterssons around here, so that makes me the original, and you the copy. And that's not up for dis-cussion. You know as well as I do that you are living my life."

"I didn't ask for this," said White Hat Jakob. He hadn't expected such resistance from someone he was trying to help. "I wasn't sitting around in some limbo wishing I existed. And if I was, do you really think I'd pick your life? Your miserable, motherless childhood and tormented adolescence, with the shit of the EMP thrown in and capped off by the execution of a starving wraith. An execution I actually feel guilty about because I enjoyed it so much. And then a life wrestling with the weed addiction you brought on me. Wrenching from hazy, forgotten highs to raging lows, alienating my friends and colleagues and living, actually living for the moments when I can be alone and get stoned. And now I find out I'm a reprint. A reprint! How do you think that makes me feel, to be not even my own self, but a copy? You're dreaming if you think I'm enjoying any of this."

Prisoner Jakob wasn't having any of it. "Yeah, well, thanks for summing up my life in such glowing terms, but at least you have that. What do I have? A chain and a wheel. So stop your bitching, you've got the best of it." His expression softened and he looked sad and lonely. "Hah. You know, I used to feel like I was trapped. Imprisoned by my need for weed, by the misery of my relationship with Ellandra, and my unhappiness with myself. Shit, I even felt caged by my own past. But now I realise how free I actually was. I made choices around all those things. I built my own prison, and I wallowed in it, lamenting the fact that no-one would ever let me out when all I had to do was walk out and be free. You only know how free you are when your freedom is truly taken from you."

"I'm going to get you out of here," whispered White Hat Jakob, affected by the sunken-cheeked visage and pathetic speech of the man before him.

"How do you think you might do that?" The cynicism in prisoner Jakob's voice was unmistakable.

"I've been into the generation room and filmed everything," said White Hat Jakob. "I'm going to expose it on Felicity."

"Ha ha ha." Prisoner Jakob laughed huskily, ironically. "It'll never happen. You'll finish up in here with me."

"I'm going to make it work," Jakob said. "You'll see."

"No, I won't," said prisoner Jakob. He looked at his reprint dejectedly, and then a sudden light gleamed in his eyes, a glimmer of unexpected hope. "Let me do it," he said.

"What?" Jakob was startled, and abruptly uneasy. "What do you mean?"

"I mean swap with me. Let me go out into the world again, and you stay here."

"No, that won't work," said White Hat Jakob a little too quickly. He hadn't thought of this particular possibility, but now that he did consider it he was stricken by a certainty that this prisoner version of him, who spent hours every day building his strength, could overpower him with ease. And they were in a soundproof room.

"Why not?" The prisoner was eyeing White Hat Jakob with an unsettling intensity, and the reprint turned his gaze on the ceiling, perhaps hoping for inspiration up there.

"Too much has happened," he said after a too-long hesitation. "You wouldn't be able to cope. There are new people in my life that weren't in yours. New situations."

"Bullshit," said the prisoner. "I've been in here for a few months, not that much could have changed."

"I've got a White Hat tied up next door, in old Edgar's house," Jakob said. "And I've been working with an Australian director, Stone Carpenter."

"Stone Carpenter? *The* Stone Carpenter?" Prisoner Jakob was impressed.

"Yep," said White Hat Jakob. "You'd be lost, and people would notice."

"But if I've got the footage you shot in the generation room, that won't matter," said prisoner Jakob.

"No." White Hat Jakob was resolute. The very idea of not walking out of this place was horrifying to him, and he felt as though he should get out of there as soon as possible, lest the urge to overpower him occur to prisoner Jakob. "It would take too long to explain the plan to you, and we'd both get caught. I can't."

Prisoner Jakob snorted with derision, and his voice betrayed a sullen anger born of suspicion and despair. "It's not that you can't, it's that you won't," he said. "And you won't be back, either, except as a prisoner. Your only purpose here is to torture me even further. As if this wasn't enough." He looked at his calloused, torn and almost unrecognisable hands. "Just fuck off," he said. He stood up and walked to the door, laying his hand on the doorknob.

"I'm going to get you out," said White Hat Jakob. "Because we're the same, you and me."

Turning to face his reprint straight on, prisoner Jakob glowered. "No, we're not. I'm me and you are you, and it doesn't matter how many times you tell me you're me, you never will be. You're just a fucking reprint, and as far as I'm concerned you ought to be in the shredder."

Without waiting for a response, he opened the door and disappeared into the darkness of the dormitory. For a moment White Hat Jakob sat trying to concoct a suitably soothing reply, but he couldn't, so he got up and walked out behind his double. Switching on the torch, he made his way out of the barracks quietly.

He stopped and had a brief conversation with the sentry to the effect that everything seemed in order, and went out to get into the electro-van. He was shaking.

To his relief, the gate opened automatically as he approached, and within minutes of the end of his unhappy interview with his doppelganger, Jakob was driving back toward his home. He'd hoped to get some information regarding this reprint program, but clearly that was not going to happen. None of it had gone the way he wanted it to, and now he didn't know what to do. He had the footage of course, and that might just be enough, but he felt the need, on a personal level, to know more. Almost without thinking, he started heading toward Ellandra's place.

36.

It was very late and the streets were deserted by the time he made it to Ellandra's place. The lights in every property on the street were out, and only half of the streetlights were glowing – an energy saving measure introduced by Major Flynt. In the gloom all the houses looked more uniform than they were. Jakob thought of Ben, pushing the beam around and around. Then he thought of the other Jakob, and tried to put himself in that unfortunate's place. He couldn't.

Jakob stopped at the front of Ellandra's place and parked the electro-van. He put Dave's white hat helmet on and jammed it down low over his face, checking up and down the street before crossing the pavement and entering the tiny front garden.

Being tired to the point of near delirium helped him. If he had been in his right mind, he would never have confronted Ellandra with what he had done and what he knew. But now it didn't occur to him that she would be less than accommodating. He rapped briskly on the front door, adjusted his helmet and stood to attention as the sound penetrated the house. Deep inside he could hear movement, and fancied for a moment that he could hear voices, but when he concentrated he heard nothing. He dismissed the idea as a hallucination.

There was a shuffling sound near the door, the porch light over his head went on, and a sleepy Ellandra opened the door, one hand working fruitlessly to tie her robe's belt. Seeing the uniform, she straightened up a bit and said, "How can I help you offic—." But, recognising in a rush that the White Hat was in fact Jakob, and instantly assessing that the situation was dire, she slammed the door in his face.

Jakob knocked on the door again, loudly and continuously until she opened it.

"Jesus, Jakob," she said. "What have you done now? Go away." She tried to slam the door again, but this time Jakob caught the edge.

"I'll keep knocking," he said. "And shouting if I have to."

Taking a step back, Ellandra allowed him to enter the darkened hallway, her face reflecting the dread and disgust she was feeling. "You're making a big mistake coming here," she said as he pushed past her.

"I've already made so many mistakes, a couple more won't hurt," he said with dark assurance.

"Don't bet on it." Ellandra closed the door behind him. She turned the hallway light on and touched his shoulder. He looked at her; she placed a finger to her lips to indicate that she he needed to stay quiet. He complied, and led the way down the hallway toward the familiar lounge room. Ellandra followed, closing the bedroom door on the way. He stopped in the lounge, but she pushed him on into the kitchen, closing the lounge room door as well. A few moments later they were facing each other across the kitchen table, a rough pine affair surrounded by ill-matched chairs and topped with several placemats, a pair of tarnished silver candle holders, and an assortment of paper bills and receipts.

"I can't help you, Jakob," said Ellandra. "There are consequences for committing crimes, and impersonating a White Hat is a major crime. I don't even want to know what you did to get that uniform."

An image of Dave, tied to his kitchen table – perhaps even suffocating – flashed across Jakob's mind. He pushed it out of his thoughts.

"I know about the reprints," he said, carefully watching Ellandra's tired, lined face for her reaction. She was startled, but in a way that told him she was familiar with the term; there was no wondering what he was talking about in her eyes, and the severe set of her lips barely changed.

"Who told you that word?" she asked.

"Prisoner Jakob Petersson." His eyes bored holes into her face. She dropped her head into her hands and shook it, as though she was trying to wake up from a bad dream.

"Jesus," she breathed.

"I've been to the Energy Directorate," he continued. "I've seen it all, and I have it all on video."

Shaking her head again, Ellandra looked up at him. There was sincerity, pity, sorrow and defeat written all over her face, and her body seemed to relax as though awaiting the final blow.

"So what do you want from me?" she asked.

"Tell me all about it," he said. "I need to know what the fucking hell is going on. How this happened, and why."

"It won't do you any good. Knowing, I mean. They can't –

they won't let you keep offending. They have ways of dealing with repeat offenders, you know. You'll never get the story out."

"Yeah that's what prisoner Jakob said. I don't care, I need to know. I need to try. And I have to do what I can to get him out of there. To get them all out."

"It will never happen," she said.

"Just tell me what you know. Start right at the beginning."

Glancing at the closed kitchen door and sighing with a kind of sad resignation, Ellandra started talking. "Back in the old days, before the EMP, Cheyenne Mountain was supposedly closed down. But as was typical of the government back then, it wasn't actually mothballed, or even shut down in a proper sense. They turned it over to clandestine programs. One of them was overseen by Tom Flynt. They aimed to create exact replicas of soldiers so that if they were injured on the battlefield, their own bodies could be used to repair them. Three-D printing was making huge advances at that time, and Major Flynt's team perfected a means of using it to create a perfect duplicate of the subject. The first step was in reading the genome, available in just about any cell in the body, and this information, along with an atomic level scan of the body itself, was fed into the printer. The scans were – are – so accurate that they can take an intensely detailed image of the entire body, right down to the neuronal and synaptic architecture of the brain. Because the scan reads from the ground up, it just happens to read the brain in a sequence astonishingly similar to that in which memories are made – starting with the hippocampus and the cerebellum, moving up through the striatum and putamen, on to the amygdala and finishing with the cortex. Now, it wasn't supposed to happen – they didn't even expect these copies, or reprints as they became known, to have consciousness – but when they animated the bodies, they found they'd not only created complete doubles of the subjects, those subjects had total consciousness. Even more remarkably – and no-one has found an explanation for this – the reprints possessed all the personal traits, habits, likes, dislikes, qualities, failings and even the memories of the originals. They were perfect copies."

She got up and moved to the sink, where she poured herself a glass of water. Without being asked to, she poured Jakob a glass too, putting it in front of him and sitting down again. He nodded thanks, and drank half the glass off in one swig. He hadn't thought about eating, drinking or even breathing for many hours, and he was surprised at how thirsty he was. He was also pleasantly surprised at how warm her gesture, so carelessly delivered, made him feel.

"But that's impossible," said Jakob.

"Agreed," said Ellandra. "And yet," she shrugged her shoulders, "that's how it happened. Some people believe they've actually replicated the soul. Others think they've somehow split it in two, so that neither the original nor the reprint has a complete soul of their own."

"Well that's bullshit!" Jakob said. He didn't feel like half a soul.

"No studies have ever been done, because so few of the reprints are even aware that they're duplicates of someone else. In fact, you might be the first," she said, looking at him with a kind of scientific interest. "When the program was adapted as a penal measure, it became a relatively simple matter to delete the last twenty-four hours or so of short term memory in the reprint, so that the reprint has no memory of the crime they've committed, or the arrest and duplication procedure. Reprints aren't meant to retain any memory of the event that leads to their replication. But apparently you do."

"I think there might be at least one more," replied Jakob, thinking of Dave. He wondered if the Dave tied up at his home knew he was a reprint. "So how did a program for fixing shot up soldiers turn into a program for turning minor criminals into slaves?" he asked.

Giving Jakob a wry look, Ellandra sipped her water and continued. "As I mentioned, Cheyenne Mountain had theoretically been closed, but then many elements of the old government pursued a very aggressive foreign policy; restarting the seemingly endless war in Iraq, attacking other countries in the Middle East, setting up a coup in Ukraine that directly threatened Russia, and assuming a belligerent posture toward China. So some of these people, who knew they were promoting wars that could turn nuclear, started talking about the potential effects – ironically, as it turns out – of an EMP generated by a nuclear strike. So they advocated reopening Cheyenne Mountain as a kind of anti-EMP haven. Although it hadn't yet been fully reopened, much of the equipment and protective structure against an EMP was in place when the sun's EMP struck, so those of us in Cheyenne were safe."

"Now as you're aware, a lot of troops, including senior officers, deserted in the aftermath of the EMP, leaving just a few of us there to deal with the mess. Among those who stayed were Major Flynt and pretty much his whole team. Their newly completed reprint technology of course remained untouched by the EMP. Colonel Martin was the senior officer, and he directed Major Flynt to manage the planning and construction of New Elysium. Being a practical man, and having few resources available for energy generation, and admittedly eager to see his technology put to use since its original purpose had evaporated, Major Flynt created the Anthropogenic Energy Reclamation Office – AERO."

"AERO!" said Jakob. "Jesus, it sounds so benign."

"It was only supposed to be a temporary measure, presenting a means of dealing with the many looters, shooters, rapists and other crazies that you'll remember were swarming around at the time," Ellandra continued. "You'll recall that they all conveniently disappeared, and nobody ever asked where they went. They were the original AERO energy source, which was, as I say, only meant to be temporary. But as time went on and the city grew, no viable alternative seemed to present itself, and it turned out to be a very clean source of energy. A lot of those original offenders have since died, but because the city continued to grow, the demand for energy kept growing as well, so Flynt and Martin decided that putting criminal offenders in there was the answer. That makes AERO energy both clean and renewable."

"But, my god," said Jakob, appalled, "it's monstrous. And you knew about it all this time?"

"Yes I did," she said. She looked defensive, and a little bit defeated. "But what was I to do? Say something and end up looking crazy, or worse, chained to a wheel? Besides, looked at in certain lights, it makes sense."

"It makes sense? In what universe?" Jakob was incredulous.

"Well it gives the personality – not the individual who committed the crime, but the personality they possess – a second chance. An opportunity to live within the laws and norms of the harmonious society we're trying to build. And it gives the offenders an opportunity to contribute in a very real way to that society. It also eliminates the social problems involved with criminal justice the way it used to be done – the families, colleagues and friends of both the victims and the perpetrators were affected by the protracted proceedings, the endless repetition of the circumstances of the crime and the trauma of the sentencing, and those associated with the criminals were stigmatised, shunned and abused. One single criminal act has a ripple effect that radiates out into society in unimaginable, toxic ways. This system allows society to continue on undisturbed – the victims recover quickly, and the rest of the world has no knowledge of what went on, so it is unaffected."

"But where's the justice?" said Jakob. His voice was rising.

"Shhh! Keep it down," Ellandra whispered tersely, glancing again at the kitchen door. She glowered at Jakob. "Where's the justice in you beating a man almost to death?" she asked. "Where's the justice in Ben practically destroying a store and leaving the storekeeper a bloodied mess?"

Jakob was white with anger. "You knew everything the whole time?"

"No, after you came to see me I made some enquiries," she said. "I wanted to make sure something really had happened, and that you weren't just losing your mind. I asked Tom to keep me updated should there be any change, and he told me about Ben."

"So you just committed both of us to a life sentence for a minor crime, is that it?"

"No, I didn't commit anyone to anything, and certainly not you – you're still running around being a criminal, while the first Jakob is at the wheel. But I don't see what you could want me to do, or what I could have done, short of ending up next to you on a wheel."

"But it's barbaric. Inhuman."

"So is almost killing a complete stranger Jakob," she said. "Don't get me wrong, I think it's sometimes excessive, but what alternative have we? Personally I'd rather live in a truly harmonious society where there is no crime and no need to punish people, no need to decide what kind of penalty is equal to what sort of crime, as if that could ever be determined fairly for anyone concerned. But that's not the case. We live in a world where idiots like you go around assaulting people and expecting some kind of slap on the wrist. Well sorry, it doesn't happen like that anymore. You commit the crime, and you pay with a lifetime of servitude for the greater good of the society. Your duplicate is allowed to go back into society to try and live a more productive life, and because almost no-one is aware that you've even committed a crime, let alone that you've been reprinted and replaced, the disturbance to society is minimal. People go about thinking that they really do live in a peaceful crime free place, and that encourages them to be peaceful and crime free themselves."

"So basically, fuck those slaves in there," said Jakob.

Ellandra shrugged. "What can I say to you Jakob? If you'd never committed a crime in the first place, you'd be none the wiser. You'd be grateful that New Elysium has the world's cleanest renewable source of energy, you'd be going home to get stoned every night, and I could get through a week or two at a time without some sort of crazed appearance from you."

"I honestly thought you were better than that," said Jakob. "All that pretence about caring about people, all that public gentleness and private evil. You're not the person I thought you were."

Ellandra was wounded, but kept her anger under control. "You're exactly the fool I thought you were Jakob. Now get out of my house." She stood up.

"I'm going to get them out of there," Jakob said as he stood.

"And what then Jakob?" she asked. "Are you and your original going to settle down and love together like some sort of demented, stoned Tweedledum and Tweedledee? And what about Ben? Is he going to go home and be the third member of his marriage? Don't be ridiculous. All you'd do is create all sorts of trouble. If you succeeded."

"Oh, I'll succeed," he said. "And then your precious Tom

and you and everyone else involved will finish up in a proper jail, with a proper sentence and a chance at rehabilitation."

She scoffed. "And I'm guessing the master of all this will be you, will it? The dopehead cameraman who can't even manage his own life will somehow run the city without screwing up everything. You are so delusional it's not even funny." She paused, and looked him in the eye. "I can't believe I ever had anything to do with you, ever had any respect for you. You know, you're going to finish up on the wheel, and your personality will be terminated the way so many other recidivists have been. And to be honest, I'll be glad to have no more to do with you." The look in her eye was pure hatred, and it hurt Jakob to see it, even though, at that moment, he despised her, too.

"You'll see," he said, and walked out of the door.

With only the light of the kitchen behind him Jakob carefully picked his way down the hall to the front door. As he passed Ellandra's bedroom door he thought he saw that it was slightly ajar again, but he couldn't be sure, it was so dark. He was seething with what he believed to be righteous anger, and more than ever resolved to carry out his plan. She'd see – they'd all see.

37.

Back in the electro-van, he thought about what Ellandra had told him. It was hard to believe that a society that professed to be so good was so rotten at the core. He wondered what other deceits and betrayals were being carried out in the name of the public good, and told himself he would not be surprised if there was a large catalogue of such atrocities.

He drove the deserted streets back to his own neighbourhood, parked in front of Dave's place, and sat in the electro-van. What to do next? He was dog-tired, emotionally shattered and in desperate need of some relief. He wondered if he should leave Dave where he was, and just go into his own place. If he had just one small reefer, he would probably drop off to sleep fairly quickly, and he could deal with Dave in the morning. The White Hat wasn't going anywhere before then. But then he thought of the awkward position he'd tied Dave into, with his upper arms secured as tightly as possible behind him with wire, and again considered the possibility that if Dave was to pass out or sleep, his weight may fall forward and he could suffocate. He didn't want his friend's death on his conscience, even if his exposé of Flynt's energy scheme was successful.

He stood on the street for a few minutes in just his shirtsleeves to allow the midnight chill to wake him up a little. It didn't work very well. He still felt drugged and distracted, but it did make him cold. Using the house keys on Dave's van key ring, he let himself into the house. Before he'd even walked in he noticed that the lights were on and he wondered, in his lightly befuddled state, whether or not he'd left them on. He thought he'd switched them off to deter any would be visitors, but he couldn't be certain.

Entering the house quietly, he stepped softly into the lounge room, expecting to find Dave asleep or perhaps even passed out. To his utter amazement and not a little dismay, Dave was sitting comfortably on the couch, legs crossed and one arm spread languidly along the back of the cushion, watching him with an expression somewhere between amusement and wry disapproval.

"Ah, you're home. Good-oh," said the Australian. "Have fun?"

"Dave!" fluttered Jakob. "You're okay, thank god."

"No thanks to you but, mate," replied Dave. He was cool and good natured, which was unnerving.

"I only did what I had to do, I hope you're not too upset," Jakob said.

Dave chuckled. "Huh huh huh, you bash me over the head, tie me up, steal my uniform and leave me for dead. What could I possibly have to be upset about?"

"It wasn't personal, honestly," said Jakob. He put his hands out in front of him palms up and his face the very picture of remorse.

"Don't worry about it mate," Dave said. "I'm sure it was all worth it. And I'll let you in on a little secret, you're not as good a tie-er upperer as you think. Although it did take me a little while to wriggle out of it. So what did you see, anything interesting?"

"I went to the Energy Directorate," said Jakob. "And I learned all about the reprints. I saw myself there, and my brother."

"Look at you, intrepid explorer. How very investigative of you," said Dave. He was mocking Jakob, but he couldn't hide a certain glimmer of admiration, too.

Jakob tried to take the offensive. "You know you're a reprint too," he said.

Dave grinned and nodded his head, as though he was impressed with Jakob's detective work. "Jeez, you're good Jakey," he said. "How could I not know? I go there a couple of times a week. In fact, I take the new reprints there. So yeah, I've seen the other me. So what?"

"What happened?" asked Jakob. He was curious that the Australian could be so nonchalant about it.

"Dreadful business," said Dave. "The other Dave let a woman go. He was sent around to a house with an emergency medical team, and they found a bloke cut up and comprehensively dead at the scene. The wife was standing there, bloody great kitchen knife in her hand and covered in gore, and she readily confessed. Turned out she'd murdered her husband because he was an abusive asshole, forever belting her, committing rape within marriage, all sorts of other nasty stuff. The world really was much better off without him. The other Dave thought that was justifiable, so he wrote a report that it was an unknown assailant who'd killed the bloke and then attacked the woman. She had plenty of cuts and bruises to back that up. But the fuckin' ambulance crew dobbed him in, and he got hauled up before the boss. He explained his concept of rough justice, but the Major didn't buy it. So now he's in there with her. And you and sundry others of course."

"Shit, that's horrible," said Jakob. He didn't know what was worse, the fact that poor Dave had been locked away for protecting a victim of abuse, or that his reprint was so blasé about it all.

"Still, it's all water under the bridge isn't it?" said Dave. "And here I am."

"Doesn't it bother you that you're living someone else's life? You've basically stolen the real Dave Belleville's identity."

"Bullshit," replied Dave in that deadpan way of his. He might have been telling Jakob the time. "I'm the real Dave Belleville. I have all the memories, I have the body, and nobody can prove otherwise. I am as real as you are. And who are you to ask anyway? Are you not Jakob Petersson? If not, who are you?"

Jakob was taken aback. It had been easy to assume that Dave would agree with him that he'd stolen the real Dave's life, but had he not recently had the same argument with the other him? He did not feel as though he was anyone but Jakob Petersson, and although it was safe to assume that the other Jakob felt the same way, he no more knew that other Jakob's thoughts than he did the thoughts of anyone else in the world.

"I am Jakob Petersson," he said. "I can't be anyone else.

But I can't ignore the fact that I'm a reprint. Worse, I can't ignore the fact that the other Jakob – the real Jakob, like the real Dave, is chained to a wheel. He's a slave. I can't live with that. I have to do something about it."

"Why? You're free, that's all that matters."

"But how can I be free if one of me is a slave? Who was it that said 'none of us is truly free while others remain enslaved'? That's true."

Dave chortled. "That, it so happens, was me old mate Desmond Tutu, and he had to say that, he was a bishop. And it's utter shite – as demonstrated by the very fact that you are free," he said. "The freedom or otherwise of the other Jakob Petersson doesn't affect you either way. That whole 'none of us is truly free' crap is a whiny statement dreamed up by the bleeding hearts to guilt the rest of us into sharing the misery equally. You know Jake, the entire progress of the human race is built on one sector of society profiting from the hardship and pain of another, right back to when the Greeks and the Romans sat on their arses while slaves did everything for them, including wiping said arses. And so it goes throughout history, right up to the present day. The Indians and the Chinese, among others, had to suffer for the growth of the British Empire. The indigenous native American population and the Africans stolen and enslaved by invaders had to suffer so that the great American empire, the land of the free and the home of the brave, could be built. The examples are legion. And until you found out about the other Jakob, you were perfectly happy being free. Although you're like everyone else. You think you're free but in reality you're a slave to something – whether it's a dead-end love affair, or a job, or the dreaded weed – we'll leave that aside for now and pretend that you actually are free. At least, you were yesterday morning. What changed? Only one little piece of knowledge. You found out that there's a bloke who looks like you chained to a wheel somewhere, and now you're all wound up because you think it somehow affects your freedom. Pull the other one mate. Sure, you can sympathise with the other Jake all you want, even empathise if you want to make yourself feel even worse. But don't kid yourself, whether the other Jakob lives or dies is of no consequence, let alone concern to you, and deep down you know it."

Jakob was frustrated. There was a certain logic to what Dave was saying, but it was a cold, heartless logic, and he wasn't sure he could agree with it. If he did, wouldn't that make him some kind of pitiless automaton? And yet he'd never thought of Dave that way, and here he was, making the callous, self-serving argument that the best they could do would be to forget about their respective predecessors. He fell back on the concepts of right and wrong he'd been taught as a boy.

"Well it's not right, and I'm going to do something about it. I'm going to expose Flynt and free those slaves."

"Don't be a fuckin' idiot Jake," spat Dave. It was apparent that he was getting fed up with this conversation. "How are all those people going to come back? Is your brother going to move into his house with his wife and kids and himself? Are you going to hand over your job, your house, your life to the other Jakob? And all live together in the darkness?"

Dave was echoing the argument that Ellandra had made, and it occurred to Jakob that this was what humanity had come to, avoiding things because they were hard. Because that was the only real reason not to try and reintegrate those people into society – it would cause friction. He didn't have time to dwell on that, though, because Dave was barrelling along now.

"You need him to be in there chained to that wheel every bit as much as New Elysium needs him to be there. Even more. The die is cast and the moving finger has writ, my friend. You can't change the past, but you can learn to live with it. Don't forget, you're an innocent party in all this. In fact, I'll see to it that they go easy on you, mate. Your memory erasure didn't work properly and it fucked you up, so you went a little off the deep end. I won't tell 'em that you tied me up, I'll say we had a few million beers together and I passed out, and you took advantage of the situation to rip off me uniform, take the van and go investigating yourself. But it's a mental illness you've got mate, and you need treatment, not punishment. Be reasonable."

"I can't Dave, I really can't," said Jakob. "I promised him."

"Him? He's the bloke who got you into all this. He's the bloke who's going to want his life back. He's the bloke who deserves to be there."

"But it doesn't seem fair." Jakob was wavering.

"What is Jakob? Nothing. I got stuck here in this shit of a country because a fucking great electromagnetic pulse wiped out practically everything above the equator in this hemisphere. That's not fair. Some lived, millions died. That's not fair. Some rule, others get told what to do. That's not fair. Nothing is fair mate, nothing."

"No," said Jakob, feeling a new resolve from he knew not where. "I'm going to do it. I've got video evidence of the whole thing, I'm going to air it on tomorrow's news, and get this whole stinking mess out into the open. Then we'll just deal with the fallout. I don't know what will happen, but I do know what's going on here isn't right."

"Well go ahead then, free the wrongdoers," said Dave. His voice was with a mixture of disgust and derision. "See where it gets you. Because that will be in a chain, next to the you that hates your guts and wants you to die because you stole his life. And you'll be in there until he kills you – and every day you're in there you'll wish he would. In fact, I wouldn't be surprised if he lets you live just to torture you."

"You don't know that, Dave. Any of it. Unless you turn me in. But I know you won't, because I think secretly you believe it's wrong the same way I do. What about that poor woman whose husband spent his life making hers a hell, and now she's in there, living in torture because she did something about it? What about all the other innocent people who've been put there because they have mental illnesses, or they went temporarily nuts like my poor brother Ben? Don't you want them to be free?"

"Well sure, mate," said Dave. "But it's not going to happen."

"It can," Jakob asserted as much to himself as to Dave. "This place is rotten, and as long as we let it remain that way, it will get worse. I want New Elysium to be a society that's just, and honest with itself. A place where we acknowledge that people sometimes need to be locked up for wrongdoing, but where they pay their debt to society and re-join it. Not a lying sham where even a minor infraction is punishable by a lifetime of slavery. We have this pretence of perfection and harmony, but it's all a huge lie."

"Even if you succeed, another lie will just take its place," said Dave. He sounded weary now. "But go ahead. Give it a whirl. I won't stand in your way. I'll call in sick for tomorrow, which I really am because you fucking belted me pretty good with that bottle, and my arms and shoulders are bloody stiff right now. So do your best, mate. In some ways I admire your courage, even if I feel sorry about your stupidity. And I promise, I won't say anything to the new Jakob when he turns up in a couple of days."

Jakob grunted at the attempt at humour, but his head hurt and he was afflicted with uncertainty and fear, hampered by hunger and exhaustion, and he really felt that all he could do now was sleep. He started peeling off Dave's uniform. "I need to lie down for a while," he said.

"Whoa, don't be taking that shit off here," said Dave. "Take it home and give it a good wash, mate. I don't want to see it until it's clean. Don't fret, I've got another. Just go home and crash."

Jakob tried to smile at Dave. It was remarkable how much of a friend, and how incredibly tolerant, this funny Aussie White Hat had been to him. He believed that Dave wouldn't betray him to the authorities, and he hoped that he'd get through all this so that the two of them could renew their friendship.

"I really appreciate what you're doing for me. I am so sorry I hit you and tied you up, you didn't deserve it. I was desperate. But you've been," he hesitated, searching for the right word. "You've been a mate." Dave grinned broadly and waved a hand in shy dismissal of this unexpected intimacy.

"Just go home, you crazy fucker," he said.

Jakob headed toward the door to the hallway, but as his hand gripped the doorjamb he turned and regarded the bruised, bloodied but unbowed White Hat. "Just one thing," he said. "You were sent here to keep an eye on me, weren't you? After the other Jakob assaulted that old man."

Dave looked genuinely surprised by the question, and even perhaps a little offended. "I came here because I was assigned this house, Jake," he said. "I knew that you were a reprint because I delivered you to the Directorate, so I made it my business to know as much as I could about you. But I kept an eye on you because you're a friend."

Beset by a kind of moral exhaustion, numbed by all that had occurred in the last few hours and upset to find that he had so badly misjudged Dave, Jakob went next door to his house, closed his own front door and stood in the dark, his eyes closed, listening to the beating of his heart. Confused, less sure of his path than he had been all night and beginning to understand the risks he had taken and was still to take, he began to be frightened. But above all he was absolutely drained of energy, so he pushed himself away from the door and walked to his bedroom in the dark.

He took off Dave's uniform and threw it carelessly on the

floor, and got into bed. For a few minutes sleep eluded him, and the idea of getting up to roll a joint popped into his mind. It would only take a couple of minutes, and it would help him drop off, if it didn't ignite a phantasm of conflicting ideas and paranoias that actually kept him awake. But eventually he agreed with that voice in his head that said that waking up in the morning would be harder, his mind would be more clouded and heavier if he was to have a joint now. He rolled over and tried to sleep, when a thought struck him like a thunderbolt. The camera! It was still attached to the hatband of Dave's White Hat, which was in the front of the van. He'd forgotten all about it in the rush to get inside and make sure Dave was still alive.

He sat up in a panic and wondered what the hell to do now. Then he realised that Dave's uniform trousers were lying in disarray on his floor, with the van keys still in them. It took mere seconds for him to have the lights blazing, Dave's uniform pants on, and himself out the front door, bare chested and bare footed. It was cold out there, but he was quick, getting into the van, retrieving the camera and leaving the helmet there, and darting back inside in less than thirty seconds.

As he again closed his front door and leaned against it, his heart thumping and his mind once again racing, he wondered if sleep would ever come. But he also silently thanked whatever gods were out there for ensuring he hadn't had a joint, because if he had, he would have left the camera there all night, and Dave probably would have found it. He knew Dave would be as good as his word not to turn him in, but if the means to thwart his mission should come to hand easily, there is little doubt the Aussie would have used them.

Shaking his head and pursing his lips, he undressed and got back into bed, sure now that he would lie awake for the rest of the night. The adrenaline rush of the last few minutes had woken him up properly, and he didn't feel at all like sleeping. In his mind he started editing the vision he'd captured and trying to write an accompanying voice over, but he didn't know where to start, and his thoughts were difficult to marshal. In any case, fatigue has a way of overcoming all obstacles when it really needs to, and in a very short while his mind was quiet, his pulse slow, his movements stopped, and he was asleep.

38.

Jakob felt incredibly well rested. He took his time waking up, leaving his eyes closed while he did so. He tried to remember what day it was so he could ready himself for the tasks ahead. Yesterday had been a day on the road, filming interviews, so today would be the day they taped the show. That must be right, although it seemed so long ago he couldn't be sure. He opened his eyes. He wasn't in his room at home. The ceiling was lower and whiter, the light much brighter than it would be in the early morning at home.

Sitting up, he cast his eyes around this strange room. Obviously it was a hospital room – small, crowded with instruments and apparatus, two visitors chairs, a tray for meals stationed over the end of the bed and a small cabinet either side of the narrow bed. Putting his hands up to his head, he found that his skull was bandaged, and that there was a cannula in the back of his hand, connected to a saline drip. The needle hurt.

Had he been in some kind of accident? The last thing he could remember was walking out of Mickey's after post-work beers with Toney and Lars. He thought he'd been headed home, but maybe he was going somewhere else – for the life of him he couldn't remember where. In fact, despite feeling so well-rested, there was a cloudy grogginess about him that was heavy, and slowing him down. He decided he'd just close his eyes for a moment to clear his head – and fell asleep again.

When he woke, a nurse was sitting in a chair beside the bed, making notes in a tablet. She looked up when he moved, made a note in the tablet, and stood. "Good afternoon Mr Petersson," she said. "It's nice to have you with us. I'll get the doctor."

"What am I doing here?" asked Jakob.

"I'll get the doctor," the nurse replied. She strode out of the room. Jakob lay on the bed feeling a little lost and helpless. His last real, tactile memory was fingering the bud of weed in his pocket. He wondered if it was still there. Then it occurred to him: he didn't even know where his clothes were.

A white-coated doctor walked into the room and greeted Jakob with a courteous but cool nod. She picked up the chart hanging at the end of the bed, and consulted it, looking up once or twice at the patient as she did so before putting it back. She picked up his wrist to feel the pulse. At last she turned her eyes, cool light blue beneath blonde eyebrows and straight greyish blonde hair, on Jakob's. "How are you Mr Petersson?" she asked.

"A bit confused I guess, Doctor," answered Jakob. "I don't know what I'm doing here or how I came to be here. Was I in an accident?"

"Not exactly," replied the doctor with a slight frown. "You passed out on the street, and you were found there by none other than Major Tom Flynt and his friend Ms Mansoor. I gather you were in the vicinity of Ms Mansoor's house."

Jakob had a vague recollection of going to Ellandra's

house, and of seeing her with Tom Flynt. Had that been when he'd passed out? He was sure he'd gone home that night. But it was all so fuzzy.

"Of course Major Flynt insisted that you get the very best of care," said the doctor, an air of admiration hanging around every sentence in which she spoke of Flynt. "So we ran some tests to determine what had caused your involuntary loss of consciousness." Here, the doctor's expression became a shade more serious, as if she was about to disappoint a child who wanted an ice-cream.

"I'm afraid what we found is not good," she said. "You have a Grade IV Astrocytoma, otherwise known as a glioblastoma multiforme, confirmed via stereotactic biopsy. The location of the GBM deep in the cerebellum makes it virtually inoperable, as the chances of intersecting with the brain stem or spinal cord are unacceptably high."

"That doesn't sound good," said Jakob. "But I didn't understand a word of it except 'inoperable.'"

"In layman's terms you have a large, advanced brain tumour nestled at the very base of your brain. It's quite unusual but not completely unknown for people not to experience symptoms of some sort prior to a collapse such as yours. Have you had any headaches?"

"Not really," said Jakob.

"Blurred vision?"

"No."

"Depression, psychotic episodes, hallucinations?"

"Well my work colleagues might tell you differently, but I don't think so," replied Jakob with a weak grin.

"Hmm, quite unusual," said the doctor.

"So what happens next?" asked Jakob.

The doctor assumed her most sympathetic, apologetic look. "The trouble is, we can't get at it to cut it out, given the location and the possibility of a negative outcome on the table. Unfortunately, the incidence of mortality in a tumour of this nature is above ninety-five percent. I'm sorry to tell you that there is little that can be done for you. An intensive course of radiotherapy and chemotherapy may arrest growth of the Astrocytoma for a while, but unfortunately the outcome is typically lethal."

Jakob swallowed and tried to assimilate what he was being told. "How long have I got?" he asked in a small voice, reluctant to utter the question because he was unwilling to receive the answer.

"A month. Perhaps three, with luck. Up to six if you follow through with aggressive treatment, but the majority of that time will be spent in, ah, severe discomfort. We generally find that most people wish to use the time more profitably, in setting their affairs straight, spending time in the company of family and friends, and enjoying experiences they might otherwise have put off. At least those they can undertake in a weakened state. Again Mr Petersson, I'm very sorry to be the one to have to tell you this. I know it's hard to take on board."

It seemed to Jakob that the doctor's sorrow at having to be the bearer of such news was mainly for herself – it made *her* day a little tough. But a feeling of bitter loss and dire helplessness was overcoming him, and he knew he would impute ill will or, at the very least, apathy to everyone at that moment. He nodded numbly and dumbly to the doctor. He knew what she was saying – he was going to die, and soon, and there was nothing that could be done. Perhaps sensing that the patient wished to be left alone to consider the prognosis, the doctor silently excused herself and left the room, stopping at the nurse's station to order that a course of sedatives be dispensed to Mr Petersson.

After the doctor left, Jakob lay back and stared at the ceiling. His mind was a complete blank, and he spent a long time watching the light burn into the plain white of the ceiling, doing nothing but blinking. At some time, the nurse came in and administered the sedative, and Jakob drifted off into a magically meaningless trance. He dreamed he was a White Hat, driving imperiously up and down the street, sharing his wisdom and authority with adoring crowds, until he realised he was actually Major Tom Flynt, and that everything in New Elysium was his, had been made by him, and exalted him. By his side was the radiantly beautiful Ellandra, smiling in the way he hadn't seen her smile for years, happy and secure, filled with laughter. It was a voluptuous reverie, and as it faded and he drifted off into a dreamless slumber, a smile played on his face.

39.

Far away, noises could be heard. The creak of a door, the scuff of a chair being dragged along a vinyl floor, and a softly polite cough. Jakob emerged from the depths of his torpor slowly, his eyelids fluttering as he opened them to find Lars and Toney standing quiet, respectful and sombre beside his bed. They were holding hands.

"Hey buddy," said Lars. "How you doing?"

"I don't know, to be honest," said Jakob. "I kind of feel as though I've just been dropped into somebody else's life. It's like I don't belong, but it's going to be taken away from me and I don't want that to happen."

"Yeah, we heard you've got a pretty bad situation going on," Toney put in with a solicitous look. "We're really sorry to hear it Jakob."

"It happens," Jakob said, trying to sound philosophical. But he didn't want to dwell on what the doctor had told him, nor share it with his friends before he could process it himself. He changed the subject. "So what's going on with you guys? Am I seeing hand holding here?"

"You are, at last." Toney was bashful but clearly very pleased with herself. "The other night when you wouldn't come to Mickey's with us we ended up getting pretty drunk and then we went back to Lars's place to smoke some weed and, well, you know…" she tailed off.

Forcing a happy face, Jakob nodded. Looking at Lars, he said, "well it took you long enough." Then a thought came to him. "Hey Toney, what do you mean, the other night when I wouldn't come to Mickey's? They told me I collapsed on Monday night after we'd been there together."

"No, that was Tuesday night, the night you wouldn't come," Lars said.

"That's odd." Jakob was wondering whether he'd mis-heard what the doctor had said, but he didn't think so. Still, he wasn't of a mind to think about it. This short conversation had made him tired. His friends prattled on for a while longer but they could see that he was fading away, so they awkwardly wished him well and left, and he slept again.

When he woke, Dave Belleville was sitting quietly on the chair next to the bed. The affable Aussie grinned when Jakob opened his eyes. Dave had a large band aid on his head, and what looked like the remnants of a black eye.

"So you are alive after all," he said.

"Only just," said Jakob.

"They tell me you got the C," said Dave. He always was direct.

"Yeah, something like that," replied Jakob. "I guess there's a lot of it about. Broken nuclear plants all over the continent, you know. Or it could have been the weed. I smoked quite a bit for a long time."

"Yeah, I know," said Dave. "Strange that you didn't have any symptoms though?"

"I suppose," agreed Jakob. "I hadn't really thought about

it. I know I was a pain in the ass to a lot of people, maybe all that grumpiness was my brain getting sick."

"Yeah maybe," said Dave. They sat for a while in silence, and eventually Jakob, the sedatives still coursing through his body, dropped off again. Dave sat for a few minutes looking at his sleeping friend.

As he got up to leave, he softly said, "It was always going to end this way, wasn't it Jakey? Still, it's a shame, because underneath it all you could have been a good man."

Epilogue

Jakob Petersson woke up in a state of fright. Was it a nightmare? The bare boards of the bunk above him told it was not. The raid had been short and brutal, personally directed by Major Thomas Flynt and observed by his ex, Ellandra. They'd beaten down his door less than half an hour after he'd fallen into shattered sleep, and caught him while he was still trying to drag Dave Belleville's uniform pants on. Nothing had been said, there was no trial or sentence. There was no need, Jakob knew exactly where he was going. The only conversation, if you could call it that, came when he was being dragged out of the front door of his home. Ellandra, looking glum but glaringly unapologetic, said, "I warned you Jakob."

The barrack lights came on and a loud voice said, "Rows one to ten, horticultural duties. Rows eleven to thirty-two, generating room."

Jakob was in row twelve. He was about to spend the first of many days chained to a wheel. Watching what the others did, he held out his hands so they could be manacled into the long chain on the floor. When everyone was secured to a chain, the lines of prisoners started shuffling forward. For a split second, Jakob hesitated. The man behind him gave him a rough shove, and he heard his brother's voice say, "Come on asshole, I've got plans for you."

307